DARING CHARLOTTE

Julie Glover

JBQ Publishing

What dare would you take to fulfill a dream?

High school drama geek Charlotte Romero loves the stage, but not her stage fright. Instead, she works theater tech and dreams of one day seeing a show on Broadway.

When her teacher announces a drama class trip to New York, the price is way too high for her cash-poor family. But not for drama queen Deedra, a rich classmate offering $5,000 to the student who best completes her nine dares.

Charlotte pushes past her performance anxiety and enters the contest. Soon, she's got an unwanted spotlight, a crush on a competitor, and increasing panic that she can't possibly win the prize.

To my Coffee & Critique Group.
I'm so grateful to have joined y'all and look forward to many more
hours of critique and companionship!

Contents

1
CENTER STAGE

I blamed Mary Poppins.

Standing at our high school theater's backstage door, I checked to make sure the coast was clear, unlocked the door with my bootleg key, and stepped inside. I twisted the bolt behind me and tapped on my phone's flashlight. Though I didn't really need it. As a backstage crew member, I had this place memorized—the sets stored behind the heavy curtain, the catwalks above and trap door beneath, that one warped plank upstage left that creaked when you stepped on it just right.

"Hello?" I yelled into the emptiness. "Anyone there?"

Silence.

Reaching center stage, I held up my phone and cast a bluish beam around the theater, scanning for intruders. "Hello!"

No response.

Safe. I closed my eyes and imagined the space filled with colorful backdrops, music rising from the orchestra pit, spotlights streaming to where I stood. A perfect world where happy people suddenly broke into song and dance. I straightened my spine. Opened my eyes. Cleared my throat. "Ladies and gentlemen, two-time Tony award winner, Charlotte Romero, is here to perform the hit song from the Broadway musical *Wolff*, 'So I'm Scared.'"

Silly, sure. But no matter how impossible it was for me to sing in public, a sliver of wistful thinking lingered. And *Wolff* was the hottest musical on Broadway. I desperately wanted our new drama teacher to choose it for the spring musical. So what if I'd cut off my big toe before having to perform for real people.

I pulled in a deep breath and sang the first line. "What is this fear inside me? Why do I tremble so?"

The first words were tight and tentative. But with no one around, I slowly found my focus, and the notes grew stronger. Every nerve in my body buzzed with excitement. My voice filled the room and echoed into the rafters. Music swelled my heart and stirred my dreams.

I kept singing, working the stage, performing to no one and nothing. Just. For. Me.

Reaching the end, I raised my arms and went all-out, singing the last lyrics to an invisible crowd. "I will persevere. Conquer my own fear. And make you learn to fear me."

"Daaaaamn."

Panic slammed into my gut, fractured my nerves.

The house lights came on. A figure loomed at the soundboard in the back of the theater. Logan Barrett, fellow theater tech student, sound guy, popularity-magnet.

Heat rushed to my cheeks. Nausea curdled my stomach.

I didn't sing in front of anyone who wasn't a Romero...*mi familia.* Not since my disastrous eleven-year-old performance as Marta Von Trapp in *The Sound of Music.* I'd had a great debut, but as soon as they'd turned up the lights and illuminated the audience's faces, I'd lost my lunch—right on the captain's spit-shined shoes.

Stage fright sucked.

Logan left the soundboard, jogged down the aisle, and vaulted onto the stage.

Room tilting. Palms clammy. *Uh-oh.*

Suddenly, he was in front of me. "Should have told you I was here, but I was listening to a track through the headphones. Took them off, and you were singing, and wow, that was wild."

"Uh-huh." My head swam. My voice cracked. "I'm...going to...class...something." I grabbed my pack, slung it over my shoulder, and took a step toward the exit.

The nausea moved up to my throat. "Oh no."

"What's wro—"

I shouldered out of my backpack, ran to the trashcan just behind the curtain, and held it to my torso like a life preserver. A good portion of my breakfast burrito landed at the bottom.

Immediately, my stomach felt better, but everything else felt worse.

Footsteps shuffled up behind me.

I shut my eyes, praying Logan would leave. Leave and never talk about this morning ever again.

"Can I get you anything?" The softness of his voice surprised me.

"Invisibility?"

"I was thinking more like paper towels or a glass of water. You know, something that doesn't require supernatural powers?"

"Nah, I'm fine." I took a deep breath, opened my eyes, and set down the trash can. "I'm sorry."

"For what?"

While I pulled out the trash bag—thank heaven for liners—and tied it up, his footsteps faded and then returned.

"Here."

I turned around to see him holding out my backpack.

His tanned face was framed by tendrils of honey-colored hair, and a gray knit beanie topped his head, giving him that common slacker look that was at complete odds with his rich, popular persona. Trying hard to look like he wasn't trying hard. "It's cool. Believe me, I get it."

I swallowed the scoff that threatened to come out. No way he understood how I felt—like I'd been flipped inside out. I accepted my bag and slid it over my shoulder. "Thanks."

"No, thank you. Clearly, I witnessed a performance few get to hear."

No kidding. Even my best friend Kat had barely heard more than a hum. "I'd appreciate if you'd keep this to yourself."

He tilted his head, narrowed his eyes, and gave a *humph*. Then he checked his watch. "Ooh, gotta go. See you later."

"Later," I agreed.

Logan backpedaled through the open curtain, stepped off the stage, and balanced on a seat arm. He smiled his made-you-swoon smile. But swooning was for prima donnas, not girls stuck in the fly gallery. "Too bad you don't perform. You sing like a freakin' angel."

My stomach dove to my sneakers. "I—I—"

He spun around and crossed to the back of the theater as if the seats were a rock path through a creek. Then he leaped to the floor, grabbed his own backpack, and passed the soundboard, shutting off the lights as he went. The back door swung open, and he walked out.

I stood there, processing what had just happened. I'd sung, Logan had heard, I'd tossed my cookies, he'd promised not to tell, and he'd said I sang like—

Wait, he *hadn't* promised not to tell. He'd *humphed*.

What kind of answer was that?

Kat found me hiding in a bathroom stall. She knocked on the door. "I know it's you. I recognize those trash scraps."

"Trash scraps?" I mumbled.

"Converse high-tops."

"Hey!" She might not appreciate my Incognito Chic, but my sneakers were top-of-the-line, molded-to-my-feet Chucks. Bought on clearance. Like everything I owned.

"Why'd you send me a vomit emoji? You know how much I hate emojis."

I'd actually sent three emojis. Words had failed me, so I'd summed it all up with a microphone, music notes, and a puke face.

Kat knocked again. "Charlotte, stop hiding. What happened?"

"I'm not hiding from you." I got up from my seated position on the floor and unlatched the stall lock. The door swung open, and I slumped back into my place. My butt had fallen asleep twenty minutes ago, and it stung when I sat down again.

Kat crossed her arms over her black Mötley Crüe tee. Today's rebellious pink streak in her short blonde hair matched the text of the logo. "Well?"

"While you were drumming away in morning band practice, I was having a repeat of my Worst Moment Ever. With the added joy of Mr. Popular as my audience."

"And how is that clearer than the string of icons you sent me?"

I took a deep breath to settle the kickline of nerves can-canning my ribs. "I sneaked into the theater this morning and sang on stage, assuming no one was there. Only someone was there."

"Ohh." She lifted her eyebrows and cocked her chin at the toilet. "And you tossed your cookies?"

I nodded. "But not here. There. Into a trash can, with him watching."

"Yikes. Him who?"

"Logan Barrett." I sighed.

Kat stepped into the large stall, locked the door behind her, and slid down next to me. "So what's the worst that could happen? He tells a few people you puked, they laugh, and that's that."

"A few people?" I shrieked. "I sang at full volume, even introduced myself, like I was performing for a sold-out show. And Logan knows everyone, Kat. He could tell everyone."

She sucked a gasp through clenched teeth. "Then the laughter might be louder."

My stomach jolted. "What if he recorded it? *Dios mío.*" I scrambled over to the toilet, expecting the retching to happen any minute now.

After a long minute, I sat back down.

The class bell rang. We sat through its echoing tones, me curled in on myself, Kat sitting casually like she spent every morning hanging out in a stinky stall. The bathroom was empty, silent—the way I'd thought the theater was going to be before school started.

"I'm going to be late," I muttered. "This is your fault, you know."

She flinched. "You being late?"

"No. The other thing." I couldn't even say it again.

"How is that *my* fault?"

"You're always saying to try new things, live on the edge, take risks."

She stared at me like I'd lost my sanity. "Yeah, but for you, that meant wearing more color or trying oysters or listening to something other than songs from *Hamilton*. I didn't know you'd expose your deepest desires in the Vortex of Doom."

"Vortex of Doom?"

"Just stepping foot on school grounds invites bad things to happen." She waved an arm around, as if displaying the doom.

"What are you, a tour guide of some dystopian world?"

"If the vortex fits..."

I huffed out a small chuckle. For Kat, school represented institutionalized brainwashing hellbent on turning out citizen automatons. Or something like that. For me, it was just a daily test of staying unnoticed in the crowd.

"Speaking of the vortex," she said, "are we skipping?"

"I've never skipped class." And yet, I didn't move.

Kat lifted one shoulder in a half-hearted shrug. "True, but you've never sung in front of Logan Barrett before. There's a first for everything."

I sighed. "Guess I could claim I'm really sick."

"Now that you mention it"—Kat stood hastily—"there's no telling what virus we picked up sitting on this nasty floor. We should both go home and decontaminate."

I stood and wiped off my dusty, and somewhat sticky, jeans. "Want to know who I really blame for this morning?"

"As long as it's not me, yes."

"Mary Poppins. That's the first musical I can remember seeing."

"Should have known." Kat rolled her eyes. "That British nanny bitch."

2
BROADWAY

I couldn't avoid Logan forever, but I didn't spot him until lunchtime the next day. He burst through the main doors of the cafeteria with his stepsister, Deedra. Deedra wasn't a theater person, probably figuring she didn't need a stage with her own personal popularity spotlight following her everywhere.

I narrowed my eyes as I watched them, Logan leaning over her shoulder with an animated expression, mouth moving quickly. Obviously arguing. When she spotted friends waving her over, her scowl switched to a smile, and she moved away.

Logan blew out a gust of air, puffing out his cheeks the way I'd seen him do when he got frustrated with sound equipment. As if he felt my eyes on him, he turned toward me.

My heart *ba-boomed* like Kat's bass drum. I turned away and whispered to her, "He's looking at me."

Kat was giving her sandwich the smell test and shoved it up to my nose. "Do you think this turkey's still good? I'm starting to believe I walk into school and things start rotting."

"Logan." I pushed her sandwich away slowly. "He's looking at me."

Dropping her sandwich, she scanned the cafeteria, fixed her stare on one place, and widened her eyes. "If he was going to target someone for ridicule, don't you think he'd start with her?" She pointed her chin where she was looking.

Loud claps and a shrill voice shot through the cafeteria. "People! Listen up, people!"

I spun around to see Deedra claiming the center of the room, as if a pedestal had been erected underneath her. While Logan Barrett knew a lot of people, Deedra Fine was known by a lot of people. She didn't care who you were, as long as you knew who she was.

Kat scoffed. "No telling what she's up to. Such an attention hog."

"Oink-oink," I muttered back.

Attention-seeking ran in the family. Her mom was Jenna O'Far-rell-Fine, feature reporter of the highest rated local evening news.

But imagining Deedra as a hog was a massive stretch. She had one of those unusual looks that marked someone as a run-way model type—statuesque body, peach-and-porcelain skin, long fiery-red hair.

She flipped her hair, *a la* photo shoot, and announced, "Starting today, I'm hosting a fabulous contest with a grand prize of five thousand dollars."

Rumbles erupted throughout the cafeteria. My jaw surrendered to gravity. Five thousand dollars? Who in high school had that kind of money?

Deedra clapped again, slipped on her mom's newscaster smile, and raised her voice. "It's called Deedra's Dares. You can find out more information from these flyers." She dangled a stack of pink neon paper in the air like it was a treat for hungry puppies, then started working the tables.

Hands stretched out to grab the flyers.

Kat rolled her eyes, then took a drastically large bite of her sandwich as if in protest of Deedra's escapades, the turkey apparently fresh enough.

I kept my butt in my chair and my hands to myself. After yesterday's perform-and-puke, I had no business doing anything with dares. Not even for five thousand dollars.

I chewed my lip and looked around the cafeteria, my eyes landing on Logan.

He was staring up at the ceiling, probably praying for relief from his stepsister.

I pulled my gaze away. I didn't think he'd told anyone about my fiasco. No videos had hit the usual social media sites. And there'd been none of the tell-tale glances, pointing, or smirks that came with high school rumors.

Eventually, Deedra reached us and tossed two pink papers onto the table. She didn't even make eye contact, just strolled away with her rhinestone flip-flops *thap-thapping* the floor.

Kat groaned—"Fine, I'll look"—and grabbed a paper.

I read over her shoulder.

What Would You Do for Money?

$5k to the Winner of Deedra's Dares

Contest Details on the Website

Next to a QR code were the words *You Risk, I Reward.*

Kat yanked out her phone, scanned the code, and started scrolling down the screen. "Listen to this. You sign up and do the first dare, and she lets the top nine people into the contest. Then there's more dares, nine rounds in all, and each week someone gets voted out. So basically, a popularity contest."

I leaned over and saw the simple website with a professional head shot of Deedra followed by a section on contest rules. "Voted off? Like reality-TV-show voted off?"

Kat read more and summarized. "People's choice rules. Last one standing gets 5K."

"How does she have so much cash?"

"I heard her dad gives her a hundred dollars every day. She makes like thirty-six thousand dollars for existing."

"My mother doesn't make that working full-time." Money had always been tight, and even more so since Mom had been going to school at night.

"Whatever this contest is, it's ridiculous." Kat clicked off her phone and crumpled the pink paper. "Who'd agree to publicly disgrace themselves just because Rich Bitch dangles a few stupid carrots?"

Five thousand dollars was more than carrots. It would buy a lot of Converse high-tops, rent payments, or community college tuition. "Think anyone will sign up?"

"Some people will do anything for money." She wadded up her lunch bag, stood, and turned toward the exit.

"Yeah, good thing we're content with being broke," I muttered and followed. But on my way out, I glanced back at Logan, who now sat at a filled table and gave a strained smile to his buddies as they pored over the pink flyer in his hand.

Even if Logan had leaked out the story of "Charlotte Romero Sings and Spews," it would have had a short life in the headlines. After that lunch announcement, our school was overtaken by nonstop discussion of Deedra's Dares.

For no good reason, I'd grabbed the wad of paper and stuffed it into my pocket. I'd throw it away later.

I reached my last class eager to leave contest gossip behind and enter my theater world. Even with my fears about Logan telling, Theater Tech was my sanctuary.

We met in the smaller of two auditoriums on campus, this one acting as the catch-all for theater equipment and drama geeks. Now and then, we cleaned up and presented a production that only required these two hundred seats, but most of our shows were held in the big auditorium where audiences reached up to a thousand-plus. In either place, I stayed behind the curtain.

Students trickled in and gathered into a loose huddle, sitting or lying on mismatched chairs, stage platforms, and the wood-planked floor. I took a spot on the perimeter, sitting on the ground and leaning against the claw-footed leg of an ornate love seat—last used for our high school's production of *The Importance of Being Earnest*.

Logan glided into the classroom wearing a Bowie Lives On T-shirt, black headphones, and his easy-does-it smile. He slid the headphones to his shoulders, took a seat on the other side, and dropped his gaze to me.

I folded my arms and lowered my head to form a protective cocoon.

Miss Holt, our new drama teacher, took center stage and clapped her hands twice. "Welcome, welcome!"

People stopped chatting and gave her their attention.

"Our next show," she said, "is Pecan Field's holiday production of *A Christmas Carol*. I understand this seasoned and competent crew can sort through the sets and costumes we'll need for that show."

The moans and groans made our theater sound haunted. I didn't join in, but I understood. Our high school always did *A Christmas Carol*, so the creative part was done. This was the boring stuff of technical theater—dragging out platforms and props, pulling out costumes, double-checking items, repairing damage from prior years.

Holt held up her hands. "I know, I know. Believe me, I've performed *Our Town* so many times, just the sight of a ladder makes me recite whole sections of that play. But this is theater, people! What's old hat to you is fresh to someone in your audience. And *A Christmas Carol* is a classic."

Our collective eye roll should have shifted the Earth off its axis, but it didn't even make a wobble. She clapped her hands again. "One final announcement."

Heads turned her direction. Was she finally yanking the curtain back and revealing her choice for spring musical? Hope hovered in my chest. Please let it be something current and creative.

"I had to twist a few arms in school administration, but I finally received the thumbs-up to put together a trip for our drama department..."

Not spring musical.

She paused while murmurs trickled around the room—probably people guessing which nearby town we'd visit for a local production of Shakespeare. Miss Holt loved her Shakespeare.

She waved her arms to regain our attention. "Class, class, settle down. I think you're going to like what I have to say next."

A hush settled.

Her mouth curved into a bow-smile. "I wish I could have given you more advance notice, but we've been approved to travel over Spring Break to Broadway. *The* Broadway in New York City."

Gasps, screams, and laughter erupted and echoed into the rafters.

I didn't make a sound. Couldn't. My breath had wilted in my chest, and my head floated about three feet above my body. Still, my brain tried to sort through what she'd said. *Broadway. I, Charlotte Romero, drama die-hard, am going to Broadway.*

"We'll be spending time behind the scenes of a production," Miss Holt continued. "Backstage. I'll have full information soon—"

"How much?" Logan's voice startled me.

Not just because he interrupted, but because that question seemed preposterous.

For him, not me. People like *me* definitely needed the answer to that question. But Logan Barrett? He might not have Deedra's money, but he had enough.

Holt tilted her head, as if her next words required extra sympathy. "Total cost? Twelve hundred ninety-five."

My heart sank to my threadbare shoes. She might as well have said a bazillion dollars.

3
Crew

At the mention of Broadway, I'd felt like I was flying on *Aladdin*'s magic carpet. At the mention of the price, the carpet yanked out from under me. I should have known it was too good to be true.

Miss Holt continued. "I know it's quick, but the first half of the money is due in four weeks and the last half eight weeks later. We'll only have time for one fundraiser..."

I tucked my knees against my chest, wrapped my arms around my legs, and dropped my head. My posture matched my defeat.

Even a fundraiser wouldn't help much, since most involved selling to a lot of people. Not that helpful when your entire customer base included your *abuela*, your mother, and the few coworkers at your mother's nonprofit.

When I tuned back into Miss Holt, she'd moved on. "...getting our costumes, props, and everything ready for the Christmas show. I'll let you choose how to spend today's class time, as long as you find something productive. If you don't get busy, I'll make suggestions."

Our circle dispersed, looking for something to keep them busy for the rest of class. The last time she'd made an announcement like that, the slackers had ended up scraping gum off the auditorium seats.

But conversations began immediately, all about the trip.

"I can't wait to go to New York again."

"Wonder what shows we'll see."

"Nothing beats Broadway."

I ignored the mini-celebrations of people already planning to go and headed to the costume closet across the hallway to sort through options for the ghosts who visit Ebenezer Scrooge. We'd use the same basic clothes, but I could add a little pizazz. Maybe I could make this year's Jacob Marley ghost of *A Christmas Carol* look more like a zombie extra from *The Walking Dead*. Or at least Michael Jackson's classic *Thriller* video.

Digging through costume accessories, I found a torn shirt labeled for repair. Tearing it a few more times would make it perfect. I scissored a small cut at the bottom of the shirt, yanked, and felt the satisfying *zzzfffttt*. Ripping things always relieved stress.

Added bonus—it kept my mind from playing rounds of *will I or won't I* about the trip. Which leaned heavily toward *won't*.

The closet door opened, and Logan's face appeared around the corner. "You all right?"

My body was near-frozen. I usually did costuming alone and didn't expect visitors, much less Logan. "Yeah, I'm fine."

"When you weren't in class yesterday..." He trailed off, leaving me to fill in the blank.

I tried to laugh, but the puff of air sounded more like a nervous tic. "Oh, that? I just had another big meeting on my schedule I couldn't get out of. You know how it is." I bit my lip, stopping myself from any more babbling.

He smiled then stepped all the way inside and shut the door behind him. "Want some help?"

A shiver tingled my spine. "I don't really need—"

"Come on." He shot me a pleading grin. "Sound equipment's good to go, but if I don't find something to do, Holt will probably have me cleaning the stage with a toothbrush."

"She does have that cool-but-tough vibe, doesn't she?" And as the only tech student who liked working with costumes, I really could use some help. I gestured to the clothing rack against the wall. "Can you pull out the robe we used for the Ghost of Christmas Present? It got torn last year, so it needs to be fixed."

He gave a nonchalant smile. "You're not expecting me to sew, are you?"

I laughed and shook my head. "No. I just need to know what I'm up against. If it's something I can do by hand or if I have to take it home and pull out my grandmother's sewing machine." The sewing machine was old, but it still made a decent stitch.

"She sings, *and* she sews," he whispered under his breath.

He hadn't meant for me to hear so I didn't answer. But anxiety spider-walked across my skin.

While Logan paced the length of the rack, I refocused and dug around for something to stain the shirt with smudges. Maybe charcoal? I sifted through a box marked Miscellaneous that could have as easily been labeled Crap We Have No Idea What to Do With. *Never mind.* I slammed the lid onto the box and shoved it back into the cabinet. "Did you find the robe?"

"Not yet."

"I can find it." I pushed clothes around on the rack and peered through the gaps. Catching a splash of green on the floor, I squatted and grabbed the robe that had fallen off its hangar. The hangers slapped closed around me, and heavy clothing buried my head.

Logan came behind me and held the offending costumes out of my way while I retrieved the robe and made my way out.

"Thanks." I grabbed a fistful of the robe and held it up. "Ghost of Christmas Present."

We stood close. His expression softened as he stared down at me, as if taking me in for the first time.

My heart kicked up to double-time, and I wanted to dive back into the clothing racks. I wasn't used to being studied carefully by any guy, much less Logan Barrett, a guy squarely in gorgeous territory.

He tucked his hands into his pockets. "So, you going on the trip?"

I took a deep breath, thinking that would shake me from my weird daze. But it only made me more aware of him so close, with that smell of rugged boy, coconut shampoo, and a dab of Abercrombie. A single curl on his forehead dropped lower than the others, brushing his eyebrow and calling my attention to his green eyes—the color of a Mountain Dew can. *Drink up, Charlotte.*

Where had that come from? I ran my hands over my temples, trying to wake up the logical part of my brain. "The price is a bit high. I'll have to see if I can raise the funds." I stepped back, put some distance between us.

"If musicals are your thing, you definitely should visit Broadway. My parents took me to see *Lion King* years back, and it was awesome."

I couldn't help but feel jealous. My mom and I had only seen community productions. No big family vacations to the Big Apple and its theater core.

"Guess you'll get to see another show on this trip." I'd bet my Broadway poster collection on that one.

"If I can make the case to my dad that it'll help my college application, yes. If it's something I just want—like a new guitar amp or my own car—he's stingier than Ebenezer Scrooge."

"That's pretty stingy."

His broad smile didn't quite hide an underlying frustration. It buzzed right there on the edges, discernible by the tension in the rest of his face. He took a deep breath. "I didn't tell anybody about yesterday."

My stomach knotted, and a soft scoff escaped my lips. "Not even your best friend?"

"Not even my therapist."

I winced.

His face broke out into a grin. "Kidding. Really, it's cool."

"I'm just a private person. Like extra private."

"I've noticed." He gestured around the dressing room. "You spend a lot of time in here. It's practically your lair."

"That makes me sound like a villain."

He shrugged. "Or a superhero."

"Someone's got to do costumes." And it allowed me to now and then imagine I was the one wearing them, pretending to be the character that went along with the costume. Not a superhero, just a stage actress. Both were out of my league.

Turning my attention back to the green robe in my arms, I flicked it out to full length. As suspected, there was a gaping hole in the bottom hem. Definitely a sewing-machine fix.

Logan's hands appeared above the robe where the fur collar lined the top, and he pulled it down to put us face-to-face, eye-to-eye once more. "If you want an even trade, I could share one of my secrets."

Curiosity plucked at me. But I shook my head. "No need."

He stepped closer, the robe between us becoming a too-thin barrier. "How about this one? I used to keep a Taylor Swift poster in my closet."

I laughed. "That's your big secret? That you were an average preteen boy?"

"Hey, I would get seriously razzed about that by friends."

"Who also secretly kept pop star posters in their closets." I slid the robe from his hands and draped it over one arm, making the barrier invisible. Or nonexistent. My toes curled. Did it bring more attention to my discomfort to stay here or to step back?

He looped his thumbs into his belt loops and leaned down. "I cheated on last year's English final. I still haven't read *The Scarlet Letter*."

I clenched my jaw, determined to be unfazed by his closeness. "I'll save you the trouble. Puritan woman has an affair, turns up pregnant, gets shunned by society. But that doesn't rise to the level of Audiences Make Me Lose My Lunch."

He eased back and made a clicking sound with his mouth. "You drive a hard bargain."

I stepped away and found a plastic bag to shove the tattered robe in to take home. "I'm not driving a bargain at all. I don't need to know your secrets. I'm the last person who would make someone share something they don't want people to know."

"Why? You got more secrets tucked away?"

My hands fumbled tying up the bag's handles. "I respect people's privacy."

He moved closer. "Still, I think I'd feel better if you knew some-thing about me. Then you'd have leverage."

"What makes you think I don't trust you not to tell?"

He pointed to the side of my mouth. "That twitch."

"What twitch?"

"The twitch you get whenever yesterday comes up."

I rubbed my palm over my mouth. "I twitch?"

"Just don't play poker."

"Thanks for the tip."

He peered at the ceiling for several seconds, then lowered his head and looked me in the eye. "How about this? Worst thing ever."

"You don't have to—"

"I caught my mom kissing another guy. Not my dad."

My face blanched. I could feel the blood bolting away. "After their divorce?"

"Nope. Walked in on her and some guy from her office." One side of his mouth turned down. "And thus began my parents' stormy breakup."

"I'm so sorry." I couldn't even imagine. My dad had never been around. Mom had met him through her friend's bachelorette par-ty, had an only-time-ever, one-night stand, and I was the result. But he'd left town before she could even tell him. She'd barely dated since.

"Yeah, well…" He sighed. "Not the best image to have stuck in your head."

We fell silent, no way out of the awkward moment.

Finally, he tapped me on the shoulder. "Now you know you can trust me."

I swallowed and gazed up at him. "But how do you know you can trust *me*?"

"I trust my gut, and my gut says I can trust you." His eyes narrowed, and that swoony smile slid onto his face. "Of course if my gut's wrong, I'm screwed."

4
Box Office

Getting home didn't ease my tension the way it usually did after a full day of overstimulation. The quiet of our apartment couldn't silence my mind.

My conversation with Logan had sparked a flurry of questions. Were we becoming friends? Did knowing each other's secrets tie us together? Was it now okay to stand closer and gaze into his bright green eyes?

I shook off that last thought and headed to my room.

Broadway. That's where my focus should be. I stopped just inside my bedroom door to wonder where I'd put souvenirs from the trip. My bedroom's walls were painted brick red with musical posters tacked in rows—everything from *Chicago* to *Grease* to my new favorite, *Wolff*. String lights hung from the ceiling, and above my bed was a vintage 42nd Street sign my mom had given me a few Christmases ago. Only a few open spots remained, but enough to add ticket stubs, photos, and playbills.

The half payment was due in four weeks, and I could probably manage that much. Digging in my closet, I found the wooden box in the back corner where I kept my savings. I'd tucked away birthday money from my grandmother, babysitting wages, and couch change. I stretched out my dollars into piles, sorted the coins, and started counting.

"*Hola.*" Mom's voice startled me.

I glanced up to where she leaned against the door jamb, arms crossed with a tired smile on her face.

"What time is it?" I'd been so engrossed in counting I hadn't heard her come home.

"Five fifteen." Even her voice was weighted with weariness.

I laid the last dollar down. $572.28, both times. Not bad. My spirits lifted. If I could snag a few odd jobs and raid my cafeteria lunch fund for the next month, I could pull together the six hundred-fifty-dollar deposit for my dream trip.

My reality-check brain pulled me back down. It had taken me years to save this much, and I couldn't get a part-time job. I had to be a theater student to go on the NYC trip, and productions took up evenings and weekends. My spirits fell into a dark pit. For the second half, I'd need a fairy godmother, a magic wand, and heaping piles of pixie dust.

Mom pointed at my stack of cash. "What are you doing?"

"Seeing if I have enough money for a school trip to New York," I answered. "But it's no big deal. I can go another time."

"New York?" Mom perked up. "Who's hosting the trip? When? How much?"

"Drama trip. Spring break. Too much." I shoved my cash back into the box.

"How much money is too much?" Her hand-on-hip, head-tilted pose made it clear I couldn't shrug off the question.

I stood and hugged her. "More than I have in my savings. And more than we can afford." I stepped back and forced a smile.

"Broadway's been there for a hundred years. It'll be there when I have enough money to go."

I made it sound like I really didn't care. Like I could wait for years, even a decade, to soak up the sights and sounds of Theater Central. *Today, tomorrow, whenever...*

"Broadway? *The* Broadway?" Mom's eyes nearly danced. "You're going to Broadway?"

"I'm not going to—"

"How much?" Mom raised a single eyebrow, a trick I could never master. "I want a dollar figure."

I regretted even bringing up the subject. Mom worked too hard already and too long, and any extra money needed to go toward her college degree so she could get a job that paid more and let her live a little.

With a sigh, I answered, "One thousand two hundred ninety-five."

"One..."

"Thousand." The two hundred ninety-five didn't matter. Pushing over the thousand-dollar mark put this idea into not-gonna-happen territory.

Her face flashed a colorless panic, but she quickly recovered. "How much do you have?"

"Not enough, Mom."

"Will you please treat me like the adult I am and let me decide based on the numbers?"

Guilt churned like sludge in my gut, muddying my insides. Mom manipulated numbers all the time, juggling the timing of her paycheck and the due dates of our bills. Calculating which debts to pay down with overtime. She had her own numbers game to play. She didn't need my impossible math.

"I have five hundred seventy-eight, which doesn't even cover the deposit." I shuffled to my bed and settled onto the rumpled covers. "I don't want to talk about this anymore. Miss Holt made it clear the trip's not required, just an opportunity."

"An opportunity of a lifetime."

"I can go another—"

"*Escúchame.*" My mother sat on my bed and grasped my hands. "I want you to go."

"Mom—"

"Don't *Mom* me. Somehow or other, you're going. We'll pay that deposit and figure out the rest."

I opened my mouth to protest, but Mom covered it with one finger. "I mean it, Charlotte. My senior year, I went to Miami with my choir. I've never forgotten that experience. I'm not letting you miss your chance."

"You don't have to do this." Tears clung to the corners of my eyes.

"I also don't have to love you," she said, "but I can't help myself. *Te amo.*"

We both laughed, but I threw myself into her arms and hugged her hard. "*Te amo también.*"

She pulled back and tucked my hair behind my ear. "Just promise to take lots of pictures and tell me everything when you get back."

"You won't be able to shut me up."

"When it comes to theater, I already can't shut you up."

She squeezed my hand and left to start dinner.

I grabbed my phone and texted Kat: *$78 more for deposit, and I'm going to New York!*

5
IMPROV

The next morning, I was covering a tiny hole in my Converse with duct tape when Kat's horn beeped. With Mom off to work early in the morning, Kat was my daily ride.

I glanced out my window and spotted her old, beat-up Kia Sportage idling at my curb and Kat rocking out inside the car like a concert goer.

I smiled, then secured the end of the tape. These shoes would have to last a while yet. All my money was going toward NYC.

Kat tapped her horn again. I tramped over my clothes from the night before and darted from the house. When I reached the SUV, she'd turned the volume down, but was still rapping the dashboard with her drumsticks and bobbing her head like music was playing in her mind. Music played in mine too, but while Kat lived in the world of rock classics, I indulged in rock musicals.

Before I'd slid all the way into my seat, she stopped drumming. "Hold out your hands."

"What?"

She gave me her impatient eye roll. "Just do it already."

I shoved my backpack to the floorboard and put out my hands. "Close your eyes."

"Seriously?" This was getting weird, even for Kat.

"Don't make me shut them for you." She added her rebellious expression that strived for bad-ass. I might have been more convinced if Kat and I hadn't been friends since Happy Meals and kiddie pools.

"You'd have made a good gang member for *West Side Story*. Jets or Sharks?"

"You're hilarious." Her deadpan tone made me hope she was at least laughing on the inside.

I closed my eyes and heard a rustle above the growl of the engine. Kat's hand touched mine and left something cool and smooth in my hands, like paper. What was she giving me?

"Before you open your eyes, you have to promise not to argue with me. I will not be challenged."

"What are you talking about?" I popped open my eyes. Then blinked and widened them more. A stack of cash rested in my palms. "What the—"

"It's sixty dollars. Not much, but you'll put it toward your trip and not make a big deal about it. Understand?"

A lump rose from my chest and filled my throat. I gawked at the money. Kat and I lived in a world of hand-me-downs, clearance racks, and enough change to order two burritos and one Dr Pepper at Taco Bell. For some kids in our school, sixty dollars was Wednesday's spending money, but Kat was giving me all she could spare. And then some.

"But my mom already said she'd cover this, and I can't just—"

"Yes, you can," she said.

"But what about gas money?"

She waved me off. "My brother gave me a gas card for my birthday."

I did a double-take. "Your birthday was last month."

"Well, belated's better than never." She pointed a finger at me. "But no more arguing. Shut up, and take the money."

I nodded once, folded the bills, and stuck the money in an inner pocket of my bag. Then swiped away a couple of stray tears with the back of my hand. "Thank you."

"No biggie." She smiled through that total lie. "But I need a favor."

"A favor?"

"Didn't finish my poem for English. I need you to drive while I write it on the way."

"Oh. Sure."

She got out, walked around to the passenger side, and we switched places.

I readjusted the seat for my two-inch shorter frame and dug the stick shift around for a bit until I found first gear. Unlike me, Kat had wheels, but her odometer was pushing 150k, the exterior was scratched and a bit rusted, and her auto parts lived to be cranky. She'd aptly nicknamed the SUV Jezebel.

While I drove, Kat scrawled out her assignment on a piece of paper balanced on her knee.

Meanwhile, I sang show tunes in my head. Mostly from *Wolff*, the all-the-rage musical that was a modern-day version of *Little Red Riding Hood*. Only Red was Scarlet who owned Hood Vineyard, and Mr. "Big Bad" Wolff was a corporate CEO trying to gobble up her family business. The rights for high schools to perform the musical had just been released, and I was aching to have it come to our high school.

"What do you think of this?" We'd almost reached the campus when Kat read what she'd written on her paper.

Life is a contest
Rigged and ruled by villains
That care nothing for human souls
Locked and loaded to kill
The very heart of us
Pitting one against another
Making us enemies
Drawing lines and walls
Blood and scars
You win, I don't
I win, you don't
Losers all.

She didn't just read the words. She turned them into slam poetry.

I gulped with the final line. "That's, um, disturbing."

"It's supposed to be disturbing. The world is disturbing. The imbalance, the—"

"Then you nailed it. It's awesome." And our English teacher would love it. She might make Kat visit the school counselor, but she'd love it.

I pulled into the school parking lot and drove down the rows looking for a good spot. We usually parked in the front with Kat's early morning marching band, but the band director had given them today off. And the parking lot was a free-for-all when you showed up at the regular time.

Seeing a spot, I drove toward it and flipped on my turn signal.

Before I could turn the wheel, a Mustang zipped in and swiped my place.

"Ugh."

I drove down another row, and another, not finding open places or missing them by split-seconds as other drivers pulled in ahead of me.

Kat shook her head. "C'mon, Charlotte. If we're ever going to park, it's might over right."

I smirked. "So forget manners?"

"Manners have no place in the school parking lot. Welcome to the jungle, Charlotte. They want to watch you bleed."

I took my eyes off the road long enough to give her a confused look. Her dark attire, dark poetry, and dark outlook made me worry about her sometimes. But I was pretty sure the girl who'd watched Disney movies with me as a kid was still in there. After all, she liked happy endings enough to empty out her piggy bank for me.

"Ooh, there, there!" Kat yelled.

I jerked my attention back to the lot and peeled around the corner to reach the spot she'd pointed out on the next row. I wasn't going to lose this one.

Thunk!

"Aaaarrrgh" I slammed my foot onto the brake. We surged forward, our heads following a millisecond behind. I landed back in place, but not my heart. I'd hit another SUV pulling out of its spot.

My lungs were empty. My hair stood on end. Nerves sizzled all down my limbs. I sucked in gasps of air and gripped the steering wheel.

"Shiitake," Kat said.

I gazed out the windshield at the other vehicle.

A fresh wave of panic rushed over me, covered me, suffo-cated me. Until I was buried in dread. Our student parking lot was filled with vehicles ranging from showroom-floor-model to rescued-from-the-junkyard. I could have hit any number of not-so-great cars. But no, not me. I'd rear-ended a Lexus SUV pol-ished to a brilliant shine with a license plate that read D33DRA.

Dread slithered into my gut and curled into a tight ball. My voice fell to a shaky whisper. "That's. Deedra's. Car."

6
DIVA

I stared at Deedra's banged-up bumper and prayed my eyes were malfunctioning.

The SUV's door flung open, and one long leg appeared, followed by the full Deedra. She was dressed like a fashion model—fitted blouse, pleat mini, sleek shoes—but she wasn't runway walking. Instead, she stomped to the rear of her vehicle. "Unbelievable!"

I cringed in my seat, wondering if I should pray harder. To every god I could think of.

"Wow." Kat's tone was as even as ever, but she had a nail-digging grip on the dashboard. "Deedra's pride and joy."

Deedra glared death rays through my windshield. "Are you blind? Or just an idiot?"

Her passenger door opened, and Logan stepped out. A shiver took a slow pass up my spine. Of course he'd be here.

"It's okay, people." He waved his hands above his head, signaling to students gawking at us. "We're fine."

Nice try, Logan. But we were not fine. If the high school parking lot was the jungle, I'd just slammed into the alpha lioness.

I stepped out of Kat's car. "I'm soooo sorry."

Deedra's SUV rested half-in, half-out of the parking space. The gap between our cars was just enough to show chipped paint, scratched metal, and crooked dents. A smashed brake light completed the mangled look.

Deedra closed the distance between us and stuck her finger in my face. "You will pay for this, or you will regret existing."

Her darkened eyes and flared nostrils shouted *loca*. So much for the sweet and smiling persona. This Deedra was a button-push from personal apocalypse.

I leaned back carefully, as if rapid movement might bump that button.

"All right, all right." A booming voice preceded the appearance of the School Resource Officer, our fancy name for campus cop.

Deedra flipped her bitch-face to pretty-pout and faced him. "Mr. Silva, thank goodness you're here. Charlotte slammed into my car, completely out of the blue." She rubbed her neck. "It's amazing I'm not injured worse."

"Injured?" My initial guilt gave way to shock.

"She's fine," Logan said. "It was a fender-bender."

Deedra flashed a scowl at him, but I doubted Officer Silva caught it. She immediately regained her woe-is-me expression. "My neck is killing me, and my beautiful car is a mess." She choked on the words, like she might fall into a heap of tears any minute.

Despite growing panic, I had to give her mental kudos for great acting. "I didn't even hit you that hard."

"Calm down." Silva smiled at Deedra and patted her arm. "We'll get this all worked out. What happened?"

Kat said, "We tapped her car," right as Deedra said, "Charlotte sped up and hit me." They exchanged glances, a brief showdown threatening to become a fight.

My mouth fell open. Sure, I'd gotten impatient, sped around the corner, rear-ended her. But Deedra made it sound like I was gunning for her.

Logan stepped forward. "Deedra pulled in crooked, so she backed up to re-park. Charlotte probably couldn't see we were backing up until it was too late."

"Are you saying this is my fault?" Deedra lasered onto Logan and pointed her finger at Jezebel. "This trash heap just destroyed my pristine car."

"Hey," Kat yelled. "I'm rather proud of my trash heap."

"Destroyed?" Logan laughed. "That's ridiculous. Besides, Daddy'll get it fixed." He said *daddy* with the same harsh tone Kat used for *school*. Definitely a story there.

"If you ever want another ride"—Deedra poked a finger at him—"you'd better shut up."

Silva stood apart, exuding the calm of someone used to crime scenes and teen drama.

"Believe me, Officer"—Deedra pointed at me now—"it was all Charlotte. It's like she saw me and raced around the corner to hit my car."

Heat rushed to my ears. "Why would I wanna to hit—?"

Kat lunged at Deedra.

I grabbed her arm to hold her back. An assault charge wouldn't help our situation.

"Bash Charlotte one more time"—Kat spoke through clenched teeth—"and I will back my car up and hit you again."

"Whoa, whoa, whoa." Officer Silva held up his hands. "Let's calm down and just gather some facts."

Anxiety tornadoed in my stomach. We could stand here arguing with Deedra's portrayal all day, but what was the point? Jungle or not, I had to be honest.

I let go of Kat, took a shuddering breath, and lifted my chin. "The accident was my fault, Officer."

All heads turned toward me, with varying degrees of surprise. Silva raised an eyebrow.

"We spotted an open space, so I came around the corner." I gestured the direction we drove. "But, like Logan said, I didn't see Deedra backing up, and I rear-ended her car."

Deedra gave a smug smile.

"But I swear I didn't hit her hard enough for anyone to be injured. It was your average parking lot bump."

Logan raised his hand. "I'll testify to that. Mildly jarring at best." He ignored Deedra's scathing glare.

Officer Silva scratched his head, then wrote on his memo pad. "All right then. Charlotte, let's see your license and insurance."

"*My* insurance?" I asked. "I was driving, but it's Kat's car."

Silva shook his head. "Liability insurance follows the driver, not the car."

My heart crashed against my ribs. "I...um...I'd have to..."

"You do have insurance, don't you?" Silva's expression was part-judgment and part-sympathy.

I looked over at Kat. She stood with her arms crossed, one hand over her mouth, and her brow creased. Uncharacteristically silent.

"No," I answered. "No insurance."

I had a license, but with no car and money tight, I'd told my mom to drop coverage of me. Kat or Mom drove me everywhere anyway.

Officer Silva sighed heavily.

"That's a ticket right there." Deedra's mini-celebration wasn't helping.

"License?" Silva remained unruffled and authoritative.

"Yes." I pulled out my wallet, found my license, and handed it over.

He jotted down some information and handed it back. "Okay, I'm going to take a few pictures, then you'll park your cars, and I'll interview you individually. Based on that, I'll put together a report."

"Saying she's at fault," Deedra added. "And should pay for everything."

Kat stared at Deedra but spoke to Silva. "Can you add to the report that Deedra's a bitch? I think that's pertinent information."

Deedra seethed. "You little—"

"Stop!" Silva yelled.

Deedra hushed, Logan snickered, and Kat rolled her eyes back to last Tuesday.

When Silva turned to take pictures, Deedra lifted her hand and raised her middle finger. Of course, she got in the last word. Then she turned and followed Silva around her SUV, making sure he took a picture of every little scratch.

With every snap of Silva's camera, my heart dropped a little more, all the way to *Hadestown*. This was bad. Really bad. I didn't want to admit it, but deep inside I knew that in a split-second everything had changed.

Goodbye, Broadway.

7
Drama

While Officer Silva snapped pics and Deedra played Poor Pitiful Me, Kat and I moved to the back of Jezebel and leaned against her rear bumper to wait for our turn.

I swiped sweat from my face. It was already muggy with our usual South Texas heat and humidity. But fear upped my inner temp to deep-fried.

Students slowed as they walked past. No one said anything, but I translated their side glances as "sucks to be you."

Logan came around the back. "Dee's not hurt. I'll talk to her."

"Would you?" I peered up at him with a thin smile.

"Can't promise anything. But I'll try."

For a moment, I felt like touching his arm to show how grateful I was. But that seemed too familiar. I crossed my arms and widened my smile. "Thank you."

I turned to Kat. "And I'm sorry. I should have seen Deedra coming out. I'll pay for your car too. Somehow."

"No, you won't." She flung her hand in the air, batting away the offer. "That scrape just gives Jezebel more character. Now the front matches the back."

"Thank you." I breathed a little easier. Although I was still steeped in worry. "Deedra's really pissed, isn't she?"

Logan tucked his hands into his pockets, casual as ever. "She's extra-stressed because she posted the first dare online this morning."

"She announced it?" Once again, the contest trumped everything else.

"Yep." He raised his eyebrows and cocked a smile. "And it's a doozy."

Officer Silva waved him over, and Logan headed toward the SUV.

I turned to Kat. "How much do you think it will cost?"

"Bumper like that? Maybe a few hundred?" Her tentative tone made me think she was sugarcoating. Paying for that bumper would easily empty my savings account. I should hand back Kat's sixty dollars right now. And forget New York.

No way I was going now.

"I should have known," I moaned. "Things were going too good."

Kat put one solid hand on my shoulder. "Life is not out to get you."

"Says the girl who swears the universe is out to get us."

"And you listen to me?" Her hand dropped. "I'm a known cynic."

I lifted my head. "Even a cockeyed optimist could see that I'm in deep doo-doo. How am I going to tell my mom?"

Kat puckered up her face. "Do you have to?"

Silva approached while Deedra stayed back, running her finger over the car's surface as if looking for more nicks to add to the list. I tried to stop thinking about her and stepped back to let Silva take pics of Jezebel in all her dented glory. But I kept darting my gaze back to Deedra's car, wondering how bad the bill would be.

"You need a distraction," Kat mumbled. "Where's Logan? You like looking at him."

I flinched and felt my cheeks warm. "What? Logan?"

Kat laughed. "Whatever. It's not like you're the only girl to notice he's hot."

"He's just a guy in theater tech." Who was barely visible on the other side of Deedra's car.

"Uh-huh." She drew out the *huh*.

"That's the same tone you used when I said 'Cell Block Tango' is as good as that Bohemian song."

"'Bohemian *Rhapsody.*' I'll give you a pass on that since you're having a hard day." She pulled out her phone. "Here, we'll distract you with making fun of Deedra. What do you think this first dare is? Logan said it was a 'doozy.'" She tapped her screen a few times, then chuckled. "Listen to this. *Pucker up, y'all. School's about to become a Kissing Zone. To qualify for the contest, you must give a memorable kiss to someone you've never met. Details on acceptable evidence are below. The top nine students with the most votes will be entered in Deedra's Dares.* Insane, right?"

"Yeah, insane." But hearing about it wasn't helping. Deedra had five thousand dollars to run a contest, and I was still going to have to pay her money.

"That's not even the whole thing." Kat snorted. "*Entrants must also submit a secret they'd hate to have shared with the whole school. If a contestant pulls out of the contest, their secret goes public. This ensures contestants participate in each dare. No quitters.*"

"Kisses *and* secrets?" My coiled stomach added another twist. "Though that's kind of the point of 'Cell Block Tango.'"

Kat shook her head. "What kind of person collects people's secrets and blackmails them to stay in a silly contest? And what kind of secrets does she expect? 'I wear fake boobs'? 'I wet the bed until I was ten'? 'I have a total crush on your brother'?"

"Stepbrother," I murmured, watching Logan round the car from the corner of my eye. He wasn't wearing a cap this morning, and his hair hung loose.

"Who does she think she is—the Tony Soprano of high school? The only memorable kisses will be all the people kissing her ass. Pucker up, y'all. Deedra's derrière is ready for your smooches."

"That sounds more *Bachelorette* than *Sopranos*." I rubbed my temples, weary from the whole morning. "But go on."

Kat was in a mood to fume. Might as well let her get it all out.

"The Vortex of Doom has become the Black Hole of Desperation. Mark my words, our school is about to get even more disgusting with everyone competing for a few tainted dollars. The powerful are never satisfied."

"Never satisfied," I muttered in robotic agreement.

Kat shoved her phone into her pocket and kept going with her rant, slipping into that tone she used when discussing Earth polluters, misogynists, and cheesy boy bands. By the time Silva had released us and Kat had parked the car, she was finishing strong with "and then there'll be justice."

I threw a supportive fist into the air. "Justice!" How could I not be for more justice?

But nothing seemed more unjust to me than getting within striking distance of a dream trip to New York, only to have it swept away in one single moment by one mistake and an IOU to the richest girl in school.

All day I heard chatter in the school hallways about some girl who ran her ugly SUV into Deedra's car. It was a good thing no one knew me.

I had three pop quizzes, started my period two days early during English, and opened my sack at lunch to discover my banana had fallen victim to the Black Plague. Even Miss Holt provided no relief in my last class, with her announcement that we needed to take inventory of every costume and stage prop. Eight people crowded into the costume closet with me, and I spent theater tech jotting down items on a legal pad.

Logan spent his class time taking stock of sound equipment, so we never got a chance to talk.

Once I got home, I beelined to the Blu-ray collection in my room. Who needed streaming when you could own the movie versions of musicals? I realized just how crappy I felt when I flipped past *Les Misérables*, *Cabaret*, and *West Side Story* and shoved *Seven Brides for Seven Brothers* into the player. A bag of tortilla chips and a jar of extra-hot salsa completed my self-soothing agenda.

When my mom got home, I was hunkered down in my bed, halfway through the bag of chips, lip-syncing "Spring, spring, spring!"

"You're watching without me?" Her tone hovered between amusement and offense.

I usually saved perky musicals to watch with Mom, who was a sucker for happy endings. I paused the movie. "Long day."

She crossed the room and sat on my bed. "Long day or Alexander day?"

Alexander day was short for a terrible, horrible, no good, very bad day. That author had nailed it—some days really were like that.

"Pop quizzes, my period...nothing I can't handle."

Her long pause made me wonder if I was twitching. That's what Logan had said was my tell.

I looked away and busied myself with a loose thread on my comforter. I'd already decided not to deliver the bad news of my accident just yet. No one had gotten hurt—no matter what Deedra said—and Officer Silva hadn't ticketed me. So it was just about the damage to Deedra's luxury Lexus. No need to worry Mom—or face her likely lecture—until I knew how much it would cost.

Mom tucked a strand of hair behind my ear. "So, pizza for dinner and *Seven Brides*?"

"I'm almost done." A couple more scenes, the shotgun wedding finale, and credits would start rolling.

"We could watch another musical," she said brightly.

"Okay, but no Doris Day." Day was her favorite, but I'd already watched *Pajama Game* ten times.

"No *Rent* or *Sweeney Todd*." A little too edgy for her.

"Don't worry. I'm not in the mood for the demon barber of Fleet Street."

She laughed. "*Guau*, it must have been an Alexander day."

I pointed my chin at the TV screen. "Let me finish this final scene, and I'll be down in a minute."

"Charlotte?" She stared down at me with her own look of defeat.

"You okay, Mom?"

She shrugged. "Yeah, but the nonprofit lost a big donor. They're scrambling to avoid layoffs or pay cuts."

Her message was unspoken, the blanks left for me to fill in—we needed to conserve savings, not spend it. "I don't need the trip deposit yet." Or ever.

Her weary smile said thanks. "I'm going to pop the pizza in the oven and take a shower. How about you narrow down our film choices?"

I nodded.

She left.

I pushed play on the movie.

The scene resumed, and my phone buzzed. The screen showed an email from username Fined. *Fined*? I swiped it open.

It wasn't Fined after all, but FineD, as in Deedra Fine: "Attached is the police report showing you at fault and the estimate for repairs to my car. Payment due immediately."

Immediately?

I bypassed the police report and clicked open the PDF of the estimate. It included details, but I simply scrolled down to the total at the bottom of the page.

My gut sank like sandbags into the ocean. Over three thousand dollars' worth of damages.

The words *The End* appeared on my TV screen. "You said it." I clicked off the movie. "The End." Where was I supposed to get that kind of money?"

8
BACKDROP

I sat on the stairs of my apartment building waiting for Kat and scrolling my phone for job opportunities. I'd spent the weekend calling contacts to ask for babysitting and pet-sitting jobs. But between a divorce, a move, and three pet deaths, my prospects had dwindled away. The online job boards didn't look much better.

Kat pulled up in her Sportage. I clicked off my phone, got in, and moaned. "I'm going to have to ditch theater, wear a paper hat at a minimum-wage job, and work every hour I'm not in school."

"Good morning to you too," she muttered.

"Sorry." I added another sigh to the pile of sighs I'd exhaled the last couple of days.

She pulled away from the curb. "What if you just don't pay her?"

"She'll sic her attorneys on me. It was in the fine print of her email." Knowing Deedra, she'd probably pay her family's attorneys a bundle of money to get even less money from me, just to make a point.

"You can't quit theater. It's the only reason you get up every morning. Besides me."

I gave Kat a quick smile. She didn't share my love of drama, but she respected my obsession. "If I work around my theater schedule, it'll take months to make enough money to pay Deedra."

Kat tapped her steering wheel as she drove, always drumming. "Too bad you can't sell your plasma. Or your eggs."

"What?" I twisted up my face.

"You have to be eighteen to sell plasma"—Kat cocked her head—"and I assume the same is true of your eggs."

"I'm not selling my eggs at any age."

"Of course not." Kat shook her head, as if I'd come up with the idea. "What about your hair? Could you sell that?"

"My hair barely hits my shoulders, and it's boring brown. No one wants it."

"You might be surprised."

"No selling of anything on or in my body, please."

Kat pulled into a *primero* parking spot, well before school started, and faced me with a mischievous smile. "Well, if you're going to limit me like that."

I pointed at the football field. "Don't you need to get out there?"

She checked the time on her phone. "Oh crap." She opened her door, and discordant noise spilled in—band members tuning up their instruments for practice. "If I come up with a brilliant idea, I'll let you know."

"Thanks," I yelled at her back as she rushed toward the band hall to grab her drums.

I took my time getting out and walking into school. Catching rides with Kat gave me a full hour before everyone else arrived. I usually spent that time finishing homework, listening to music, or from time to time, pretending to be a Broadway star.

Not that I'd do that last one ever again.

The chill of air conditioning hit me as soon as I entered. Security lights let me see enough to stroll through dim hallways. The walls were institutional white with posters and flyers tacked up every-where.

My footsteps echoed in the emptiness.

Neon pink caught my eye.

I backed up and stared at Deedra's flyer.

What Would You Do for Money?
$5k to the Winner of Deedra's Dares
Contest Details on the Website

Five thousand would pay for all of New York and my debt to Deedra.

My chest clenched. That was a crazier idea than egg-selling.

With a sigh, I walked away.

I didn't even know where I was going until I stood in front of the theater door. That place was like a super magnet, pulling me back again and again.

I dug in my backpack for the bootleg key and let myself in. This time, I bypassed the stage and walked down the main aisle toward the soundboard. A small light illuminated the area, and a shadowed head peeked above the wooden half-walls. Logan.

My mouth went dry, but I kept going.

He didn't see me until I was only a couple of rows away. "Back for more singing?"

I gave a nervous laugh. "No, thank you. What are you doing here?"

"Mixing a song for my band." He pointed to one of three monitors on the table in front of him.

"Your band?"

"I'm in a garage band with a couple of guys. I play guitar and sing lead."

My interest perked up. Not because I was a guitar groupie, but *music lovers unite* and all. That's all it was, right?

Keeping my reaction in check, I simply nodded. "What do y'all play?"

"Classic rock." Of course. I'd seen him in that Bowie T-shirt and an Aerosmith one too, both artists Kat had in her playlist.

"Can I have a listen?"

"Um..."

I circled around the soundboard to his side. "You heard me sing. It's only fair I hear you."

"Good point." He pushed a few buttons and passed me a pair of headphones.

I slipped them over my ears. First came a strong drum beat, then a moving bass line, and finally a wailing guitar and vocals. After a few seconds, I looked up and smiled at his wary expression. "This is good."

He flinched.

I pulled off the headphones. "Did I yell at you?"

"A little. Hard to hear yourself. Noise-canceling headphones." He took them back and shut off the music. "How did you even get in? The theater's locked."

"How did *you* get in?"

He narrowed his eyes. "Impression of the lock."

I raised my chin. "Bootleg key."

A grin spread across his face, as if he was impressed.

With *me*.

Should I confess that our last drama teacher loaned me the key, forgot to ask for it back, and no one had come looking for it? Nah. "Bootleg key" sounded much better.

"I should let you finish mixing the song."

"You're welcome to stay. Do whatever you came here for. Unless I'm in your way?"

"No, I have a paper to proofread. Just came here for a quiet place to work."

"Then have a seat." He gestured to the back row. "Make yourself at home."

With a chuckle, I sat, pulled out my folder, and started reading. Behind me, I heard him shuffling around and clicking with his computer mouse.

My foot caught on something on the floor and slid a few inches. Looking down, I saw yet another copy of Deedra's Dares flyer. I picked it up and peered at it for a long time.

"That stupid contest," Logan said.

I turned around. "It's not just crazy. It's expensive. Why is she doing this?"

He scoffed. "Dee doesn't need a reason to do something crazy or expensive."

"Everyone has a reason for what they do, no matter how crazy." Like my self-performance the prior week, or the throwing up afterward.

Logan left the sound booth and sat beside me.

My body tensed.

He ran a hand through his tousled hair. "What's said here stays here?"

"Yes, but if you tell me two big secrets, and you only know one of mine, then—"

"Then you'll owe me one." He smiled. "When you're ready."

I just stared at him.

He seemed to take that as agreement. "Deedra's got this theory she doesn't need college. She wants to go into business for herself. And she thinks all you need to be successful is a great social media presence."

"This is about a business?"

"Not the dares part." He chuckled. "But Deedra made a bet with her mom that she could get a bigger number of followers on social media sites. If Deedra can outdo the highest-rated local news anchor, she gets to use half her college fund to launch a business."

Forget crazy. The word *ludicrous* made jazz hands in my brain. "Her mom agreed to that?"

"She was in the middle of something when Deedra caught her off guard and made the deal, but yeah, she agreed."

"Does her mom know about the contest?"

"Not yet. But even if she doesn't like it, it won't change the bet. Believe me, my stepmom sticks by what she says. Deedra knows that."

Their family worked so differently from mine, I could barely compute what he was telling me. "So the contest is about getting social media followers?"

He shrugged. "It's Dee's first effort at going viral. She probably has other ideas up her sleeve. Trust me, it's a magician's bag of tricks up there. No one connives like my stepsister."

"What kind of business?"

"Shoes."

"Shoes?" I instinctively wanted to hide my poor, needy Chucks.

"She's got super-thin feet. Says she can't find nice shoes and wants to design for narrow feet. Already has a name registered: Fine Nine Fashion."

"Catchy." I didn't know what I'd call a business if I had to use Romero. "So is that the reason for nine dares?"

"Probably."

"Are the dares going to all be public?"

"Why, you thinking of entering?"

My mouth opened to give a big *No Way*, but I shut it again. A prickle ran up my neck and circled my head.

"Charlotte?" Logan's voice awakened me from my daze.

I shook my head. "No, no, no. Of course not. No."

He drew close, seemed to study my face.

I peered up at him. "What are you doing?"

His eyes narrowed. "Looking for that twitch."

"I'm not twitching." At least I hoped I wasn't. "You've seen the result of me trying to perform. I couldn't compete, much less win."

He leaned back and folded his arms. "Actually, I have this feeling you could do all kinds of things. Might not be easy, but I think you could get there. Not that I'm trying to throw you to my sister, with her sharp fangs and her stupid contest." He cocked his head back. "But it would be a beautiful thing to see you take Dee's money."

I gave a soft chuckle. "Sharp fangs, huh?"

He just smiled. "Better get back to mixing. I need to make us sound better than we are."

"Sounds like you have your own business plans."

He stood, winked, and walked back to the sound booth, leaving me with a funny tingle in my tummy and a question in my head: Did I want money bad enough to do something *that* crazy?

9
CASTING

I couldn't put Deedra's contest or Logan's words out of my mind. But the first dare was kissing someone you didn't know. I hadn't even kissed someone I did know.

Plenty of people had no such hang-up. By the time I reached lunch, our school had become Lip-Lock Central.

Kat appeared at the table. "Tongues everywhere." She drew out the word *everywhere* like the kissing spree was a CDC-worthy epidemic. "I swear if someone tries to put his mouth on mine, he'll be kissing his own nuts."

"Thanks for that mental image." I pulled out the leftover pizza I'd brought. "Though I have seen a few slaps."

"Ya think? I wouldn't be surprised if someone files harassment charges."

I shrugged. "It mostly seems innocent."

"Innocent?" She yanked a sandwich from her bag and started to peel away its wrapper. "I saw a guy kiss a cheerleader's butt. I mean she let him, it was her spankies, and it's not the first time a cheerleader has had her butt kissed, but still."

I set my pizza down and rotated to face her. "Okay, so not everybody is handling it well, but some people are just giving polite pecks and having fun with it. Is that so bad?"

She stopped chewing. "Whether it's bad or not, it's stupid. If I don't call out stupid, then who will?"

"Maybe someone's doing it not because they're bad or stupid, but because they're desperate."

She squinted and rearranged a lettuce leaf in her sandwich. "What are you talking about?"

Did she know what I was talking about and just making me say it aloud? Did *I* know what I was talking about? "I want to enter the contest," I blurted out.

Kat froze mid-bite, every muscle in her body tensed. Even her hair seemed to come to attention, her pink streak leaning toward red.

I wrung my hands and waited.

Then wrung my hands some more.

She wiped her mouth with her napkin and lifted her head. "Not only is this contest the brainchild of an enemy, you have no idea what the other dares will be. Kissing someone you don't know is bad enough, but it's probably the tip of the humiliation iceberg."

"Everyone's played truth or dare. What's so different about this?" Actually, I'd played truth or dare exactly once. At age nine. When our dares were more like *eat a lima bean.*

"You don't do public performance. Not without..." She mimicked puking.

"I know, I know." It's not like I could forget. "But you could help me."

She tilted her head and gave me her sad-puppy eyes. "Charlotte, I know you need money, but the odds of you winning are really low, and the odds of you—"

"Upchucking," I offered.

"—are really high," she finished. "What kind of friend would I be to help you do something that will just make you feel worse?"

"You've seen all these people kissing." We couldn't get away from it. "Some of them have no more chance than I do. But they're entering. You never know. What if by some miracle I did win? Then I'd have five thousand dollars. Five thousand dollars of Deedra's money. Come on, Miss Rebel, think what a coup that would be. I'd get Deedra to pay for her own car repairs *and* my New York trip."

She leaned back from the table. "I'm sorry, but how could you win a popularity contest?" Sympathy oozed off her now, like she was a parent breaking it to her child that they weren't going to Disneyland after all. "You've spent years at our school cultivating anonymity. You're less known than a covert operative, and suddenly you're going to turn that around and take the prize in a public dare contest?"

"It's not just a popularity contest. You have to actually perform the dares in an entertaining way. And who has been around entertainment her whole life?" I punched my chest with my finger. "I know what audiences enjoy. It's just like any other performance."

With every word, I was trying to convince myself as much or more than I was trying to convince Kat.

Her hands settled on the table, still for once. She shook her head. "Is this your out-of-the-box idea?"

I straightened up and smiled. "I prefer to call it my Pandora's Box idea. Since I have no idea what it will unleash."

"You got that right."

"But what if I won?" I whispered. "You have to admit that would be quite the plot twist. And we could order a second drink at Taco Bell."

One side of her mouth flirted with a smile, and her fingers started drumming again. "If you're going to do this, you have to go all in."

"Are you offering to help?" Shock shot my voice to a high pitch.

"Well, if you're going to do it, I can't let you do it half-assed."

I threw my arms around her. "Thank you, thank you, thank you."

She laughed and hugged me back, a short squeeze. "You're welcome. But you have to promise not to embarrass me."

I pulled back. "I promise to only embarrass myself."

In fact, that was pretty much guaranteed.

10
DEBUT

I tugged at the blue-and-red spandex suit, far too aware of my curves on melodramatic display, then wistfully scanned the closet filled with theatrical costumes. Costumes that didn't have spider-webs crisscrossing in neat lines and beady eye-holes limiting my sight. I should have known when Kat decided to do something, she really didn't go halfway.

"You think this will work?" I stage-whispered. As if whispering would balance out the loudness of my outfit.

"It better. Dizzy said that Jeremy's a superhero movie nut who goes to comic book conventions and he'll eat this up."

Dizzy was the nickname of a guy in Kat's percussion section. She was always first chair. He was always second. They weren't friends exactly, but they had a healthy respect for each other's drum skills. Jeremy played saxophone for our Fearless Falcons Marching Band.

And as it turned out, they were the other two members of Logan's garage band. Kat's brainchild was to use one of them, figuring Logan would then use his popularity channels to push for my entry into the first round. I'd already met Dizzy once, but Jeremy was fair game.

I didn't like the idea of making my first kiss Logan's buddy, but it was going to be a peck, not even a real kiss. It didn't really count.

Did it?

I pulled the full-head mask over my face. "And no one will know it's me?"

"Not until you pull off the cowl and pose for my camera phone. If you don't make the cut, the video clip will die a painless death."

"The entire marching band will be watching, and this is going on Deedra's website. That's not painless."

"Do you want to do it unmasked?"

"No." My stomach did a full building leap. "I can't believe I'm doing this at all."

I'd been watching people kiss all week, and every smooch had tripled my nervousness. This was the last day to enter. Now or never.

"Well?" I spread out my arms, palms out, and spun in a circle.

"Why, Charlotte Romero, you have a rockin' body when you're not wearing jeans and over-sized tees."

"What?" Panic crawled across my skin, in whatever teeny space there was between my body and the sticky suit. I wrapped my arms around myself. "I can't wear this in public. It's so tight you can see what I ate for breakfast."

"Do you want in this contest or not?"

Umm...98.4% of me did not want to be in this contest—not at this cost. The other 1.6% of me screamed, *Need this money!* "You're sure no one will recognize me?"

"Do you regularly dress like Spider-Girl when I'm not around?"

I cocked my head in answer.

"Then. Stop. Bitching. We're good."

I tugged at the spandex licking my torso. "This suit should have bought me dinner first."

"Ready?"

"I am a million miles from ready. Ready is a distant planet in a distant galaxy in a distant time," I complained.

Kat just raised an eyebrow and waited.

I straightened, imagined liquid metal pouring into my spine and hardening to steel. "*Vamos.* Let's go."

It took one hundred twenty-two steps to reach the exit that led to the football field, my heartbeat stomping in my ears the whole way.

Kat led me out with a confident stride, the way she walked to marching band practice every weekday morning at the crack of dawn. She assured me her band director wouldn't freak about our plan, even if it meant Kat showing up with her tom-toms and drumsticks late, after my deed was done.

We passed a few students in the parking lot, but I kept my head down and tried to ignore their stares and snickers. Some catcalled. Others yelled.

"Where's the Green Goblin?"

"You can crawl up my wall, Spider-Girl!"

"How limber are you?"

Shock waves prickled down my spine. If I had actual Spider-Man powers, I'd be tempted to wrap those slimy guys in a ball-breaking web.

"Ignore them." Kat stopped and pointed. "Orange shirt. There. Perfectly positioned."

My gaze followed the invisible line from her forefinger to the guy sprawled in the middle of the football field. I'd studied the photo of him on Kat's phone—a decent-looking guy with a full head of straight black hair, naturally hooded eyes, a scruffy-hair-spotted jaw. Today, he wore a bright orange shirt and dark green jeans. He looked familiar, but I definitely hadn't met him. Dizzy had sworn that Jeremy was laid back and would love the movie reference kiss.

I swallowed, but the hard lump in my throat bobbed right back into place. "Maybe we should have tipped him off."

Kat shook her head. "While you practiced calming techniques, I read all of Deedra's contest rules, twice. Telling someone ahead of time counts as meeting them, even with a go-between. It's got to be a surprise attack."

"Of course it does," I mumbled.

I stared at Jeremy's back. He'd set his saxophone on the ground next to him, waiting for the band director to call everyone to attention. My nerves quivered and quaked. If this was my spidey sense, the superhero thing had overpromised and underdelivered.

Kat nudged my shoulder. "Sooner you kiss, sooner it's over."

I exhaled. "My first kiss. Here I go."

She grabbed my hand and leaned close. "Your real first kiss will feel completely different. Promise."

I turned back to her, a surprising bit of extra moisture in my eyes. "Thank you."

But she was right. I'd come this far, and it was one little kiss.

One. Little. Kiss.

As Logan had said, I could do all kinds of things, if I wanted it bad enough.

Kat let go and shoved me forward. "No more procrastinating. People are staring."

I glanced back with a grimace but walked in the right direction. From the corner of my eye, I saw her moving into position in the stands so she could capture the whole thing with her phone.

As I advanced, the attention multiplied with murmurs and a few whistles. Everything weird happening this week had been contest-related, so everyone knew why I was here. Phones lifted, and laughter pealed through the air. But Jeremy didn't budge, oddly oblivious to my approach.

Cheers erupted around him as it became clear who I was headed for.

I remembered the meditation techniques I'd worked on—deep breath in, deep breath out, rub palm with thumb, count back from one hundred—and moved into place, right behind him. *Seventy-eight, seventy-seven...*

He lifted his head and saw me. Surprise widened his eyes, and his face flushed. He had a nice face. Nothing spectacular, but kissable enough.

Before I could change my mind, I repositioned behind him, bent at my waist, and leaned over his head—my face right in his, upside down—and bunched the mask up to my nose. Exposing my mouth. *Seventy-six, seventy-five...*

His lips curved into a grin.

Applause rumbled through the crowd, a few instruments blasted, and a snare drum rolled.

My stomach rolled too. I flinched back, swallowed hard, and licked my lips.

No one knows you. No one knows. No one...

My heartbeat slammed against my ribs. I closed the distance between us. When my lips hit his, I felt his smile beneath the kiss. A snort came from his throat, like he was about to break into laughter. The kiss lasted one second. And five million years.

A cymbal crashed, and our audience whooped and hollered.

I pulled back, yanked the cowl back into place, and rasped a quick "thanks."

Jeremy raised a high-five hand. "Hope you get in."

On autopilot, I slapped his opened palm, though my own hand was clammy beneath my glove. Blood rushed from my head, leaving me feeling as if I was hanging upside down. Like the famous Spider-Man movie kiss.

"Show yourself!" someone yelled.

Others followed.

"You're not Peter Parker."

"Who are you?"

"Let us see your face."

"C'mon, reveal your secret identity."

In one quick burst of motion, I spun around and ran full speed ahead, my heart in my throat the whole way.

"Wait." Kat sprinted behind me, in hot pursuit. "Stay where I can see you."

I paused at the corner, waited for her to catch up, and we ran through school toward the theater. Heads turned as we jogged by. I didn't break stride. They'd know soon enough why Spider-Girl streaked by in a flash.

When we reached the costume closet, I tore off the mask, bent over with my hands on my thighs, and gasped for breath. Nausea swooshed into my stomach. Sweat soaked my skin.

Kat kept her phone camera trained on me. "Sit down. Head between your knees."

I sat on the cold floor and dropped my head between my legs. I took slow breaths in and out, while my head spun like a carousel. When I could finally speak, I glanced up to where she stood. "I did it." My voice sounded small, like all the confidence I possessed was tucked into a tiny space.

"And you are?" Kat asked.

"What?"

"Tell us your name." She remained focused on the end goal. Which was probably a good plan, since I sure didn't want to have done this for nothing.

I raised my head a little higher, making sure the video saw my face. Regardless of the jitters still crashing through me, I had to make this moment count. "Charlotte. Charlotte Romero."

11
Upstaged

All afternoon, the hallways were clogged with students sucking on each other and school staff trying to pull them apart. Phones were held at arm's length to capture videos for proof and for social media. Our school needed its own hashtag: #LipsGoneWild.

I could tell my kiss was starting to make the rounds by the number of glances I got in the hall. Some people pointed fingers. And a few of the creepier guys slid right into suggestive gestures. Two different times, I had to pop into a bathroom, lean over a toilet, and wait until I was sure nothing would come out.

When I walked into the cafeteria, it was with the plan of suggesting that Kat and I find somewhere else to eat lunch. I scooted along the wall and made my way to her as invisibly as possible. I leaned over the table and whispered, "Can we get out of here? I'm really rattled."

She looked up from her carrots and hummus and made a face like she'd eaten a pickle instead. "What are you going to do when the video comes out on Deedra's website? Check yourself into a nunnery?"

"That sounds very appealing right now." Especially since my entire knowledge of nuns was based on *The Sound of Music.*

"Okay." She sighed and gathered her lunch items. "You get today and today only. By Monday, we're back in this cafeteria."

"Because you love it so much?" She couldn't miss my sarcasm.

She tilted her head. "Because we're not going into hiding. We should be proud of who we are, and you should be proud of our entry."

Proud was a bit of a reach. I was just aiming for not-physically-ill. Which leaving this crowded cafeteria would help.

We were headed toward the door when Logan rushed across the cafeteria, dodging people as he went. I stopped moving when I realized he was aiming for me.

"Charlotte," he panted, clearly out of breath. "You didn't tell me you were going for it."

I cringed. "You saw the video?" I knew he would, but I hadn't mentally prepared to look him in the eye afterward.

His face broke out into a grin. "That was a heck of a performance, Sexy Spider-Girl."

Whatever I'd imagined, that wasn't the response I'd anticipated.

Kat nudged me from behind, reminding me she was there, we were supposed to go eat lunch somewhere, and I was probably looking like a lovesick idiot right now.

I kept my eyes on Logan. "Thanks. I think."

He laughed. "It's a compliment. I promise."

Jeremy strode up behind him. "Yo, it's time." Then he grinned and pointed at me. "Hey, it's my Mary Jane."

Logan sneered at his friend. "Just get ready, okay?"

Kat leaned into my ear and whispered, "Jealous."

My palms went slick. So she thought Logan was flirting with me too?

Jeremy studied Kat briefly, as if trying to figure out if he needed to acknowledge this third person, but then wandered off with a shrug.

Logan returned his attention to me. "Anyway, I didn't think you'd enter. Because...you know."

Yes, I knew. "I wasn't sure I'd do it until I did it."

Kat buzzed with impatience, tapping me on the shoulder and saying, "Can we leave yet?"

The speakers in the cafeteria crackled. Almost as if they were responding to the electricity radiating off Kat.

"Gotta go." Logan ran across the cafeteria and disappeared into the crowd.

What had just happened?

Guitar music came through the speakers, followed by a drumbeat.

Kat and I exchanged what's-going-on glances.

Our question was answered when Logan slid down the middle aisle of the cafeteria and started singing.

"Oh, hell no," Kat said.

I recognized the song. "Kiss" by Prince. Even I knew that one.

Logan toured the cafeteria, singing and dancing like he belonged in a boy band. Based on the cheers from the girls in the room, maybe he did. He smiled and worked his way around, stopping now and then like he might kiss a girl, then moving on.

The room tilted. He was entering Deedra's contest. Why? And if he expected me to tell him about my plan, why hadn't he told me about his?

Logan kicked off verse two, beelining toward the corner.

I spotted his bull's-eye. The girl had short dark hair, a pretty face, but thin legs that angled to the side in her wheelchair. I didn't know why she was disabled. She was new to school this year. We didn't have any classes together, but I'd seen her around.

Logan beamed, sang, and pushed her in the wheelchair from the table. The girl's eyes widened, and her friends at the table gasped and squealed.

My heart pounded like timpani in my chest. Some small part of my brain registered that the song was pitched too high for him, but that's not where my focus was. My gaze bounced from him to her, back to him, then her, again and again. He twirled in a dance in the middle of the cafeteria, stopping now and then to sing right at her and smiling like he couldn't think of anyone he'd rather be with.

Maybe he hadn't been flirting with me. Maybe he was just that way with every girl he talked to—making a girl feel like she was the only one he saw.

The girl laughed and started dancing too, waist up—her torso shifting back and forth, her shoulders shimmying, her hands waving in the air.

Logan trotted around her, playing up every moment.

The rest of the cafeteria went wild, clapping and singing like they were really at a concert.

Well, not everybody. Kat groaned next to me.

I scanned the room for Deedra, wondering what she thought of this performance, and finally spotted her. She was pressed against a column, her arms crossed, her jaw set, her cheeks almost as red as her hair. It wasn't hard to figure out that she was feasting on fury with a side of venom.

The song came toward a close. I knew what would come next. Everyone knew what would come next. It was about him kissing someone he didn't know. Getting into the contest.

I vise-gripped my own hands, letting all the tension flow into them.

He sang the final words, "And your...kiss," then bent over and paused, as if asking for the girl's permission. She nodded, and he planted his lips on hers.

It wasn't a peck, like I'd given Jeremy, but a full-on-the-mouth kiss.

My heart twisted.

The room roared.

He pulled away and spoke to the girl. I was at just the right angle to read his lips. *Hi, I'm Logan. What's your name?*

The girl nodded and spoke back. But I couldn't see her answer.

Logan spoke again. *Thank you.* Then he said something in her ear.

She grinned and giggled.

Finally, he turned to the crowd and yelled, "Meet Bailey, every-one. I've heard she's cool, and you should get to know her. And vote for me! Logan Barrett!"

I glanced where Deedra had stood, but she was gone.

Good idea.

Spinning on my heels, I walked to the exit. Kat followed and started on a rant—something about stealing spotlights—but I couldn't process her words past the fog clouding my mind.

12
ROLES

Heading to last period, I turned a corner and bumped into yet another couple snogging in front of the door to the drama studio.

"Sorry," I mumbled and squeezed past.

When I walked into the room, the whole theater tech class was chanting, "Logan, Logan, Logan."

My lungs seized, and heat flooded my body.

He stood in the middle of the group, wearing a cocky grin and accepting high fives and accolades from his new fan club. "You gotta vote, though," he reminded them. "I need support to get into the contest."

"And win!" It was Marita who spoke—the girl who spent as much time as possible playing with theater makeup. She could Lady-Gaga her face in three seconds flat. The way she was looking at Logan, I kinda wanted to jam her extra volume mascara up her nose."

Soy loca. I was losing it.

I stole into the corner, dropped my stuff, and curled into a sulk.

Miss Holt's stage presence arrived a millisecond before she did. She waltzed into the room, saw the hip-hip-hooray, and merged into the mob. Clapping her hands, she called everyone's attention to her. "Now, now. I also witnessed the official entry of one Logan

Barrett into this interesting contest endeavor hosted by the young red-haired lady."

"Deedra," someone added.

"Yes, of course." Miss Holt's flippant tone conveyed it didn't matter to her who Deedra Fine was. Clearly, Miss Holt wasn't a student. And hadn't hit Deedra's car. "Kiss aside—"

Whoops and whistles filled the room.

Logan smiled and gave a thumbs-up, playing to his audience. So much for my performance.

Miss Holt turned to Logan. "I want to know which part you'll be trying out for in our spring musical. That was you singing, yes? Or do you just captivate an audience with your charm?"

He laughed with her, easy and cavalier. Like the next break-out star being interviewed on a late-night talk show.

I wanted to spear him. Multiple times. I was sure we had swords somewhere in the costume closet.

Dios mío. What was with this new violent streak?

At least I wasn't feeling nauseated anymore.

"I sing," Logan answered. "But here, I prefer to run sound."

"I'll be working to change your mind on that." Miss Holt turned her attention to the rest of us. "All right, class, have a seat somewhere, and let's talk sets for *A Christmas Carol.*"

I plucked at loose strings on my backpack while the class discussed the plans for our next play. I usually cared about this stuff, but today I didn't care whether they recreated a nineteenth century street in London or painted a yellow brick road.

Was it that Logan entering the contest made me feel like I didn't have a chance of winning? Was it watching him plant a kiss on someone other than me? Was it how stupid I felt thinking he was interested in me?

When we finally broke, I was past eager to get to the costume closet. Maybe I could figure out how to install a lock on the door or erect a barricade with the clothing racks.

Logan jumped in front of me. "You okay?"

I bit my tongue for a few seconds. "Why wouldn't I be okay?"

"Well, you know, because..." He pointed back out toward the cafeteria, now properly known as Logan's Debut Venue.

I gave him a relaxed smile, channeling my acting skills. "I'm just tired. All the buzz about this contest and my video getting shared everywhere." Plus, you stabbing me in the back with your entry.

"It's good to have a worthy opponent."

I searched for sarcasm in his tone or a smirk on his face, but found none. "Could you at least tell me why you're entering? I need the money, but you..."

Logan gestured with his head to follow him to the costume closet. Where I was already going before he interrupted. Guess he wanted the privacy. When we got inside, he closed the door but left a gap. It was back to the two of us again, but escape in sight.

I dropped to the floor, cross-legged.

He sat too. "Deedra told her dad the car was ruined. He took it literally, and he's buying her a new one."

"He's *what*?" My whisper sounded way more like a scream in my ears.

"Sucks, I know."

"Wait." I halted and tried to sort out the family tree in my head. "So she stayed with her mom and you stayed with your dad and..."

"My mom remarried, Deedra's dad moved out of town. He tries to make up for his absence with money." He sighed. "Anyway, I have her dad's number, so I texted and offered to buy Deedra's SUV for five thousand dollars, which is a lot less than it's worth. He said okay, if I can get it in the next few weeks."

"You're in the contest to get money to buy her car?"

"Which infuriates her to no end." He grinned at that thought. "Although I don't see why she cares if I get her hand-me-downs."

"Surely your dad could buy you a car."

"Could? Yes. Will? No." He raked his hand through his hair. "But if I had my own SUV, not only would I not need her to give me a ride to school, I'd have room for my gear and could take myself to gigs."

"Your band has gigs?"

"We're working on it."

I could hardly blame him for wanting something he couldn't buy on his own. I knew the feeling. "Does your band have a name?"

He snorted a laugh. "We're working on that too."

"So I guess this is a case of *may the best person win.*"

"It's pretty stiff competition." He winked at me. "But I think I have a shot. I've been told I'm a pretty good kisser."

"Oh, yeah." I sighed. "Bailey."

"I picked her because I heard she was having a difficult time getting to know people. I think some people are nervous about the wheelchair. Stupid, right?"

I plucked at a stray string on my jeans. "Was she a good kisser?"

Why had I asked that? Immediately, I wanted to take it back.

He lowered his head, then peered back up through his curly bangs. "She was fine. Probably make some other guy very happy."

"Like Jeremy?" I offered.

Logan laughed. "Jeremy needs a special kind of woman. I'm not sure who. But not your basic nice girl like Bailey." He stood, walked to the door, and turned back around. "And definitely not you."

With that, he walked out, leaving me even more confused.

13
ASIDE

Kat said I'd gotten into the contest for three reasons: the high population of band people, the prevalence of superhero fans, and the creativity of the kiss.

She had to stay after school to work on a drum solo, so I had thirty minutes to kill before we headed home. I stood by Deedra's car, waiting to deliver the first payment for repairs and the secret to guarantee I'd stay in the contest. The longer I waited, the slicker my palms became.

I kept my head down, avoided eye contact. All day long, I'd been the subject of double takes, pointed fingers, and congratulations. Suddenly, people knew my name.

"Great entry, Charlotte."

"Nice outfit, Charlotte."

"I voted for you, Charlotte!"

I couldn't wait to get home, crawl into bed with the covers over my head, and recuperate in silence.

"Hey!" someone called. "Congratulations!"

I lifted my gaze and smiled at Logan, the only person besides Kat I was glad to see. "I'd say *you* deserve the congratulations, for coming in first."

Deedra had posted vote totals online, and Logan had been the clear winner with me coming in ninth. But ninth put me ahead of the fifty-two valid entries that didn't make the cut.

"Waiting on Deedra? Or me?" Logan's hopeful look made me think, once again, that he might be flirting.

But we were competitors now. I had to stay on track. "I've got her money. Well, all that I can pay her. And…" I took a deep breath. "I have to give her my secret."

Logan groaned. "Yeah, that was stupid, right? I had to dig up something she didn't already know."

"Deedra knows all your secrets? Even the…?"

"Nah. Not the stuff about my mom." The way he leaned casually against the car, his hair fell in tousled waves, and he spoke so nonchalantly all signaled he was Mr. Easygoing. But the tightness in his jaw gave his tension away.

I wanted to change the topic and save him the discomfort. "Guess you came up with something."

"Went with cheating on a test." He toed the parking lot gravel with his boot. "May seem like a small secret, but Deedra knows my dad would flay me for unprincipled behavior." He said *unprincipled behavior* like it was a direct quote.

"Well, you already know my secret," I said.

He leaned in and whispered, "And I won't tell any—"

A loud whistle cut him off, followed by some guy shouting, "Webalicious!"

I cringed.

Logan looked up at whoever was walking by and yelled, "Hey, show a little respect!"

Their laughter faded away.

"Thanks," I said, "but do you really think I'm going to hang onto my respect? Who knows what the next dare is."

"Oh, she just posted it. You haven't seen?"

My insides swirled. I shook my head.

He opened up the website on his phone and passed it over to me.

Your admission into the contest also earns you admission to my annual Invitation-Only Halloween Bash. Costume required. Your dare this week is to impress me. Impress all of us. Don't even bother showing up with some party store staple. Make your costume worth getting into the next round.

"Interesting," I mumbled and handed back his phone.

On one hand, costuming was my wheelhouse. On the other hand, wearing and showing it off. At a party. With a crowd. So many eyeballs and cameras.

"Speaking of the dare diva..." Logan pointed toward the school.

Deedra was strutting toward the car, red tresses flying out behind her. Even at the end of the day, her hair looked like it had been styled five seconds ago. She strolled straight up to me. "Charlotte Romero." The way she said my name, she didn't like it. Or didn't like me.

I pulled out two envelopes and handed her the first one. "This is all the money I have right now for your repairs. As you know, I'm working on getting more."

"As if you're going to win my contest." She peered inside the envelope. "This is barely a deposit on what you owe me."

"Just call it done, Dee," Logan said from behind me. "You're not even using the money for repairs."

She glared at him. "Stay out of this, traitor."

"Buying a car you don't want is not betraying you."

She stabbed the air with her finger. "You went behind my back and texted my dad."

"You were getting a new car anyway. What were you planning to do with this throwaway?"

I winced. Not only was it uncomfortable watching siblings fight, the very idea that a banged-up bumper made a car a "throwaway" stabbed my gut. And I'd just handed this girl my life savings.

Logan turned to me. "You should get a receipt."

Deedra cocked her head at him. "You're my witness. I accept partial payment." Then she turned to me. "And she should be grateful I'm keeping both insurance and police out of this."

Grateful didn't match how I felt toward Deedra, though I was relieved. The more I thought about it, the more I concluded my mom didn't need to know about the accident *or* the contest. Every time I imagined telling her, my mind showed me an image of tears rolling down her cheeks. She'd feel guilt for not having more money, worry about how to get the funds, or steep herself in sympathy for me.

"Whether or not I win, I'm in the contest." My hand shaking, I shoved the second envelope at Deedra. "Here's my secret." I couldn't believe I'd even written it down, much less that I was handing it to her. But then, desperation is quite the motivator.

She ripped the envelope and pulled out the notebook paper.

Logan stepped to my side, adjusted his backpack over his shoulder, and watched me. His sad eyes said he empathized, and his half-smile said he wanted to make his sister behave, but couldn't. She was like an untrained Doberman.

Deedra barked out a laugh. "Seriously? This is your secret?" She shook the paper at me. "You get scared in front of crowds? Big whoop."

My shoulders sank.

"Besides," she said, "I don't buy it. You had to kiss in front of an audience, and you did that."

In. A. Mask. And I wanted to die after.

Logan stepped toward her. "It is a big deal. And she doesn't want everyone to know, so maybe you could lower your voice?"

She tilted her head. "If it's such a big secret, why aren't you surprised? Must be that you already knew." She turned and passed the paper back to me. "Which means it's not even a secret."

I searched my brain for a response. But my head was swimming.

"I won't tell anyone about your little fear. But you have to do better than this. A bigger secret. Something you'd never, ever want out."

Logan shot her a dagger glare. "Do you have to be such a bully?"

"Deedra's Dares is a big deal to me. I don't need people in my contest who bring no new followers." She flicked out her hand at me. "Charlotte's not going to help my numbers."

Logan shut his eyes, like he couldn't even look at her now.

But he'd been right. This contest had an end goal for Deedra—beat out her mother's follower base, skip college, start a business.

She slid past, opened her driver-side door, and threw her bag in the seat. "I'll just call the girl who came in tenth. She's a popular sophomore. She'll get me followers."

Heat surged up my neck. Tears stung my eyes. Had I gone through the humiliation of that first dare and come in ninth for no reason? With nothing to show for it?

She got in her car and started up the engine. "You coming, Log-head?"

Logan's face flashed anger. But to me, he simply said, "It's not fair, but do you have something else?"

"Maybe."

He slung off his backpack, pulled a pen from a pocket, turned around and bent over. "Use my back. Write something new."

Deedra moaned. "Fine, but hurry up."

I grabbed the pen and laid the paper on Logan's back. All I had to do was tell a secret. One little secret. My brain churned and churned, searching for possibilities.

Apparently, Kat was right—I needed to take more risks. If I had, I'd be able to come up with something I'd done worth others not knowing about.

"C'mon!" Deedra stepped out of the car. "I don't have all day."

The only thing I could think of was my dad. Mom had told me the whole story, but it wasn't something we talked about or shared with others. I supposed to others it would seem like a huge deal.

I took a shaky breath and quickly scrawled: *I'm the product of a one-night stand with a male stripper.* I folded the paper and handed it to her, my hands trembling almost as much as my stomach.

Deedra opened the paper. As she read, a smile curved slowly across her face, as if my deep secret fed a need inside her.

"Good enough?" Logan straightened and asked.

"Oh yeah," Deedra said. "And Charlotte, I can't believe your dad—"

"Secret." Logan slapped his hand over Deedra's mouth. "Remember?"

My breath withered. I went numb.

She peeled his hand away, leaving a grin in its place. "I thought you already knew all her secrets."

"You say one more word to anyone about what Charlotte put in that note, and I'll not only tell your mom what you're up to but a few other secrets you don't want her to know about."

She pinched her mouth shut, got back in into the car and slammed her door, revved the engine.

I was stiff as a statue. Eyes frozen. Breath gone. *What had I done?*

Logan sighed then turned to me. "Get that costume ready."

"Costume. Yeah." No time to recover before the next dare arrived.

"You'll figure it out." He grabbed his bag and walked to the other side of the car. "Just make sure you're at the party. Our house is the one at the end of the cul-de-sac with an angel sitting in front of a big fountain. Completely over the top, but I didn't pick the house."

I nodded. "I'll be there."

No backing out now. Even if I didn't need the money, I'd just given Deedra my mother's secret as collateral.

14
WINGS

Kat and I sat in Jezebel and watched early party goers—dressed as anything from aliens to superheroes to zombies—make their way up to Deedra's house.

The home was exactly what you'd expect for a popular princess. The two-story brown-brick structure was half-English cottage, half-castle with turret-shaped corners and a cone-shaped roof. The landscaping looked like it had been maintained by Edward Scissorhands—lush and impeccable. An ornate fountain spewed water in a front courtyard. And just as Logan had described, an angel statue sat at the front of the fountain, spreading protective wings over the home's entrance.

I barely fit in Kat's front seat with all my gear. "Two costumes in a row. If I can do every dare without showing my face—"

"Don't count on it." Kat studied the house through binoculars. "Deedra's not doing you any more favors."

"I hardly think she was doing me this favor. She was ticked off I got in."

Kat lowered the binoculars. "Can you even pull this off? I can't stand at attention that long in marching band."

"When I was a kid and the drama coach called 'freeze frame,' we competed to see who could hold our pose the longest. I always won." I hadn't realized then it was a technique used to draw attention to a focal point on stage where action was still happening.

Kat swung toward me, and her pink streak flared in the moonlight. "So you freeze-framed years ago. I bet it never lasted thirty minutes."

That's how long we figured it would take for enough people to see me in costume to make my reveal worthwhile.

"You're not helping."

My stomach curled into knots, right underneath the latex-paint-doused sheet I wore like a toga dress. A pair of painted wings rested on the floorboard, ready for me to add to my costume. My silver feet were tucked into slippers I'd remove as soon as I reached the fountain. But the kicker was the metallic silver body paint that covered me from head-to-toe, including several layers in my hair. Not only did I have to stay still for a half-hour and pretend to be a statue, I had to somehow get all of this off in a shower when we were done. Before Mom's radar pinged, and she started asking questions.

"Sorry," Kat muttered. "I just want to get this over with. I'm breaking out in hives just being in this stinkin' rich neighborhood."

"Do not try to get out of this party. You're coming with me." Deedra's invite included a plus-one.

Kat closed her eyes, but the eye roll underneath fluttered her lids. "Why did I agree to this?"

I slid my hand into hers and squeezed. "Because you love me?"

"Oh yeah, that," she said flatly. But underneath, I knew she cared. If she didn't, she wouldn't be here. You couldn't *make* Kat do anything she didn't want to do.

I pulled back my hand and fidgeted with my outfit, not because it needed it but because I needed something to keep my mind and fingers busy until we were ready.

She raised the binoculars again, looking for a break in the stream of cars arriving. For an exclusive party, there sure were a lot of people here. A couple minutes later, she said, "Go time."

We shot from her vehicle, ran as quickly as my costume allowed, and reached the fountain. I settled onto the small patch of grass circling the stone structure. Kat took my shoes, attached my wings, and arranged my toga dress.

Headlights appeared down the street. "Go, go," I told Kat.

She bolted off with a whispered "good luck."

I leaned against the legs of the existing angel and rested my head on its lap.

The first people to approach the house included one contestant I recognized, a freshman named Kirk who wore rings around his body with various hues of green and a red bulbous head. Like every other kid in America, I recognized the Very Hungry Caterpillar from the popular children's book.

"...coolest party of the year," shrieked the girl with him, who was dressed as a large green leaf.

"I know!" Kirk answered.

They moved past with eager faces, excited voices, and a spring in their steps, celebrating the contest that awarded Kirk and his date an invite to Deedra Fine's Halloween party. Another group passed, then another, and another.

The cool night wind brushed my face. I wiggled my toes tucked deep under the sheet but froze every other muscle. The rushing water behind me seemed to whisper encouragement. I could do this.

"Hold on." A familiar female voice spoke near me, but all I could see from my vantage point were strappy gold stilettos with flowers woven in. "Your eyebrow's crooked." Who was she talking to?

"Can you fix it?" A low rumble of a voice.

Logan.

My heart jumped.

"We'll make it look great." The girl's voice sweetened and smoothed, like honey spread on toast. "Just like you."

My gut lurched. Marita—our drama makeup artist.

I couldn't see above their hips, but Marita's bare legs flanked either side of Logan's leg like a tango hold. It would be tough to insert more than a sheet of paper between them.

"Thanks for coming with me," Logan said. "And making this costume awesome."

Resisting the urge to see what he was wearing was like pushing a balloon under water. The urge popped up, and I dunked it again and again. *Stay still.* Kat would tell me when time was up.

"My pleasure," Marita answered in a whisper.

Had I misread Logan flirting with me? Was he into Marita? Crushing on him was heartbreak territory. It was—

A lip-smack crashed my pity party. Made it a funeral.

Marita moaned, letting me know she was definitely into that kiss. The kiss Logan was giving her. The kiss Logan was giving her right in front of me.

"Uh." Logan's breathless voice made me want to whack him with my wings. "Why don't you go inside? I'll follow in a minute."

I raised my eyes as far as they could go, just in time to see Marita grab Logan's butt cheek and squeeze. "Don't be long."

He chuckled. A shaky chuckle, like he wasn't sure he could hold out. Like he wanted to grab her back and fling her into his arms. Carry her up to his room. Shed those inconvenient shoes. Entangle their legs in the horizontal tango hold.

Chale! Get a grip, Charlotte.

Marita's feet disappeared.

Logan's feet shuffled closer. "Something here doesn't belong." He bent down, and suddenly a wolf face was in mine. Teen wolf to be exact. "Only one angel guards the Fine Fountain."

My eyes widened, but I tightened my muscles to stay in my pose.

His stage makeup was good—Hollywood-special-effects good. Hard-spiked hair, a harsh widow's peak and sideburns, a thick and crinkled nose, ominous yellow eyes, and fear-worthy fangs. Marita had outdone herself. Probably through hours of leaning over him with her boobs in his face as she applied the makeup. No wonder he was returning the favor with a slurpy, pre-party kiss.

I clenched my teeth so hard, my gums ached.

"Nice costume," he whispered. "You plan on staying out here all night?"

Another group passed, and someone shouted, "Talking to statues, Logan? You need a head doctor." They laughed.

Logan tilted his head and gave a *ha ha* smirk.

"You're messing with my plan," I muttered, trying to speak like a ventriloquist.

"Your plan being...?"

I clamped my mouth shut, increasingly annoyed by his presence. He was a contest competitor, Marita's smooch-boy, and on his way to being the guy who blew my cover. Why wouldn't he leave me alone?

Logan held up his hands in surrender. "You don't owe me an explanation. I just wondered."

"Wonder elsewhere." The piercing words jumped out of my mouth before I could gain control. I had no right to be jealous, and this was his house, but I was still peeved.

He sighed and leaned against the stone fountain's edge. "Look, about Marita…"

The front door swung open, and party sounds poured out from the entrance behind us.

"There you are." Deedra's machete-sharp tone made mine sound like a butter knife.

Logan stood quickly, his feet still touching my dingy silver gown. "What do you want?"

"What are you doing out here?"

He paused, long enough to make me think he was weighing possible answers. "Apparently, pissing you off."

"You do that by breathing," Deedra retorted, her voice retreating into normal range. "But everyone's here, including all the contestants. Except you and that whatever girl."

"Charlotte?"

"Yes, Charlotte," Deedra said. "Which means she's disqualified, and I have to reveal her deep, dark secret. Not the way I wanted this contest to go."

My anger shifted. I was the one covered in stiff paint, hanging out with a stone angel, and ignored by at least a hundred students passing by. But Deedra thought *she* was being put out. All because she was too self-centered to see a second angel in her own front yard.

I wasn't waiting on Kat any longer. I stood, and my wings rose with me, spread out on either side, curved around me like a frame.

From the corner of my eye, I saw Kat holding her phone out. Recording more video.

Blood rushed to my cheeks, making me sure I'd look beet red, if not for the silver paint. But I faced Deedra with a pasted-on smile. "I'm here."

Deedra's jaw dropped.

Around her, party goers peered through the doorway. Murmurs started.

"Wait, I walked by her."

"I thought she was another statue."

"Who is that?"

"Cool."

Logan stepped back from my imposing costume, but his musical laugh echoed into the fountain. "You didn't even see her, did you, Dee?"

Wait, did that mean Logan had seen me before he started tonguing Marita? Or after?

I wanted to run—tuck my toga dress into the crook of my arm, sprint back to the car, and drive away. But I had to go into that party, become the conversation piece of the night, secure votes for Team Charlotte. Get five thousand. Save my mother's secret.

Deedra crossed her arms, decorated with gold bangles to match her Egyptian goddess costume. "Is Logan your plus-one?"

"Um, actually—" Logan started.

"He's here with Marita." I waved Kat over. "This is my plus-one. She'll email you the proof."

Deedra scanned Kat. "No costume?"

Kat smirked. "When you're me, why pretend to be anyone else?"

We slinked past Deedra. I tried to ignore her haughty-as-a-goddess glare as we passed.

But when I entered the house, my confidence swayed. The party was elbow-room only, and everyone had turned their eyes to me.

At least I wasn't singing.

I fisted my hands and pushed myself forward. Tonight, I had to hope I wasn't dressed simply as an angel, but as my own guardian angel. I needed all the divine help I could get.

15
CHORUS

On Monday morning, while I sat at a picnic table outside school, a sanitation crew was probably hauling away my crumpled wings. Even my costuming skills couldn't repair the beating they'd taken at the party, so they'd ended up in our apartment dumpster.

A tragic fate for my angelic appendages.

Kat was at early band practice, and I was trying to finish my homework. Trying, but not succeeding. I lifted my chin to the sun and breathed in the crisp morning air. Something flashed in my eyes, and I squinted out at the parking lot. The sun's rays reflected on the gleaming red surface of a brand-new sports car, with a license place that read LUVDEE.

Deedra stepped out, clicked her fob, and the sparkling car beeped back at her. Like her own personal servant answering, "Yes, ma'am."

My spirits sagged. Here I was paying for her old car, and she was already driving a new one. An expensive, new one.

Logan strolled behind Deedra, bopping his head to something on his headphones. Completely oblivious.

I slammed my book shut, shoved it into my bag, and zipped it closed. A shadow fell on me, and I looked up.

A small, dark-blond girl hovered with a tense smile and a death grip on her backpack strap.

I gave her my own hesitant smile. "Um, yes?"

She dragged in a long breath, then sputtered out, "Y-y-you're Charlotte, right?"

"Yeah...?" The pitch of my voice swung up, making that *yeah* a "why are you here"?

"Your Spider-Girl thing was awesome, and that angel was incredible. I totally voted for you. Both times."

"Thanks." I smiled and stepped sideways to go around her.

She mirrored my movement. "I've told all my friends to vote for you. Not everyone knows who you are, but they will. We're getting the word out."

Was she fangirling? Over *me*?

"Tell your friends thanks too." I took another step toward school.

She matched my step.

"My name's Georgia." She giggled. Literally giggled. "I'm in marching band with your best friend. I play clarinet. But I'm a freshman. I doubt Kat even knows who I am. Because she's like...and I'm like..." She gestured with her head as she babbled.

"Oh, I'm sure Kat's seen you." I patted her on the upper arm, friendly-like.

She glanced at where I'd touched her, and a bright red flush flashed across her face. "Wow," she breathed.

My skin crawled.

Maybe I'd seen *Phantom of the Opera* too many times. Surely, this girl wasn't the type to kidnap me and stick me in a cellar.

She leaned forward, all wide eyes and broad smile. "You're the best!"

"Thanks. I need all the votes I can get." I smiled, added a thumbs-up, and sped away, before she could block me again.

A simple walk through the hallways confirmed that details about Deedra's Halloween party were spreading, whether Georgia did her part or not. Heads turned, chins lifted, hands waved.

"Great costume!"

"How'd you stay still so long?"

"Can I touch that heavenly body?"

My stomach lurched. Why were some guys so creepy?

I'd just opened my locker when Kat popped up. "You're not going to believe this."

"What?"

She didn't seem to have a clue about the attention I was drawing, too caught up in whatever had lit up her eyes. "Dizzy wants me to try out for their rock band."

My brain clunked through a few gears. Dizzy, the guy who'd lined up my contest entry kiss with Jeremy, had asked Kat to try out for the rock band that included... "The band with Logan?"

She gave a lightning-eye roll. "Yeah, well."

"You want to join a band with the guy you called—and I quote—a 'man-hussy with mouse parts under his wolf pants'?" She hadn't appreciated Logan kissing Marita either.

"Okay...but Dizzy says that Logan's a really good guitar player. And you don't have to like the people in your band. You play together for a while, break up, move on. Just look at rock-n-roll history." She hadn't looked this excited since the Guns N' Roses reunion tour.

I stared back and sighed. "You should do it."

"Are you sure?" She rubbed the back of her neck. "Because Logan was really—"

"Yes, I'm sure. I'm over Logan. He's out of my system."

She dragged out a long eye roll. "Oh, please. Next thing you know, you'll be singing that stupid song from that stupid musical."

"What stupid song from what stupid musical?"

"You know." She waved a hand impatiently. "That one about hair."

"The musical *Hair*?"

"No, no. The song"—she pointed at her head—"about the hair."

I sifted through possibilities, until it hit me. "*South Pacific*. 'I'm Gonna Wash That Man Right Outa My Hair.'"

She snapped. "That's the one."

"How did I figure that out?"

"The better question is, why have I even seen that musical?" *South Pacific* landed squarely in the Perky Musical column, among Mom's favorites. Definitely not Kat's style.

"Because you're a good friend who watches musicals with me and my mom."

"At least you can name all the Beatles," she muttered.

"John, Paul, George, and Ringo." I ticked them off on my fingers as I went.

"Look at my girl. I'm so proud."

I snickered.

She straightened up and looked past me. "Speaking of the guitar-playing man-hussy..."

I spun around, just as Logan reached us. My heart skittered. I'd avoided him at the party, but sidestepping him here would look petty. I should have rehearsed the role of nonchalant friend. *Line, please.*

"Charlotte." A warm smile eased over his face. "I want to explain about Saturday night."

Kat gave a two-finger wave. "See you later."

I nodded at her, then turned back to Logan. "Explain what?"

He leaned against the locker beside me. "Marita and I went out some last year. We have history."

Seemed more like a current event to me.

"Huh, I didn't know that." I delivered the line so smoothly, he couldn't possibly know how hard my heart was thumping. "She did a great job with your makeup. You looked exactly like a teen wolf."

And acted like one too.

"Thanks. Your angel was..." He glanced down at my body and back up. If he was even thinking something about my 'heavenly body,' he deserved to be slapped. "Your angel was inspired."

Inspired? What did that mean?

Now I was just confused. Confused about his relationship with Marita, confused about his newfound interest in me, confused about my feelings for him.

The first bell rang.

"I gotta get to class." I pointed. In the wrong direction.

"Okay, but I want to talk to you. Soon. About the contest and stuff."

He was back to staring at me like I was the only girl in the world, with those mesmerizing green eyes. Marita probably had that color memorized. Or maybe not, with her eyes closed during their kiss.

"Later then," I said. "Good luck with the contest."

He reached for me.

And I bolted. I had no idea where his hand would have even landed.

Was he planning to give me the same friendly arm pat I'd given my first real fan? Was he planning to stroke my arm, with the hopes of adding me to his girlfriend list? Two girls had tried sharing a boyfriend—a senior heartthrob named Hunter—at our school last year, but that had turned into a *Show Boat* sized catastrophe.

And I definitely was not interested in a cliché love triangle with Marita, Logan, and me.

I merged into the flow of hallway traffic, veered toward the outer wall, and ducked my head. I even slid a knit cap out of my backpack and shoved it low on my head. I needed exposure to gain votes, but not right now. Right now, I needed my comfortable cocoon of anonymity.

And a scalp-scrubbing to wash away the Logan thoughts that kept running through my brain.

16
CALLBACK

Eight more minutes until my next refresh.

I leaned back in bed and stared at the Deedra's Dares home page on my phone's screen. I'd promised myself to only refresh it every ten minutes until results showed up. Any more frequent, and I'd be obsessing.

Each round took two weeks. One week to complete the dare, one week for voting and tallying results, and *boom*, you were in or out.

I opened a new tab and hunted through video performances of *Wolff* songs, from whoever had posted to YouTube, then studied images of the stage costumes. The songs were amazing, and the costumes would be easy to assemble from our wardrobe inventory, with the exception of a man-sized wolf that showed up as a shadow from time to time to make the fairy-tale connection clear. But Marita had proved her ability to make someone into a wolf—literally and figuratively—so even that wasn't a stretch.

Between Marita's week-long Logan-helicoptering and my intentional avoidance, Logan hadn't talked to me about "the contest and stuff." Which worked for me. I needed to focus on what was doable in my life, not chasing fantasies.

Oh, the irony.

I flipped back to Deedra's website and clicked refresh. Nothing.

My phone buzzed. A text from Kat, which was unusual. Friday night meant football. Although I went to a couple games each season to watch her perform, she sat with the band. I wasn't going to sit alone for three hours watching padded guys slam each other on measured-out grass. So she hung with her band friends on Friday nights, and we had the rest of our weekends together.

Her text read: *Coming to get you. Be ready.*

At nearly 10:00 o'clock, what did she have in mind? I sent back: "Where are we going?"

No response. Ten minutes passed, meaning it was time to check Deedra's site again. But nope—just more silence from her and now from Kat.

I texted Kat again: *Hello???*

Dead silence. She was probably still in the band hall with a storm of noise. Two hundred people putting away instruments and plotting the rest of their evening. Kat typically ended up at a pizza or hamburger place with a few friends, but sometimes a band member threw a party. She didn't seem to like those parties either. Without a live band, Kat wasn't into crowds.

I hoped it wasn't a party. But I changed my shirt from boring charcoal gray to slightly less boring purplish gray. Then I washed my face, brushed my hair, and added a thin coat of lip gloss.

Moments later, the doorbell rang, followed by an impatient knock.

As I walked downstairs, Mom glanced up from the living room couch. "Who's knocking on our door at this hour?" She was holding a romance novel with a woman in a gorgeous red ball gown on the cover. Despite everything, my mother had not given up on love. At least in the fictional world.

"Kat." Ignoring Mom's confused expression, I opened the front door.

Kat looked like she was going to a heavy metal concert—cut-off shorts, Black Sabbath tee, leather jacket, and combat boots.

Before either of us could get out a single word, Mom yelled, "Kathleen! Come see me, *cariño*."

I cracked a grin and opened my mouth, but Kat lifted a single finger. "Not one word. Your mother gets a pass. *You* do not." Kat rarely let anyone call her Kathleen, but my mom had been like a second mother to Kat growing up, so she let it slide.

She beelined to my mom. They traded hugs and *how's it goings*.

Mom asked about school, band, her family, then finally got around to "Where are you two going at this late hour?"

I turned to Kat. Because I certainly didn't know the answer.

She grinned. "I knew you'd ask. But it's a surprise for Charlotte, so I texted you details. Didn't want you to worry. We'll be safe. Promise." Her sappy smile and bright tone reminded me that her tough exterior once held a Disney-obsessed little girl. Street fashion aside, this Kat looked docile, sweet.

Not that I'd say that to her.

I scoffed. "You're telling my mom, but not me?"

Mom dug in the cushions for her phone and read her screen. A slow smile spread across her face. "Interesting."

Frustration settled in my gut. They were teaming up, and I was left on the sidelines. How was that fair?

Mom looked up at Kat. "And you're sure these people aren't into anything bad?"

Kat held up three fingers. "Girl Scout promise." Never mind that Kat's Girl Scout days had lasted all of two weeks, since her mother had been unable to force Kat into the same uniform twenty other girls were wearing.

"Okay." Mom dropped her phone and returned her attention to her book. "If it goes past midnight, let me know."

And with that, Mom delivered me into Kat's greedy hands. "Let's go."

I followed her out the door, clueless about our destination but relieved to have something else to occupy my mind. Minutes later, we were on the road, driving through a less populated part of our suburban town. I studied the landscape for clues to our destination, but I was stumped.

Kat didn't talk, just played a Heart CD—among my favorites from her collection—and jammed out as she drove. My fingers fidgeted on my phone, resisting the urge to check Deedra's website again.

She glanced down at her phone, probably an address, and turned into a neighborhood with large lots of several acres and horses, goats, and even one llama grazing on some lawns. The moonlight beamed bright here with little artificial light competing.

I stopped mouthing song lyrics. "Where are we?"

"You'll see."

Finally, she pulled into a driveway. Or rather, a gravel path. The yard was large, but the brick house sitting back off the road was small. Several cars sat in the driveway and the lawn. Chicken cages peeked out from the backyard.

"Who lives here?"

Kat shut off the engine. "Dizzy."

"Why are we at Dizzy's? Is this a band party?"

"Nope." Kat opened her door. "C'mon."

I got out but stayed with the SUV. "What's going on?"

She swung her keys around her finger in a casual move that didn't match her narrowed eyes and pinched lips.

Music crept toward us from the detached garage. "Wait." Realization shot through me like a flaming arrow. "Is this their band practice? Your audition?"

"No." She waved off the accusation with the flick of her hand. "They're just jamming out, and Dizzy and Jeremy asked me to come by."

"Jamming out?" I gritted my teeth. "Then why am I here?"

"Why am I helping you with the contest?"

"What does that have to do with anything?"

She jutted one hip out to the side. "Answer the question."

I shrugged. "Didn't think I could do it alone."

"Fine." She walked over to me, boots kicking up dust on the gravel drive. "Let's go with that. I can't do this alone."

"Kaaaaat," I whined and got back into the car, my heart slumping along with my shoulders. "You dragged me to where Logan is?"

She squatted beside me. "I've watched you pining for that boy all week long, even though you swore you'd shampooed him out of your—"

"*Washed* him out of my hair."

"Whatever. You're going to walk in there with your head held high and show Golden Boy you don't care. Even if you have to fake it. He's not good enough for you. He only *wishes* he could have someone as good as you."

"But—"

"If you're going to be in this ridiculous contest, you have to soak yourself in self-confidence, Charlotte. This is a good time to practice."

"Self-confidence is not my thing." I stepped out of the SUV and straightened my spine. "But for you, I'll fake it."

"You just need to get out there more, let other people get to know you like I do."

"Yeah." I chuckled. "Because the world needs a teenage girl obsessed with musicals and stage fright. I'm a deadly combo."

"You are one of eight people still in Deedra's freak show."

"Now I'm a freak? Wait. Did you say *eight*?" I fumbled with my phone, opened the browser, and typed in Deedra's website.

"You made it." She shrugged. "Knew you would."

"When did you—"

"Dizzy texted a couple of minutes ago."

So that was what had drawn Kat's attention to her phone. "Why didn't you tell me? Immediately?"

She smiled, true to her name, with a feline-looking smirk. "I'm telling you now."

"Diversion tactic." I slowly scrolled down my screen. Logan was at the top of the list, easily advancing to the next round. Was it that wolf costume or his charm?

Moving down one name at a time, I noted other contestants still in the running. Walker, a football player who'd dressed as a walking shower and invited every girl to join him for a private scrub-down.

Shay, who'd dressed as a belly dancer and given a little veil dance to boost her chances. People were right—sex sold.

Although next was Alec, a brainiac whose Sherlock Holmes costume had been historically accurate down to his chain pocket watch, and Robin, whose Maleficent costume was entirely home-made. I should ask her to join theater tech and help with costumes. Kirk, the hungry caterpillar freshman. Matt, medieval knight, and...

Me.

Last on the list again, but I was there. I was a full forty-two votes behind number seven—it was a popularity contest as much as anything—but I'd made the cut at number eight. Maybe I should send that Georgia girl a cookie bouquet.

"Satisfied?" Kat stood up. "Now get moving and walk into that garage. If for no other reason than I spent two hours at Deedra's house listening to everyone *ooh* and *aah* over costumes and who's dating who. There was even a twenty-minute conversation about whether Marita's costume was sexy fairy or sexy woodland creature."

"Fairy," I murmured.

"Whatever. You owe me."

I stepped forward and gave her a hug. "Thank you."

She gave a low grunt that I translated as *you're welcome*.

When I pulled back, her mouth was slightly upturned in a reluctant smile.

"So"—I grinned—"does me going in there make us even?"

She barked out a laugh. "Not even close. You have seven dares left."

My gut went back to churning. "Don't remind me."

17
Audition

The quake in my stomach was matched by the quake inside Dizzy's garage. A blast of music seeped through the rickety overhead door. Drums and guitar boomed at a blow-out-my-eardrums volume, and Logan's voice came through the thin metal too muffled for me to get a good sense of it again.

Kat shook her head. "Boys. An extensive discography of ZZ Top songs, and they choose 'Tush.'"

I had to strain to hear her. "The whole song's about butts?"

She raised her eyebrows. "This surprises you?"

"Guess not." Given the taunts I'd heard in the last few days, it so did not surprise me.

The song finally finished, and Kat banged on the garage door, rattling the metal with her fist. I cringed at the noise, or more likely at the realization that there was no turning back.

The door screeched, and I recognized the face peeking out, since I'd kissed it a couple of weeks ago. Jeremy held the garage door halfway up. "Inside."

With a deep breath, I ducked under and entered the band's sanctuary.

From behind the drums, Dizzy yelled, "You came!"

"Charlotte?" Logan's arms dropped from his guitar, and his face went flush. Like I was the last person he expected to see. Had he known Kat was coming?

Jeremy wagged a lazy finger at me. "I know you."

Kat looked at Jeremy like he was gum on her shoe. "Are you kidding? She kissed you."

Jeremy's eyes widened. "Spider-Girl."

Kat pulled me past him.

Logan's gaze followed me all the way in.

The garage was empty of vehicles but neat as a well-stocked warehouse with large shelving units lining three walls. The shelves were labeled and filled with tools and household items. A light bulb hung from the middle of the ceiling, helped by two long fluorescent fixtures above each lane of the two-car garage.

"Hi." My all-points greeting was lame. But I attempted a smug smile at Logan to communicate *whoever you date is fine with me*. Not that I believed that. But I was getting there.

I would get there.

I smelled gasoline, but it mixed with other odors like lawn clippings, teenage boy sweat, and the faint smell of...of...urine? I turned up my nose and looked for the source of the stench. An orange tiger-striped cat lifted its head off the top shelf of one of the storage units and stared down as if I'd personally insulted him. A large litter box was tucked away in the corner. Apparently, the garage was not just a makeshift studio but also kitty's turf.

"Welcome, Charlotte." Dizzy bounced in his seat, his legs fidgeting and his hands twirling his drumsticks around like a nervous tic. "You jamming with us?"

I shook my head. "Just listening."

Kat had told me he was nicknamed for Dizzy Gillespie. From what I could tell, his only resemblance to the famous jazz trumpeter was being black. Otherwise, he was thin, gangly, and overwhelmed by his massive drum set. Though he did have a grin wider than his bass drum.

"You like rock-n-roll?" He drummed a quick solo, then flicked his drumstick around in a final flair.

"Classic rock, yes. Death metal, no." I wasn't going to add that I preferred rock musicals. Or that my knowledge of The Who came entirely from the musical *Tommy*.

Logan tapped his mouth with a guitar pick and smiled at me with his eyes. "We play classic."

Kat moved closer and studied the instruments. In addition to the guitars Logan and Jeremy held and the drum set where Dizzy sat, there was a two-tiered keyboard, a saxophone, and two more guitars. "What's the name of your band?"

Logan said, "Lovecraft Aliens."

Dizzy said, "Double Dare.

Jeremy said, "Brain Abduction."

All at the same time. They traded annoyed looks.

"So"—I gave a quick nod—"still working on a name."

"Kat," Jeremy mumbled. "Pretty sure the last thing we need in here is another cat." His slow head shake made the languid orange tabby cat seem lively.

Kat jerked up her chin. "What's her name?"

"Hendrix." Dizzy stepped away from his drums. "And it's a he."

Logan waved a hand. "I named him."

Kat gave an appreciative nod. "Jimi'd be pleased."

Jimi Hendrix. I knew that one—a big-time guitarist back in the '60s. Kat's rock obsession had leaked onto me over the years.

She pulled drumsticks from her jacket's inner pocket. "Although, the way he's hanging off that shelf, you should call him The Edge."

They laughed, and I whispered to Kat, "The Edge?"

"U2 guitarist." Jeremy sprawled on an old corduroy couch in the middle of the garage and picked at strings on his guitar.

My cheeks warmed. My whisper had echoed.

Kat pointed at the drums. "Can I give it a go?"

"Sure." Dizzy shoved his own drumsticks into his back pocket. "I'll move to keyboard. Let's see what you got."

Logan pulled his guitar strap over his head. "Kat will need time to settle in. Let's take a break."

Kat adjusted the seat and tapped the drums.

Logan walked over to me. "Let's talk."

A jolt of surprise streaked up my spine, but I didn't have time to react.

Logan was already nudging me toward the garage door with his hand on the small of my back.

I looked back to Kat, but she was near-hypnotized by a new drum set.

Once we stepped outside, Logan pulled the door down, cutting me off from the safety of numbers.

Just me and him. "Where are we going?"

He kept his hand on my back and led me through a side gate in the fence to the backyard, where there were wire coops but no sign of chickens.

Behind a large tree, we reached an unexpected trampoline. "Up here."

"Logan, why are we—"

"Give me three minutes." He smiled a *pretty please*.

I sighed and sat on the trampoline. Three minutes. But. That. Was. It. And I was going to lay into Kat later for letting him corner me. Was she so wowed by a few drums that she couldn't stick close?

Logan sat cross-legged in front of me.

The trampoline jiggled. I tipped toward him and had to lean back to right myself.

He tilted his head. "Why are you avoiding me?"

"Avoiding you?" I scoffed. "I'm not avoiding you." *Lie much, Charlotte?*

"Yeah, you are." His tone was calm and even, yet more insistent. "You're obviously pissed."

The night air added to the chill creeping up my arms, and I hugged myself. "I'm at your band practice on a Friday night. That's hardly avoiding you." Never mind that Kat lassoed me here with a rope of guilt.

"So you're not mad?"

"Why would I be mad?"

He narrowed his eyes. "You're a good actress, but not that good. You're mad."

"I just said I wasn't mad." But my huffy tone sounded mad. Hurt-mad.

I expected a sharp retort. Instead, he leaned closer and propped himself up on fisted hands, striking a casual pose. "I kinda like that you're mad."

My heartbeat skidded to a stop. "What?"

"Do you want me to repeat it?" He added a cocky smile.

Heat rose up my neck, crept over my ears, reached my cheeks. "I heard. I'm just trying to understand." Was he happy that I was jealous? Did he know that I was jealous?

"Charlotte, I—" His gaze darted sideways. Back to me. Away again. His smile fell. His hand jerked off the trampoline and onto his lap. Then he shot forward, wrapped one arm around my waist, and yanked me toward him.

We tumbled back onto the trampoline and landed near the edge. Our bodies bounced, but it was nothing compared to the bounce of anxiety in my chest.

I froze in place, my face right over his. "What just happened?"

His face flushed. "I...had...to..."

"Had to toss me around a trampoline?" I pushed up on my elbows and shifted to the side to wiggle out.

Logan turned out of the hold to let me go. But moving in the same direction at the same time, our combined weight just flopped us over together. The trampoline shook beneath me.

He hovered above, eyes glazed over, his breaths coming out in gasps.

Oye! What was he doing? If this was some play, it was awkward at best and more in the range of *way to piss me off more.*

I pressed my palms against his chest. "Get. Off."

"Okay." He curled his fingers around one of my wrists, lowered my hand, and sucked in a long breath. "I just need a minute to—"

"You heard her!" Kat's voice peeled into the backyard. "Get off!"

Logan glanced up. His breath withered again.

Kat vaulted onto the trampoline and pushed him off me. And shoved him once more for good measure.

"Yeow!' He scrambled away from us and touched his cheek. "You scratched me." He seemed to remember something, looked behind him, and fumbled back toward me.

"Don't you dare," Kat warned.

Dizzy came running, and Jeremy lagged behind.

Logan dismounted the trampoline like an Olympic gymnast. "I didn't do anything."

"You were on top of her," Kat screamed.

"I wasn't attacking—"

"I saw you, Wolf-Man!"

"Hey." I held up my hands. "I'm fine."

Kat planted her feet on the ground and her fists on her hips. "'Cause I got here in time."

Logan opened his mouth, but I pointed my finger at him. "You, shut up. And you"—I turned to Kat, and her smirk disappeared—"if I need your help, I'll ask." It turned out that I could be confident. But sometimes self-confidence came with a price.

A wounded expression flashed across her face. "Charlotte."

A lump formed in my throat. I didn't want to hear the explanation—not from either of them. Not right now. I jumped off the trampoline and strode by Logan, Dizzy, and Jeremy. All the way to Kat's car where I slid inside and slammed the door.

A few minutes later, she got in and started the engine without a word. We pulled away in silence.

A million thoughts invaded my mind on the way home. That weirdness with Logan, my tiff with Kat, how much I still owed Deedra, another dare coming. Nothing good came from them. Just a sick feeling in my stomach.

18
OFFSTAGE

Logan walked into theater tech on Monday with three nail scratches on his face. And not small ones. More like Wolverine had scraped his claws across Logan's cheek.

No matter how many times I'd gone over what happened on the trampoline, I couldn't figure out what had motivated Logan to suddenly drag me on top of him. It was the kind of move you'd expect in a movie where an explosion erupts and the hero yanks his love interest away from danger. But we'd just been sitting, talking, maybe arguing.

Still, I couldn't quite bring myself to believe he was a player. Maybe he had a decent explanation. Even if I couldn't imagine one.

Logan walked to the other side of the room and sat down.

Marita settled beside him and began fawning like he was her favorite pet.

I watched from the corner of my eye, mentally slapping myself for caring. *Forget him, Charlotte.*

Logan closed his eyes, whispered something to Marita, then looked over at me and moved away.

Marita folded her arms and shifted her stare to me—angry and accusing.

Prickles rose on my neck. What had he told her?

Miss Holt waved her arms, making her colorful caftan float around her. "Today we'll start assembling the set on stage. Rehearsals begin next week."

We had three performances of *A Christmas Carol* scheduled in early December. I had costumes lined up, but I still wanted to make the Ghost of Christmas Present more than the typical green fur-lined robe. To avoid thinking about Logan and the latest contest dare Deedra had posted, I'd spent the previous day researching ideas for the head wreath. If Miss Holt would let me beg off set assembly, I could hole myself up in the costume closet and work on my own project.

It definitely beat wondering and wallowing.

As soon as Miss Holt clapped her hands for us to get moving, I approached her. "Can I—"

"Charlotte!" She beamed a purple-lipstick smile. "Your angel costume was divine. If only this Deedra would let faculty vote, you'd have my support."

"Um, thanks." I'd been thinking of students watching social media posts, not faculty. At least I was sure—pretty sure—my mom wouldn't see. "Did you see Logan's?"

Miss Holt rotated her head, as if searching for eavesdroppers, then leaned closer. "His wolf was very convincing, but your choice was original. I'm still learning everyone's talents in this class, but your interest in costuming is clearly matched by great skill."

I let her words wash over me, infuse me with new energy. "Thank you. That means a lot." She had no idea.

She patted my shoulder. "Now what do you need, dear?"

"Permission to finish working on the Ghost of Christmas Present wreath? I want to add icicles."

"Just like Dickens's description in the original story. Do we have plastic icicles? I don't recall that on the inventory list."

"I'm going to make them. With plastic bottles and hot glue from home."

"How clever." Her eyes brightened.

So far, I really liked Miss Holt. She could be tough, but she also trusted our talents. What would it be like to act under her direction?

I wrestled that thought away. I was a behind-the-scenes girl. "So it's okay?"

"Of course. Just be sure to let me see the finished product. I'm eager to see how bottles and glue become icicles."

I spun away, ready to duck out of the room and head to my familiar port in the storm.

"Charlotte."

I turned back to Miss Holt. "Yes?"

"What about Broadway? I haven't heard from you on whether you're coming."

"I'm working on it." I swallowed. "But the first deadline is pretty quick."

Her face turned serious, and she whispered, "Am I right to believe that finances are an issue?"

I bit my lip and nodded. "I had just enough for the deposit, but I, um, rear-ended someone's car and had to pay for that. I'm still figuring out if I can get the money to go to New York."

Two contest rounds did not equal five thousand dollars. And the odds were still against me securing the money for New York. Basically, the contest was a Hail Mary pass.

"I'll get an extension for your deposit." She winked. "But let me know if you need help with the contest. I wouldn't mind providing a little advice so you can get enough money to come with our group."

My jaw dropped, but before I could respond, she strolled away.

I glanced up to see Marita still piercing me with her gaze.

Scanning the room, I located Logan lifting a wooden set of stairs to take to the auditorium. His forearms tensed, and his loose T-shirt couldn't hide the definition of muscles through his shoulders and back. His jeans hugged all the way down through his thighs, showing off a pretty squeeze-worthy butt. No wonder Marita had ass-grabbed him.

Clearly, I was addicted to wanting the impossible—winning a contest, going to New York, being with Logan.

With a sigh, I headed across the hall where the costume closet welcomed me with nonjudgmental arms. I pulled my glue gun and empty plastic bottles from my backpack. I cut the bottles into strips, heated them with hot glue, then twisted them into plastic icicles. Once dry, I'd hot glue them to the wreath, making it more crown-like.

After the plastic strips were heated, twisted, and drying, I pulled out the dare I'd printed from Deedra's website.

You are what you eat. Let's hope not. Because we want to see what you're willing to eat for five thousand dollars. As usual, make it public, keep evidence to prove you did it, and don't hurt yourself. It can be a lot of food, something unusual, or whatever you can come up with. Just eat something that makes us all say, "Wow."

The door burst open, and Marita marched in on stiletto boots. "Why you?"

My lungs seized. "What?"

She huffed then slammed the door behind her. Grabbing a chair from the corner, she sat and faced me.

I stuffed the paper back into my backpack.

"Logan was this close..." She pinched her index fingers together. "And I would have had him. But whatever you did, he's changed his mind."

Logan? "I didn't—"

"Did you have sex with him?" Her leg crossed over her knee and bounced impatiently. "You got to watch out for the quiet ones. Sometimes they're the most willing to put out."

I shirked back, as if she'd shoved the hot glue gun onto my chest. "What? No. What are you talking about?"

"I'm talking about *mano a mano*. You or me." She flipped her hair back over her shoulder. "And for whatever crazy reason, it's you."

She might as well have grabbed an icicle and stabbed me in the throat. Because no words came.

She waved her hand in front of my face. "Hello, are you listening?"

"Um, yeah." The blood rushed from my face, and I had the distinct feeling that I was becoming whiter than Jacob Marley's ghost. "You think Logan likes me?"

Her eyes widened. "You didn't know?"

Hoped? Yes. Knew? Nope, *nel, nada*.

I stretched out my legs and caught a sizzle from the plugged-in glue gun. "Ouch." I yanked the cord out and set the glue gun aside. "I thought y'all were reviving last year's romance."

She scoffed. "We went out a few times, and then it was summer and we didn't see each other. When school started, I was dating another guy, but that didn't last. A couple of weeks ago, Logan asks me to help him with the wolf costume, invites me to be his party date, and I figure we're back in business."

"Yeah, I saw y'all kiss at the party." The thought of it made my teeth clench.

"Whatever." She sighed and ran her fingers through her hair. "I kissed him, but he didn't kiss back. At the time, I blew it off, figuring he didn't want to get busy around his sister and parents."

"He didn't kiss back?" And it was *stepsister*, not *sister*.

"He told me he had a thing for someone else. He didn't say you, but he looked over at you. And that look was unmistakable." She was much less animated now, more resigned—the way I'd felt before she'd entered and thrown my world upside down.

"I had no idea." My head was floating, all the way up to the ceiling. "I thought maybe he was flirting before, but then I thought that was stupid, that of course he wasn't flirting with me."

"Then you like him too?"

"No." *Yeah, right.* "Maybe."

She stood and brushed off her clothes, as if the costumes had shared their dust while she sat. "At least I know you didn't go after him all *femme fatale*."

"Do I look like a *femme fatale*?"

She tilted her head. "The good ones don't. Makes for a good plot twist." She smiled, winked like we were friends now, and walked out of the room.

Left alone again, I checked my icicles—dry—and hot glued them to the wreath. The bell rang, and I bolted from the room with an overture playing in my heart. Logan liked me, I liked him. Everything in my life wasn't so impossible after all.

I just needed to find him. Then he could explain what had happened at the party and at the trampoline, and it would all sound perfectly reasonable, and we would talk and flirt, and he'd ask me out, and we'd kiss, and I would not think about what his tongue had done with Marita, and it would all be like the Act III finale when the hero finally kisses the woman he loves and the curtains come down with their lips molded together.

I caught him as he was walking out of the studio room. Eye on the target, I yelled, "Logan!"

Turning to see who'd called him, he took one look at me and shifted his expression to a steely glare. "Stay away from me." He stomped away.

I watched him go, my heart falling like he'd dropped it from the catwalk into the orchestra pit. What. The. Heck. Had. Just. Happened.

19
SPECIAL EFFECTS

Kat's family might've had a house and a yard, but the rest of her home was as lower middle class as mine. The Jamisons and Romeros weren't so much poor as broke.

And we were broke a lot. If it wasn't for used music stores, Kat wouldn't even have a drum set.

"Sorry about the band," I muttered. Dizzy had let her know she was not welcome back at the garage. Apparently, clawing the lead singer had made a poor impression.

"No biggie. Sorry about Logan." She only looked about half-sorry.

I couldn't blame her. "That was so weird." I still couldn't figure out what happened—why he'd behaved so strange on the trampoline.

"Yeah, boys, whatever." Kat stared in her mirror and played with the pink streak in her hair. "Purple or blue? And we need to look at this strategically."

"Wait—the band, Logan, or your hair color?"

"The contest." She gave me a *keep up* look, like I was the one veering off topic. "There may be seven other people in this contest, but you only have to beat out one each time. You can be last in every single round, except the final one."

I propped myself up on her bed with my elbows. Since Kat never made her bed, her sheets and blanket crumpled underneath me. Her walls were decorated with vintage Rolling Stone covers, song lyrics art, and concert tour posters. Right above her keyboard was a sign that read "Keys to my Kingdom," and the drum set in the corner had another sign with drumsticks that read "Weapons of Mass Percussion."

"What do you suggest?" I brushed my hair out of my eyes.

"Answer my question first—purple or blue?" For someone with such a sharp tongue, Kat could be such a girl.

"Blue. But if it mixes with the pink, it might come out purple."

She gave a curt nod. "Back to your problem." She grabbed a piece of paper on the way to her bed, then set it on a textbook and started writing. "Walker will sew up the football and cheerleader contingency, so he's in for a while. Kirk's got a lot of freshmen in his corner but nobody else—he'll last another round or two. Shay's willing to play up her looks for any dare, and since guys vote with their eyeballs, she can just eat something in a sexually suggestive way and advance another round..."

I watched a flow chart unfold under Kat's hand. It was like witnessing Napoleon come up with his battle strategy. She detailed how each would fare, working toward whoever she believed to be the weakest link.

"Which means," she concluded, "your best bet is taking out Matt or Robin."

"How does that help me figure out what to do for my dare?"

"Luckily, you have a spy in the camp." Kat grinned and tapped the paper with the tip of her pen. "Matt's in band. He's staying entirely because of the band vote. But I found out what he's eating."

"You found out what he's eating?"

"Cow tongue."

"Gross." I shuddered. "I don't want to taste anything that can taste me back."

"He thought about rocky mountain oysters, but—"

My stomach clenched. Fried bull testicles? "Even worse."

"Yeah, but Matt's not doing it because he found out that's what Alec's eating."

Of course. *Boys.* "Everyone's leaking their dare plans now?"

"Not you. And I've got your ace in the hole."

I fisted my hands and dug my nails into my palms. "Please do not tell me I'm eating monkey brains. I just can't do it."

"Nope." The doorbell rang, and she glanced at her alarm clock on the night table—3:01 pm. "Right on time."

"Who's right on time?" The conniving spark in her eyes worried me.

"Friend of Keaton's." Kat's older brother, Keaton, was off at college. "Keaton's senior year in high school, Wes was a newbie on the baseball team."

She dragged me downstairs to open the front door while my stomach threw a full-out nausea party. Whatever Kat had planned, it was bad enough that she wasn't even giving me a chance to protest. Or wiggle out.

"Hey, Kat." A tall guy entered, strode over, and held out his hand. "I'm Wes. You're Charlotte, I presume?"

"Yeah." I gave him the proper handshake. "Am I going to regret this?"

He laughed, then turned back to Kat. "You didn't warn her? What kind of friend are you?"

"The kind who wants her to win this contest. Telling her ahead of time will just make her buck me on this amazing plan."

She led us to the backyard.

Wes set a large case on the patio table and popped open the fasteners. He pulled out two sticks with fabric bulbed ends, a jar of something labeled Flammable, and a butane lighter.

This was not calming my freaked-out nerves. "What is that?"

Wes shrugged. "Tools of fire-eating."

"Fire-eating?" I shrieked. "I can't eat fire."

"Not now." He smiled. "But once I teach you my tips and tricks, you'll be able to swallow fire with nothing more than a slight sizzle on your tongue. And that goes away."

Kat raised two fists. "Charlotte Romero eats fire. Guaranteed crowd-pleaser."

I turned to Wes. "How did you learn—"

"He's a magician," Kat answered. "Works at birthday parties, Renaissance fairs, corporate events. Juggles and does Houdini escapes too."

Wes shrugged. "Haven't mastered the Houdini escapes, but I'm working on it. My assistant's better than I am—more flexible."

"You have an assistant?"

Something in his expression sparked, like this subject particularly delighted him. "Every excellent magician needs a quality assistant."

"Can I have an assistant for my trick?" I glared at Kat. "One who'll do the fire-eating for me?"

My evil eye didn't faze her one bit. She stretched into a full yawn, then headed back to the patio door. "Well, kids, I'm going to leave you to it. Your part, Charlotte, is learning how to eat fire. My part is convincing Matt's band contingent that beef tongue is no big deal. It's used all the time in Mexican cuisine for tacos and burritos."

"True, but no one in my family eats it. I've never once had my *abuela* say, 'Your tongue is served.'"

"Are you absolutely sure you know what's in her tamales?"

Kat left me with that disturbing thought, and I turned to Wes. "So Matt's eating cow tongue while my tongue will be getting third-degree burns. I don't think this is going to work."

Wes patted me on the shoulder, big-brother like. "Just listen, follow my directions, and you'll be fine. If I can teach Chloe how to eat fire, I can teach anyone."

"Is Chloe your assistant?"

He smiled again—a small smile that ran deep into his features. "She prefers *partner.* Anyway."

That was likely all I'd get out of him, so I let it drop. My latest dealings with guys demonstrated I had no idea how to read their species. "Where do we start?"

"We start with me demonstrating." He dipped the fabric end into the flammable liquid, then lit it with the butane lighter. "Watch the movement of the torch and my mouth. Focus on exactly what I do, and then I'll explain it all to you." Lifting the torch, he leaned his head way back and opened his mouth. The flames flickered toward sky, and scorching heat warmed the air around him.

My gut puckered. Should I pull out my phone to dial 911? Just in case?

He lowered the fire to his mouth and closed his lips over the bulb. Pulling out the torch, he grinned. "See? Nothing to it."

I was tempted to throw my hands in the air and yell, *I quit! I'm out.* Was Broadway really worth shoving an inferno down my throat?

Instead, I asked, "You didn't burn your mouth?"

"Nope. Could use some water, though." He pulled a bottled water from his case and swigged half of it in a single gulp. He passed me the other torch. "All right." Wes smiled. "Your turn. But we'll start with it unlit."

I stared at the fabric bulb. There had to be something else I could eat. Escargot? Frog legs? Spam?

No, if I had any chance of moving on, I had to do something no one else would have the bravery—or stupidity—to do. My muscles tensed. My gut hardened.

Time to swallow fire.

It wasn't easy to practice shoving a torch bulb into my mouth over and over without Mom catching me. I rehearsed about a thousand times with an unlit bulb in my room—which I'd learned was made of Kevlar—and several flaming versions outside when she was gone. I had to scrub scorch marks off our small apartment patio before she returned home. But there was nothing I could do about my mouth blisters.

The alarm to head to the cafeteria for lunch started a buzz inside my stomach, like a hive of wasps circling. By Friday, the only others who hadn't performed their dares were Walker and Logan. Who knew what they had up their sleeves, but according to Kat's flow chart, it didn't matter. They could eat bacon-flavored ice cream and advance to the next round.

I double-checked the supplies in my backpack, then wandered over to our table, not bothering to order lunch. Not only did I have no appetite, I didn't want to give my stomach extra content to get rid of later.

Kat arrived, drumsticks in hand. She tucked them into her pocket and sat. "You got this, but just in case." From her other pocket, she pulled out a folded paper bag. "There's a plastic bag tucked inside, so if you puke—"

"When." After all, this would be my first face-exposed dare.

"If you puke," she continued, "it will be contained in the plastic but unseen through the brown paper."

With a sigh, I accepted the bag and slid it into my pocket. Better safe than sorry. "Thanks."

She squeezed my arm. "You got this, Charlotte. No singing. Just a quick announcement, and then you'll be so focused on the trick, you won't have any headspace for your nerves."

I gave her a grateful smile. "Now who's the cockeyed optimist?"

While I laid my head down on the table and tried to settle my stomach, Kat monitored the room's capacity. I wasn't supposed to do my dare until the cafeteria was filled, since more witnesses likely translated to more votes.

And more vomit.

After several minutes, Kat nudged me. "You're up."

I stood, looked around at the large crowd, and sat back down. "I can't."

Kat palmed my cheeks, focused my eyes on hers, and glared at me. "Stop thinking about what you can't do. Think about how much you want this and how much Deedra deserves to have you win it. Plus, Broadway. Don't you want to go to Broadway?"

At this particular moment, Broadway wasn't that motivating. But I remembered the secret I'd given Deedra. Stupid, stupid Charlotte.

I stood, rolled back my shoulders, and walked toward the middle of the room.

Logan beat me there.

"You are what you eat!" he yelled.

The crowd fell silent, turned their attention toward him, and went wild. I shoved my fingers in my ears against the cheers around me. When the noise died down, I removed my fingertips and scanned the cafeteria.

Deedra sat off to Logan's side—a front row seat—tall and proud. She jostled her hair with a slight shake, like a swan preening herself.

"And what am I?" Logan paused. "I am hot!"

Hot? My heart caved. If he did the same dare I'd planned and practiced, I'd have nothing—*nada*, zero, zip, zilch. I'd be stuck with no ideas and no shot at staying in the contest.

Girls screamed the loudest, and one behind me tapped my shoulder. "Can you move?"

I sighed out a long breath and moved aside to lean against the wall. It was first come, first serve, and Logan had jumped ahead in line.

Dizzy appeared by Logan's side. "How hot are you?"

"I don't know," Logan said. "Am I bell pepper hot?"

Dizzy shook his head and gestured to the audience. "No!" they all yelled.

"Am I jalapeño hot?"

Another head shake. "No!"

"Am I cayenne hot?"

"No!"

My wasp hive was still buzzing, but more quietly now. Maybe he wasn't stealing my idea. All the hots he mentioned were peppers.

"Well, Logan," Dizzy said in a scripted, wooden tone. "These ladies seem to think you're habanero hot, but habanero peppers are more than twenty times hotter than a jalapeño."

Logan shot a gun finger and winked. "Bring it on! I can take it!"

Music came on, booming through a speaker—Buster Poindexter's "Hot, Hot, Hot." Wails and whoops joined the sound. The teachers, who seemed to be getting used to this being part of our school experience, traded a few glances and shrugs and let it all unfold.

Logan sat in a chair and pulled out an orange-bulbed pepper. I winced at the thought of him shoving that into his mouth. Habanero was an add-in, not a pepper you ate on its own.

Logan pulled out a second one. And a third.

Say what?

He drew out the moment as he puffed out preparation breaths, shook out his shoulders, and let audience excitement build. My gut clenched tight when he bit into the first pepper. He discarded the stem, ate the second, then the third. It would take a moment for his tongue to feel the heat, for the seeds to unleash their fire, for his body to absorb the pain and react.

His face turned hard red, and he growled out a massive yowl. He stood and jumped around, as if shaking off the flames.

Concerned murmurs trickled through the crowd.

Dizzy stood by with a tall glass of milk—about the only thing that counteracts a too-spicy pepper—but Logan waved him off. As if this was a test of his manhood, and he would show he had the *cojones* to take the heat.

My lungs took my breath captive.

He was sweating, profusely. His eyes squinted. His mouth curled.

Our health teacher marched toward him, clearly ready to take him to the nurse's office.

He held up a palm and pulled out an *I'm fine* smile, the kind even I almost believed.

She paused a moment.

The crowd cheered. "Lo-gan! Lo-gan! Lo-gan!"

He waved for the milk, and Dizzy handed him the glass.

Relief washed over me.

But as Logan drank, his gaze scanned the cafeteria and landed on me. Over the top of the glass's rim, his rich green eyes smiled. Was he gloating?

My wasps went crazy—no longer from fear but a readiness to fight.

I jumped onto a table and yelled, "Ya think that's hot?" Attention swooped toward me. *Dios mío,* what was I thinking? I cleared my throat. "I'll show you hot!"

21
PERFORMANCE

Looking out at the crowd, my mouth went bone-dry, my pulse pounded in my head, my stomach rumbled with anxiety. Their eyes were all on me. Logan's eyes too, but his were questioning. Curious.

"What's hotter than habanero?" My voice was shaky this time, but still loud enough for them to hear.

And they were listening. Hanging onto my words, waiting to see what more entertainment the cafeteria would hold today. Besides the guy eating three habanero peppers with a milk chaser.

Sticking my hand into my backpack, I grabbed the stick with a torch bulb on the end, a Tupperware of lighter fuel, and a butane lighter. Bringing this stuff to school would totally get me detention, suspension, or a call to the parents or police on any other day. At least I hoped on any other day.

I dipped the torch into the fuel, then yanked it out. Flicking the lighter, I lit a flame and moved it toward the torch.

"Oh no! No, no, no!" came a decidedly authoritative voice.

I swallowed a lump the size of my torch bulb.

Principal Dixon surged through the crowd, accompanied by *boos* and "party pooper!" He kept coming. "I cannot let you light a fire in the school cafeteria, young lady."

I clicked off the lighter, squatted down, and met the principal eye-to-eye. "I promise, sir, I practiced and nothing will happen. I totally know what I'm doing." *Totally* stretched it a bit. Or a lot. "I only need a couple of minutes, and then you can confiscate every bit of this." I paused. "Except the torch. I borrowed that from a magician."

His sour-faced expression made it clear that I was skating on ice so thin, one misstep could crack my high school career. "I cannot allow you to light fire on the campus. Can you even imagine what would happen if this was caught by the local news? Parents would be calling me day and night. Not to mention the fire marshal."

Panic swelled inside my chest. If I didn't do this, I had nothing. I had to deliver.

Kat's voice yanked me out of my stupor. "Wait a minute!"

I lifted my head and looked to where she had jumped onto our table. "Thirteen minutes of lunch left," Kat shouted. "Open campus for juniors and seniors. Everybody up and join us across the street. *Off* school property."

"What?" I asked.

She jumped down and began walking out. The crowd watched her go, looking like they wanted to follow.

"You can't just—" Principal Dixon started. "That's getting around the rules."

And then Logan was there, addressing the principal. "Actually, sir, the rules are that we can leave campus during lunchtime. The school doesn't control where we go and what we do, as long as we're back, ready to attend class, and attentive. Which we will be. Promise."

Logan's face was still pink, his eyes watery. It would be a while before the habanero stopped making him want to spit and die. But he held out his hand to me.

Confused, yet relieved, I grabbed it for him to guide me down from the table.

Students packed up and streamed out the door.

I joined the flow.

From behind me, I heard Dixon yell, "I'll need that butane lighter from you, Miss Romero! You cannot bring fire starters to school!"

I cringed but kept walking.

"You're really going to eat fire?" Logan asked.

"Hotter than habanero," I repeated with as mischievous a smile as I could give. I appreciated his defense of me, but I still didn't know where we stood—except that we were contest competitors.

We ended up on the other side of the street, in a parking lot outside a neighborhood shopping center. If what I was doing wasn't allowed there either, it would take a while for anyone to figure it out. A circle of people formed on the asphalt, with me in dead center, blocking the view of any passersby.

The weather was in my favor, with no discernible breeze. I'd pulled back my hair in a ponytail, having learned the hard way this trick could singe stray hairs.

I yanked two large water bottles out of my backpack and handed them to the people on either side of me, who turned out to be Jeremy and another contestant, Shay. "In case we need water."

Phones came out, and videos started recording. Kat gave me a thumbs-up from across the circle.

This was actually better. I was more comfortable in this smaller circle than the massive cafeteria. I steeled myself a second time and began again. "What's hotter than habanero? Fire!" As Wes had said, it wasn't enough to do the trick—you had to be a showman. Or show-woman.

I lit the torch and tucked a stretched cotton ball in my hand. Then I grazed my hand over the flame, grabbed hold of the now-flaming cotton ball, and waved it around a bit. From the audience's point of view, it would look like I'd picked off a lick of fire. I smiled, opened my mouth, and dropped the cotton ball in. Closing my wetted mouth carefully, the flame extinguished.

Before it was all out, I made sure to breathe out my nostrils, sending out plumes of smoke like a dragon.

Scattered applause showed they were somewhat impressed.

But Kat looked a little worried that one tiny plume of smoke was all I had.

I reassured her with a nod. Then I cocked back my head, raised the flaming torch above, and lowered it toward my mouth, trying to remember every single thing I'd learned. *Head way back, wet mouth, straighten torch, flame toward the sky, embouchure, count 1-2-3, sweet spot, close mouth.* I only had to get it right once, but getting it wrong would make habanero peppers seem like marshmallows.

The heat bore down on me as it neared my mouth. My nerves shook, but I couldn't let my hands do the same. I manufactured a new wad of spit inside my mouth, then opened wider and wider.

"Charlotte," Logan whispered behind me. "You don't have to do this."

His voice seemed to tremble, like my nerves, as if he was gen-uinely worried about me getting hurt.

Around us, the crowd began to chant, "Fire, fire, fire, fire..." Even if Logan cared, the rest of the audience wanted a show.

And you want five thousand dollars.

A shiver coiled up my spine. But I dropped the torch head and flame into my mouth, shifted my tongue and lips around to find the right place, counted *one elephant, two elephant,* and closed my mouth, praying I wouldn't die in a fire-eating incident in a shopping center parking lot across from my school with numerous eyewitnesses.

The flame singed the edge of my tongue, then extinguished. I pulled out the torch and held it high. The audience cheered and cheered and cheered and—

I did it.

I felt a hand on my shoulder, then heard Logan's voice. "Are you okay?"

"I'm fine." My mouth smacked as I spoke. "Though if you still have milk..."

"Here." Jeremy shoved a water bottle at me.

I gulped the sixteen ounces in seconds. It took the edge off the heat. The roof of my mouth and part of my tongue were lightly scorched and would hurt for a while. But Wes had assured me that the mouth heals quickly.

Suddenly I was the target of hugs and fist-bumps and shoulder slaps and "way to go!" Beside me, Logan was getting more of the same. For this round, we seemed to be the contest favorites.

Finally, Logan clapped his hands. "Hey! We'd better get back, or Principal Dixon's going to kill me."

The gathering broke up, and everyone started toward school. Kat approached and held out her hand. "Give me the fire stuff, and I'll store it in the car. You know they're going to search that backpack."

Good point. If he found this stuff on me, AP Dixon would not only confiscate it—he'd call Mom. I was still keeping her in the dark, even more now that I'd moved to fire-eating. No telling what she'd say about that.

I handed my stuff over, and Kat wandered ahead.

Logan fell into step beside me. "The hottest salsa is nothing compared to three habaneros. I'll never do that again."

"Likewise." Was this a truce?

"Really?" He nudged my shoulder playfully. "You're not choosing circus fire-eater as a career?"

I chuckled. "So you think I'll finally beat you in a round?"

He stepped ahead, spun around, and walked backward. "Let's call it a tie." Then he gave me the full-fledged grin. "Well played, Charlotte. Well played."

Before I could answer, he turned and jogged back to the school, leaving me hanging with heat in my mouth and in my chest.

Deedra appeared at my elbow, shifting the atmosphere altogether. "You've surprised me. Your entries have been pretty good."

I blinked a couple of times while making sure I'd heard that right. "Um, thanks."

"But I wouldn't get my hopes up. We're barely into the dares, and you don't have what it takes to win this contest." She pointed to Logan ahead of us. "You don't have what it takes to win him either."

I stopped short, and she kept walking. Just as I was thinking how she'd pushed my confidence off a cliff, I heard a crinkle in my pocket and pulled out the brown paper bag Kat had provided. I hadn't needed it after all.

The tightness in my chest loosened. So what if Logan wanted or didn't want me? Charlotte Romero could do the impossible—swallow fire and compete in Deedra's contest. Win or lose, I had every reason to feel good about myself, to feel and to be confident.

At least until the next dare.

22
Rehearsal

I sat in the back row to watch the play. It was Monday, first evening rehearsal of *A Christmas Carol*, and only halfway through this contest dare's voting period.

I'd barely seen Kat at school, since she was schmoozing everyone she knew, campaigning for votes. Kat's battle strategy was starting to scare me a little. What could she accomplish if she decided to use her powers for ill?

"But why do spirits walk the earth, and why do they come to me?" Ebenezer Scrooge bellowed his line from the stage.

I winced. His British accent was a miss. Although if you could get past the Texas drawl, Clay was doing a solid job. It was hard to bring anything fresh to this overplayed role.

Logan sat behind me at the soundboard, making notes on microphone volumes and listening to music from his headphones whenever Miss Holt stopped rehearsal to give the actors direction.

We hadn't spent time together, but we'd been friendly enough. I wasn't sure where we stood. Or why I still wanted to stand near him.

Miss Holt stopped practice again, and I shoved my earphones in. There was no music in *A Christmas Carol*, but I had a great playlist of show tunes on my phone. "Helpless" from *Hamilton* came on and sent me back from 1843 London to 1776 America.

While it played, I clicked over to Deedra's social media accounts and checked her follower numbers. They were increasing fast, at least slightly helped by video of me with a fire stick in my mouth.

My row of seats jiggled.

I jerked my head to the side.

Logan had settled three chairs down. He lifted his chin—another casual hello—and smiled.

A bit reluctantly, I paused my music and took out my earbuds. "You interrupted a really good song."

His mouth spread to a grin. "By sitting down?"

Bueno, sí. It was hard to ignore his swoon-worthy smile that close. "I thought you were doing sound stuff."

"Was." He moved down the empty seats and took the one right next to me. "But I have a question for you."

"So you *are* interrupting me?"

He gave a palms-up surrender. "You got me."

"What's the question?" And could I ask a few of my own—like why my heart was pulsing in my ears like Kat's snare drum?

He licked his lips, as if gathering additional nerve. "Is Kat more than a friend?"

"Well, yeah." I tilted my head and squished my brows together. "Kat's my best friend. We've known each other since—"

"No, no." He shook his head, making his loose curls caress his cheek. "If you don't want to tell anyone, you know I can keep a secret. I just want to know if you two are an item."

"An item?" *Ooohhh.* I was seriously slow on the uptake—woefully, stupidly slow. An awkward laugh spurted out. "No, we're both straight."

"You sure about Kat? She doesn't have a crush on you or something?"

"Kat's lead singer crushes are all guys." I paused, reflecting on this odd line of questioning. "Why would you think Kat has a crush on me?"

He rubbed his palms over his jeans. "For one thing, she's always protecting you. Like a boyfriend or girlfriend."

Yes, but Kat was always about protecting the vulnerable—lower classes, social outcasts, wounded animals, and her one self-effacing best friend.

"Also, the way she's talking about you to everyone." He cocked his head back at the school hallways. "Apparently, you're smart, sexy, and super fun."

My ears burned with embarrassment. "She's just trying to get me votes. When Kat takes something on, she goes all out."

He nodded, as if processing all the pieces.

I was doing my own puzzling. "Wait, is this why you were mad and wouldn't talk to me for a while?"

He grimaced. "I was mad because your friend clawed my face off. And you let her."

"I let her?" I faced Logan head-on. "I don't let Kat do anything. She does what she wants."

"You could have told her I wasn't doing anything wrong."

"You were on top of me!" My words came out so loud they echoed.

Laughter filled the theater, and someone yelled, "Way to go, Logan!"

Heat rushed to my ears, scorched my cheeks.

"It's not what you think," he yelled back.

"In case you don't realize," Miss Holt said from the stage, "we're conducting a rehearsal. Perhaps you could keep your conversation to a mild roar?" Her tone was half-sarcasm, half-warning.

I called back, "Yes, ma'am," at the same time Logan answered, "Got it."

Miss Holt gave an eye roll Kat would be proud of and returned her attention to the actors.

I slumped, buried my head in my hands, and considered crawling under the seats.

"I was moving us across the trampoline," Logan murmured, "and got tangled. I wasn't trying something."

"I know." My voice was muffled by my hands, coming out more like "I-moh."

"Besides, I'd never start something with a jerk move like that. I'd do something subtle, like hold your hand."

My lungs petered out. Was he playing *what if*? Or dropping hints?

I forced a long breath into my chest and lifted my head.

Logan wasn't looking at me at all. He sat with hands clasped, face blank, body language unreadable. "In case you wanted to know what it would look like," he muttered, stood, and walked away.

Leaving me with a gaping mouth.

Did he think I was hand-holding material?

The rehearsal continued on stage, but I slid in my earbuds and clicked play on my phone again, just in time to hear the word "helpless" sung one more time.

I knew the feeling well.

23
COMPANY

When the votes were counted, Robin was the one to fall off the list, her dish of rattlesnake not being nearly enough to impress a bunch of Texans. Even I'd shrugged, having eaten rattlesnake sausage before. Which does not taste like chicken.

Once again, my name was last. But my fire-eating—and Kat's relentless schmoozing—had kept me going. Even if she hated this competition, Kat loved to win. Or at least stick it to the "popular schmucks who garner votes by breathing."

Kat drove Jezebel onto the gravel drive identified as the location of our next dare. "Are you sure this is it?"

I glanced at the address on my phone that Deedra had texted. "This is it. I double-checked the address with Logan."

"I'm thinking haunted house. There's probably an abandoned building at the end of this road where a serial killer used to live."

I jerked my head toward her and stared. "As if I'm not already freaked out enough?"

"I'm just saying."

"You're not just saying. You're making me panic." I slammed my head back on the headrest. "What if it's like a documentary and we're pawns in a whole scare night?"

Deedra had given little information about our next dare.

See you all next Friday night, 11:00 pm. Address will be texted to you thirty minutes before. Plan to stay overnight. CONTESTANTS ONLY. All others will be escorted off the property by security and charged with trespassing. The website will provide streaming video of the event.

Kat dodged a pothole but kept the vehicle crawling down the bumpy road. "Remember, final girl, the killer is always in the basement. Don't go there."

"Great pep talk. *Gracias.*" No way Kat could dodge my sarcastic tone. It was far bigger than a pothole.

We reached a barbed fence with a sign that read Private Property: No Trespassing, but its gate was wide open.

Kat shrugged and drove through.

The dirt-and-gravel road ribboned through a huge piece of land marked only by trees and scrub brush. At the end of the winding path stood a large red barn with a man-made pond for livestock. This place was only a few miles outside the suburbs, but we were in farm country.

At the barn's entrance stood a man and a woman sporting black Security T-shirts, walkie talkies on their belts, and a serious case of *don't mess with us* expressions.

"What do you think this is?" I asked.

"Who knows?" Kat put the SUV into neutral and stared out the windshield. "I suspect Deedra was once a Defense of the Dark Arts teacher."

"I'm insane to be in this contest." I grimaced.

She covered her eyes with the heels of her hands, as if to stop herself from delivering her biggest eye roll ever, then looked over at me. "Charlotte. You have a freakin' fan club."

I shuddered at the reminder.

This past week, my superfan Georgia had set up an Insta account for Charlotte's Angels, an obvious nod to my Halloween costume. The moniker already had sixteen followers—sixteen more than I was comfortable with.

I tried to blow out all my tension in a gust of air. "Okay, I can do this."

"Pep talk over. Now get out and face the music." She lifted her chin. "Before those bouncers reach my car."

I twisted and saw the two guards striding toward us. Other cars and trucks were parked, but I'd needed a ride. Plus, Kat was my alibi. As far as Mom was concerned, I was sleeping over at her house.

I stepped out, grabbed my backpack, and leaned back in. "Thanks for covering for me."

"See you in the morning."

I shut the door, and Kat drove away, gravel kicking up behind her tires. My lifeline was gone, and I was on my own.

The security duo pivoted to return to the barn.

I started that way as well, slapping at insects that landed on my exposed skin. It being a warm night, I'd gone for jeans, short sleeves, and a just-in-case jacket tied around my waist. Maybe I should have worn a mosquito net instead.

Seven contestants huddled together at the barn entrance.

Logan waved at me, and my heart fluttered. Nothing more had happened since that odd back-and-forth in the theater, but since then, he'd been amiable. I didn't know how else to describe the friendliness that hadn't quite reached flirting.

Or had it?

I was starting to think my steady diet of musicals had set unrealistic expectations. Unless Logan stopped traffic to sing me a love song, how would I know he liked me?

I strode up to him.

"Hey." He nudged me with his elbow. "You're the last to show."

I checked my phone's clock. "And yet, it's only 10:59."

"Ready?"

I shook my head. "I have no idea what this is, but I'm not ready."

Logan laughed.

Deedra stepped out from the barn, grabbing our attention. She took a commander stance, feet spread shoulder-width apart, arms crossed behind her, chin lifted high. She even wore olive-green pants and a black shirt, as if infiltrating enemy premises instead of running a high-stakes game in the sticks.

Logan pointed to a pole behind our group. "Camera," he whispered.

Sure enough, a camera was mounted on the pole and directed right at Deedra, already filming.

"Rules," she announced. "Nothing comes inside but you and your clothing. No survival equipment, no food, no supplies, no phones..."

Some contestants groaned, a few protested, and I caught several curse words.

Apparently, I wasn't the only one who'd packed provisions. So much for my backpack loaded with a flashlight, hand sanitizer, water purification tablets, a blanket, snacks, and a change of clothes.

"No. Phones," she repeated. "We'll hold onto your stuff, keep it securely stored overnight, and it'll be returned in the morning."

She cocked out her hip and squinted. "And don't try to stash something away. You'll be thoroughly checked before you enter."

Deedra's long red hair lifted in the breeze, and she tucked a few strands behind one ear, showing off a pair of statement earrings. "Line up, get searched, then I'll tell you the rest."

We shuffled closer, amoeba-like, and kicked up a cloud of dirt as we approached. We took turns getting our TSA-worthy body search. Security discovered a few items of food, electronics, and other supplies in pockets, and socks. Though she probably could have gotten away with it, Shay made a big show of pulling lock-picks from her bra and boasted, "The rest of what's in this bra is all mine."

I winced.

Kat was right—Shay was playing the sexy angle to get more votes.

Not my plan.

Once everyone had been searched, Deedra took charge again. "Rules are you stay in your stall all night long. If you leave or try to leave, you're disqualified. There are cameras watching every space in the barn. Don't try to disable them. We'll know, and that will also get you disqualified."

I couldn't imagine how she even pulled off stuff like this. Getting permission to use this land, hiring security, running cameras, streaming video on the website. This dare experience had to be costing her more than the five-thousand-dollar prize. She was seriously motivated to avoid college and start her own business.

"If you have a medical emergency," she said, "bang on the door, and a guard will answer. Otherwise, we'll see you in the morning."

Logan narrowed his eyes, suspicion lining his features. "That's it? Stay in a barn? That's the dare?"

"That's the dare." Her coral-hued lips spread into a *gotcha* smile, one that seemed reserved for him. But it flashed by quickly, and she turned to open the barn's door.

"How will people vote?" Walker asked. "Despite the totals last time, my dare was the best, but how do we do best at staying in a barn?"

I wouldn't call his last dare the best, but I had to admit that licking the cafeteria room floor was even riskier than eating fire. His immune system must be made of steel.

"People will figure out how to vote." Deedra smirked. "Just don't lick this floor."

She waved us inside.

I walked through, and stopped.

"Holy—" Walker held his sleeve up over his mouth and nose. "It smells like a crap factory."

"Maybe because it is a crap factory," I murmured. The smell of animal dung matched the *moos* and *snorts* and banging of tails on stall doors.

Deedra held up a hand to get our attention. "I'll assign you to your stall. All you have to do is stay overnight. That's it. That's all." She looked straight at Logan, then grinned.

I whispered to him, "Why does she keep looking at you?"

He leaned into my ear and spoke low. "I don't know. She still doesn't want me in this contest. But I'm good with animals."

"Walker and Shay," Deedra said, "you're in the cow stall. Watch out for the patty."

Walker scowled. "I'm happy to spend the night with Shay, but cows?"

Shay folded her arms over her tight T-shirt. "Like you're not used to bullshit?"

Deedra held out her arm and pointed toward the stall, *a la* Ghost of Christmas Present. "Matt, Kirk, and Alec, you three are in the horse stall. Please don't get kicked."

Matt had outdoorsman written all over him. He strode confidently toward the horses' whinnies, and Kirk and Alec followed.

"Logan and Charlotte, you're in the pig stall."

"Great." Logan's chipper tone oozed confidence. "Piece. Of. Cake. Pigs are my favorite."

Deedra fought a smile tugging on her mouth.

Logan might want her to believe he wasn't concerned, but as we walked toward the back of the barn, I had an unmistakable feeling she'd planted more than pigs in our stall.

I pinched my nose and followed Logan into the small space.

He held the door open for me, then closed it to keep us and the swine from escaping.

Moments later, the barn's main door opened and shut. There was a loud rattle of the padlock being secured.

Logan winked. "How did I get so lucky to have the prettiest girl in my stall?"

Heat seared my ears and burned my chest.

No love song, but that was unmistakable flirting.

"Compared to...?" I gestured to our present company of pigs.

"Hey, I'm sure this one"—he pointed to a ginger-brown pig in the corner—"is a real babe for her breed."

I laughed, scanned the stall, and noted a security camera tucked into a ceiling corner. I flinched then pointed. "Um...look."

His gaze followed my finger up to the camera, and he nodded. "Yep, we're on display." Like it was no big deal. Like a video of him saying I was pretty was perfectly fine to stream to the entire world.

Logan kicked at the hay on the floor and walked over to the three pigs in the corner curled into a pile. They hadn't even stirred when we entered. "I don't know why she thought we couldn't handle a few pigs."

One pig lifted its head and snorted.

Logan rubbed its ears, like he'd done this a million times. "That's right. We're your bunkmates for the night. And tomorrow, we'll both be put out to pasture."

I strolled over warily. "You know something about pigs?"

"Farm field trips in elementary school. A few friends in FFA. Not much."

I squatted and rubbed my hands over the pig's ear. It was bristly yet soft. Another pig lifted its head, and Logan moved to pet her. The third pig rose, and soon we had a trio demanding our attention. They were like puppies, rolling around on the hay and reveling in our pampering. We couldn't help but laugh.

One popped up and rotated around us. "Hey, they want to dance," Logan said brightly. "Let's do it."

My lungs pinched. "Dance?"

"Someone is getting eliminated after tonight." He pointed to the camera's eye. "I bet it won't be the people who make friends with pigs and turn their stall into a dance floor."

Kat would likely agree.

Logan grabbed me around the waist and pulled me close. "Ready?"

One side of my brain said *no, I'm not ready to dance in a pig stall with you for the whole world to see.*

The other side said *yes, put your arm around me and pull me close.*

What came out of my mouth was "There's no music."

He lifted his chin and sang out the chorus of "I Saw Her Standing There," loud and proud.

Laughter bubbled up inside me and broke out in a giggle—partly for the fun I was having, but also the embarrassment I was feeling. People were going to watch this.

A yell came from somewhere else in the barn. "Shut up, Barrett! This ain't a Beatles concert."

Ignoring them, he twirled me around and sang at the top of his lungs while I followed and dodged pigs' feet when we got too close.

Kat would be proud of me for recognizing the song about a guy falling in love with a seventeen-year-old girl on the dance floor. Meanwhile, I was trying not to put too much stock in his song choice. Still, a girl could hope...

He dipped me, and I squealed like a pig myself, shocked by the move. We both laughed.

And then, his arms stiffened, his face went white, and his whole body froze.

"Logan?" I was still in the dip, kept from falling only by Logan's locked arms.

He didn't answer. Couldn't answer. His gaze was stuck on something above me, and his breaths came out shaky and uneven.

I dropped my head back to see what he was looking at.

A nest of spiders clung to the stall's corner, and webs stretched across wood planks and beams. Spiders crawled up and down the wall.

One more look at Logan, and I knew why Deedra had given him this stall.

"Logan, pull me up."

He didn't move.

"Logan, listen to me. You have to move."

I tried to slide myself out from his arms, but he was like stone, unable to shift a single muscle. My best option was gravity. I let my footing go and yanked him toward me.

We tumbled to the ground, barely missing a pig. It scurried away to a small haystack.

Still, Logan kept his eyes trained on the corner and the spiders, his jaw clenched and his throat tight.

Arachnophobia. A paralyzing fear of spiders.

No wonder he was sympathetic about my stage fright.

24
Scene

Logan lay beside me on the hay, eyes wide, face pale. We were a few feet from the spiders' nest—not nearly far enough for a guy with arachnophobia.

With every ounce of strength I could muster, I pushed him from the corner. "Just get away. I got this."

I spotted a bucket, scooped it up, and went back to the corner, nudging a pig aside with my foot. I stretched on my tiptoes and swiped at the nest with my hand.

"No!" Logan yelled.

"It's okay." For once, I was the cool and collected one, my tone smooth and reassuring. "They aren't black widows or brown recluses. Just your common, everyday barn spider."

"I'm s-s-sorry." His voice was breathy, but he could make words now. "It's no big—"

"You don't need to apologize." I made sure to keep my voice down. The whole barn had heard our singing, but Logan's fear of spiders didn't need to be everyone's business. "Everyone's afraid of something."

He bobbed his chin once.

I scraped at the wall, sliding every spider I could find into the bucket. They scurried around the metal bottom and crawled up the sides, but when they got too high, I shook the bucket and they dropped back down. I shucked off my jacket, covered the opening, and cocked my head toward the entrance. "Open up, and I'll get rid of them."

"You can't leave the stall."

"I won't leave, but I need to get them out of here." He exhaled a shuddering breath, opened the door, and scooted aside.

I peered out and saw a rake propped just outside our stall and a water puddle beyond it. I'd rather take the spiders outside and free them, but we were stuck and Logan would probably be a nervous wreck all night if he thought they were still alive. So I reached out with one arm, grabbed the rake, and positioned the bucket on its wooden handle. With the bucket dangling from the rake, I stretched out and dumped the spiders into the water. At least, I hoped they landed there.

I tossed the bucket and rake away, closed the stall door, and turned back to Logan.

He sat in the opposite corner on a rough blanket he'd found somewhere, his head and its messy curls tucked into his hands. He looked up when I entered. "Are they gone?"

"Drowned." Or at least too waterlogged to crawl back to the stall quickly. "And if you see any more, I'll get rid of them. Just let me know."

He threw his head back, clonking it against the wall. "There's no way I'm sleeping tonight."

I slid down next to him. "So Deedra knows?"

"She knows." He blew out a gust of air and tried to smile. "Confession? That's why I fell on you on the trampoline."

I scurried back in my brain to that night when he'd fallen on top of me. "There was a spider?"

"Yeah." He visibly shuddered. "On the edge of the trampoline. I had to get away from it. And protect you."

"Protect me?" Surprise rippled through me. "I let a tarantula crawl on my arm at the zoo."

He made a half-grimace, half-smile. Disgusted but impressed. "You let a tarantula crawl on you?"

"Obviously, we have different fears."

He sighed then wove his fingers into mine.

My heart skipped a beat, two beats, maybe more.

His thumb stroked my hand. "You think you'll ever get over yours?"

Would I? Could I get over my stage fright? I'd accepted it as my sucky lot in life. But I'd also performed three dares, and I was still in one piece. "I'm trying."

With his other hand, he brushed my hair from my face, then tilted up my chin. The stall's stink faded a little to the smell of him so close, that fresh-yet-manly scent.

His mouth was near mine, his breath warm and inviting.

Anticipation twirled in my chest.

"I want you to sing for me." His words were only a whisper. "Just to me."

"Now?" My inner tremble reached my voice.

He shook his head. "Not now. But sometime. At least think about it."

I nodded slowly, warily. I couldn't promise to sing, but I could consider it.

"What I want right now, Charlotte Romero, is to kiss you. May I kiss you?"

My heart caught in my throat. I hadn't misread him, hadn't imagined it, hadn't concocted an alternate reality. He truly liked me and wanted to kiss me. And I definitely wanted him to kiss me, but—

I tilted my head back toward the camera. "They're listening and watching."

"Not listening. I know my audio-visual equipment, and those are just cameras. No microphones."

So they hadn't heard him saying I was the prettiest girl or singing a Beatles song. But they'd seen plenty.

"Okay, but you want to kiss me in front of everybody?" And how did I feel about that?

He caressed my cheek with his fingers, the pads softly callused from playing guitar. "I want to kiss you in front of everybody, nobody, and all the time."

His closeness melted my heart, his touch seared my insides. Swallowing fire had nothing on this heat.

His mouth folded into mine, lingered for a long moment, and then parted my lips and softly explored.

Somehow I managed to kiss back, not thinking about how I was doing, just lost in the tangle and tenderness of the kiss. For just a moment, he'd made the world around me disappear.

He pulled back. "I've wanted to kiss you for a long time."

I couldn't have been more shocked if you'd cast me in *Hair* and asked me to disrobe on stage.

He laid me back into the blanket of hay. "How many votes do you think we'd get if we made out all night?"

My eyes popped open. "You're doing this for votes?"

"No." His tone conveyed insult at the suggestion. "I'd kiss you no matter what. But as long as we're here…"

Another excellent point.

Of all the first kisses in all of time, I was certain this first kiss had the best premiere. And I wanted an encore. "Two birds, one stone?"

"Birds, pigs, and spiders. Quite a night we're having."

"I'll say." The words came out before I could stop them. My cheeks warmed.

But he gave me a soft peck. "I should ask you on a date after this, you know. Dancing with pigs isn't the best way to woo a girl."

A pig snout appeared between our faces, followed by a snort.

We fell apart in laughter.

I shoved the pig's face out of our way, then scratched its ears. "Yeah, I guess not."

A different pig approached for Logan's attention. He rubbed its back. "So, Charlotte Romero, will you go out with me?"

25
Lines

When the dare finished, I had just enough juice in my phone to text Kat that I was catching a ride home with Logan. And then, my phone died.

I slid into his borrowed-from-Dad car, noting only that it was dusty outside and pristine inside. "Nice wheels," I murmured.

"Yeah." Logan sighed. "I'd take you for a spin, buy you breakfast and all that, but I promised to have this baby back early, and I have to find a car wash on the way home."

"No worries." I tilted my head back, breathed in the morning, and let my eyes shut.

Logan's hand slipped into mine, and his thumb brushed over my skin. The soft reassurance of his touch made my heart both settle and soar.

He dropped me off at dawn with a quick-yet-tender kiss, and I tiptoed into my apartment with *My Fair Lady*'s "I Could Have Danced All Night" playing in my head. After showering off the pig stall's muck, I crashed, hard.

Mom awakened me with her palm on my forehead.

"What are you doing?" I mumbled while keeping my eyes half shut.

"Checking you for a fever." She folded her arms. "Did you sleep at all at Kat's?'

My throat tightened. "No."

"*Ay*, to be young again." She sighed and left.

I buried my face and the truth in the pillow. If she'd had any idea her daughter had not only lied about a sleepover but had snuggled with a boy in a barn all night...? Actually, I didn't know what would happen, but likely nothing good.

The door flung open and shut again.

I peeked out, this time to see Kat standing in my room, hands on hips. "Now let's see. Was my favorite moment when Walker mooned the cameras, every hour on the hour, as if showing his butt would get him votes?"

I stared at her through squinted eyes. *Walker had mooned people?* Suddenly I was glad I hadn't been on the other side of the camera. I didn't need that image imprinted on my brain.

"Was it when the horse lifted its tail and pooped right onto Kirk's boot?" Whatever point she was trying to make, it upped her sarcasm several degrees.

I moaned and pulled the covers over my head.

"Or was it when you had your first kiss on camera in front of everyone?" She punctuated each word like a drum beat.

I flinched and covered my ears. "Stop yelling."

"How. Could. You!" Cue the cymbals.

"I don't knoooow." I sat up and rubbed my eyes.

"Uggghh." She rolled her eyes back so far I was pretty sure her eyeballs had circled around like a slot machine. "Don't you know how this works? You have your first kiss, and the *very next person* who finds out is your best friend."

I crinkled up my face. "That's why you're mad?"

She stomped over and took a seat on the edge of my bed. "You were the first person I told about my first kiss."

"You didn't even like it." It was some guy in eighth grade band who'd planted one on her behind the stadium. "Said you needed a HazMat crew to clean up all the spit."

She waved a quick hand. "He was a saliva factory. But that's not the point. I've told you about every one of my kisses—some delicious ones—and I learn about yours from a video on Deedra's stupid website?"

"Don't remind me." I pressed my hand over the twist in my chest. My first kiss in a stinky pig stall with a spider's nest nearby, and I'd let a video camera record the whole thing.

"This contest has made you crazy."

Was it the contest? Or Logan? Because I was definitely crazy about Logan. "The thing is, when we were kissing, it felt like just the two of us."

Kat *hmphed*.

I yanked off my covers, exposing my musical notes pajama pants. "How long did you watch?"

"The whole thing. Every boring minute."

"You stayed up all night?" I knew why I'd stayed awake, but I couldn't imagine Kat hooked on our barn-themed reality show. And she looked far more awake than me. "Isn't Deedra posting highlights? Why would you watch it live?"

Kat stretched out her mouth, like words were hanging in there, protesting the idea of coming out.

I gestured a *c'mon, spill.*

She looked away and scratched behind her ear. "I might have hosted a watch party with a few band friends."

Her confession hit my gut. "You hosted an all-night watch party? Why didn't you tell me!"

"You would have freaked out."

"Duh."

"Don't judge." She brushed imaginary lint off her jeans. "I needed reinforcements. I was worried about you. Not that you were thinking about me while tasting Logan's tongue."

My cheeks heated, but I smiled as I remembered that first kiss, talking for hours, dancing again, killing three more spiders, more kissing, falling asleep in his arms. When Deedra had opened the barn door and let in a shaft of light, I'd awakened to a golden boy with hay in his hair, a grin on his face, and a good-morning kiss.

"Well." Kat sighed heavily. "How was it? As if I couldn't tell by your expression."

"It was...perfect."

"Good for you. And if you want to make it up to me, you'll tell me everything you two said, because we couldn't hear anything. Seriously, you'd think Deedra would have invested in audio." She made it sound like a personal affront that Deedra hadn't spent even more money to let her listen in.

But I was happy our conversation had stayed private. "Who was at your party?"

"Besides the usual?" She shrugged. "Dizzy was there, chattering the whole time. Jeremy too, but he didn't say anything. Barely moved on the couch. I think he's legally dead. He should get that checked out."

I laughed. Jeremy definitely had that laid-back vibe.

The doorbell rang. "Charlotte!" Mom called from downstairs. "You have a visitor!"

My heart swan dove toward my stomach. "Oh my gosh, what time is it?" I dug frantically for my alarm clock, then realized it had fallen off the shelf. Wedging my arm between the bed and the wall, I flailed around to find it.

Kat announced, "It's five-oh-two p.m."

"Aaaah!" I screamed and yanked myself upright.

This was bad. Bad, bad, bad.

Mom walked in.

Why was everyone barging into my room? As if I hadn't lost enough privacy with the video camera last night.

She shut the door behind her, raised her eyebrows, and stage-whispered, "Why is there a boy in my living room saying he's here to pick you up for a date?"

I couldn't read her expression. Angry? Confused? Proud?

Based on the laser-focus of her eyes, I could scratch *proud* from the list.

Flinching inside, I smiled hopefully. "Can I go out tonight? On a date?" That's how I'd originally planned to ask—when I'd expected to wake up on my own with plenty of time to ease into the subject, discuss any concerns she had, and still have a full hour to get ready. Why hadn't I set an alarm?

"So you know this boy?"

"I'll say," Kat muttered.

I glared at Kat, and she pressed her lips together guiltily. To Mom, I said, "He's in my theater tech class." And waiting downstairs, while I'm here with sheet marks, bed head, and morning breath.

"When did he ask you out?"

"Last night?" Or really 3:00 a.m. this morning when he'd asked to pick me up at 5:00 p.m. for our first official date.

She narrowed her eyes, searching. Without my guard up, Mom could read me like a playbill. "You're not telling me everything. And I don't know this kid. I can't send my daughter out the door with a strange guy."

Worry pinwheeled in my chest. Her tone sounded very much like not happening, case closed, *The End*. I reached out and took her hand. "Mom, Logan's not a strange guy. I've known him for a while. And you just met him. Didn't he seem nice?"

Her jaw clenched, and a muscle there jumped. She turned to Kat. "Do you know this boy?"

Kat looked at me, then back, and pointed at her chest. "Me?"

I gave her the *please help me* eyes.

Kat probably would have announced a date to her parents, not asked to go. But Mom had every reason not to trust men. Unless they were safely on the movie screen wooing Doris Day. I needed Kat to reassure her.

Kat sighed. "His name is Logan Barrett. I don't know him well, but he's nice and definitely doesn't run with a bad crowd." She added, "His stepmother is that TV reporter Jenna O'Farrell-Fine."

I didn't have a clue how that was relevant, but it put a pause on my mother's face.

"Mom." I jerked my head toward my movie musical collection on the bookcase. "You raised me on Gene Kelly and Fred Astaire. I know how to spot a gentleman."

"I don't know anything about—"

"He's a senior, works sound and lighting for theater, doesn't do or deal drugs, and he's taking me out for dinner and a movie."

"Why didn't you tell me?"

I darted my eyes over to Kat. I couldn't lie again, but I could stretch the truth. "Kat and I pulled an all-nighter." Just not together. "When I got home this morning, all I wanted was my bed. I thought I'd be up in time to talk to you about this." I pointed toward my door. "But he's been waiting a while. If I'm going to go, I need to get ready."

She didn't move or respond. Which I took as not-a-no and started grabbing fresh clothes, a hair brush, shoes. Crossing in front of my mirror, I stopped long enough to gauge how bad I looked. *Crap.* Not good.

I heard a moan from Mom and glanced over to see her massaging her temples. "All right, but keep your phone on and text me if you need anything."

"Thank you!" I threw my arms around her. *"Gracias, gracias, gracias."*

If she'd said no, that wouldn't have been the end of me and Logan. But it would have required postponing our date and more convincing Mom. Maybe another Doris Day movie and mint chocolate chip ice cream. This way, I got to see Logan tonight...now.

She sighed under my squeeze. "And how long is this date?"

"I can be home by midnight."

"Midnight?" Disapproval pricked her words. Little did she know I'd been out with Logan all last night.

"Eleven?"

Kat smirked at my immediate surrender. But I'd still have six hours with Logan, and if it got Mom to agree—quickly—it was worth a little backtracking.

Mom gave me half a nod and left the room.

When the door shut, Kat laughed. "Did she give you The Talk already? Because if you want, I can cover that in the next few minutes."

"Shut up." I flew into action.

Eight minutes later, I emerged from my room with dry-shampooed and brushed hair, a touch of face powder and lip gloss, and the blue blouse I usually wore with my black skirt to usher musicals but paired with dark jeans instead. I wasn't runway ready, but I looked decent and, thanks to last night's shower, I no longer smelled like pig and hay.

Kat followed me downstairs.

The moment I reached the living room, Logan looked up. And smiled.

My muscles loosened like a pulled slip-knot. He was still into me, still eager to see me. "Hey."

"Hey." He stood from the couch, where my mom sat across from him.

I hoped she hadn't interrogated him. More importantly, I hoped he hadn't given anything away about last night.

Everyone stood awkwardly until Kat announced, "Alrighty then, I guess I'll be going."

Logan kept his focus on me. "Are you ready?"

I shifted my attention to Mom, looking for what I didn't know. But when she nodded, I felt a surprising rush of relief. No matter how her love life had turned out, maybe she could believe there were good guys in the world. And one of them was standing in her living room ready to take her daughter on a date.

"I'm ready," I told Logan.

He turned to my mom. "What time would you like her home, ma'am?"

Ma'am? Way to back up my claim about him being a gentleman.

"Eleven-thirty," my mom answered.

My jaw about dropped. Apparently his politeness had earned me thirty extra minutes. "Thanks, Mom. You're the best."

Might as well keep up these good manners. Maybe I could get a pony.

Logan gestured for me to move ahead of him, and we walked out together to the Mercedes.

"Borrowed your dad's car again?" I asked.

"With the promise of a full vacuum and wax this time." He shrugged and opened the passenger door for me.

I stepped forward, but he stopped me, slid his hand to the back of my neck, and kissed me slow and soft. "I missed you," he whispered into my mouth.

"You saw me this morning." I glanced back at my apartment, making sure no eyeballs were peeking through curtains.

Spectator-free.

"It was a nice view to wake up to." Up close, his green eyes were like speckled jade and he smelled like sandalwood.

I ran my hand up his jaw to his brows then stroked down his cheek, as if I had permission now to touch him freely. And I suppose I did, because he leaned into my hand.

He kissed me again. Then pulled back and smiled. "Mmm. You could send me home now, and just for that, I'd be glad I came."

I squinted at him. "Do you practice these lines?"

He shook his head and ran his thumb over my mouth. "Not lines, Charlotte. Just how I feel."

"About *me*?" Did he realize how mismatched we were? Hard-rock guy and musical girl, rich guy and poor girl, popular guy and nobody girl, first place in the contest guy and last place in the contest girl.

He pressed his lips together. "Don't question my impeccable taste."

"Maybe you just like me because I kill spiders."

He laughed. "That put an extra point in your column, but you were already winning."

"Winning?"

"Yep. Charlotte, a thousand. All other girls, zero."

Guau, this guy was good. He was spitting out lines Rodgers and Hammerstein could turn into hit songs. Even if I didn't advance another round—if I couldn't go to Broadway and had to flip burgers for minimum wage to pay Deedra back—I already felt like a winner.

I was officially on a date with Logan Barrett.

26

INGENUE

Logan's idea of "dinner and a movie" turned out to be getting take-out Chinese and heading back to his house for a double-feature. Just my style.

As he parked the Mercedes-Benz in the four-car garage beside Deedra's new sports car, a shiver zipped up my spine. When I'd been to his house before, I'd had an official invitation from Deedra, but I'd felt like an intruder. This time I was Logan's personal guest. And I wanted to show I could feel comfortable here, that I could belong in his world.

Even if I didn't.

Carrying the take-out, he led me to the flagstone sidewalk that wove from the garage through the garden. As we walked, motion-sensor lights popped on, illuminating our path like a traveling spotlight.

He unlocked the back door and announced, "Welcome back to Chez Barrett."

We entered a mudroom the size of my bedroom.

"Not Chez Fine?" I peered around a corner.

"No Deedra. I promise." He squeezed my hand then let go. "She's out schmoozing with our parents."

"Schmoozing with your parents?"

"She finagled an invitation to a party hosted by her mom's station. Some anniversary or something. Basically rubbing elbows, drinking champagne, hobnobbing with high-profile leaders in the community." He took us to the kitchen and pulled out plates and drinks.

I walked past him into the large living area beyond. Without a crowd, I could better see the soft leather furniture decorated with ornate pillows and an intricate area rug. It was homey, but in that featured-in-a-magazine way. "Are you sure it's okay to be here alone?" My voice echoed to the ceiling two stories up with a massive chandelier hanging from a peaked rafter.

"I'm not throwing a party, just having my girl over."

My heart jumped. *His girl?*

He looked up. "I mean...I'm not saying... " His face was pale, his jaw shifting. Logan was flustered, about *me*.

Heat fired up my ears. "Are you asking me to be your girl?"

He stepped out from the kitchen and raked his fingers through his hair, making it messier yet somehow better. "My timing is majorly off."

"So you're not asking. Sorry, I just—"

"No, no. I'm asking." He met me in the middle of the living room, slid his hands around my waist, and pulled me close to his chest. "But that's not how I should have asked. And I'm pretty sure I ruined last night."

"Ruined last night?" Being in his arms, nothing felt anywhere close to ruined.

He blew out a gusty breath, sending a whiff of teriyaki my way. Someone had sneaked a bite of the Chinese food. "I've been thinking about last night, and I have a question."

"Oh-kaaay?"

"Was last night..." The muscles in his arms tightened. "Was that your first kiss?"

I pinched my eyes closed. Had it been that obvious? Had I done something wrong? Although if it was that bad, would he have kept kissing me over and over?

"Charlotte." His breath rustled my hair. "Was it?"

I opened my eyes and bit my lip. "Do I get to count Jeremy?"

"Jeremy." He scowled. "I try not to think about that. Do you know how jealous I was?"

"Jealous? Back then?"

He laughed and pushed my hair off my face. "One of my best friends was putting his lips on a girl I was crushing on. Of course I was jealous."

"Trust me, no comparison." Jeremy's kiss was like a single note on the piano while Logan's was the *Les Misérables* soundtrack.

"Good to know. But back to my question: Was last night your first kiss? First *real* kiss?"

I tugged on his shirt, stalling. "Maybe. But does it matter? It certainly wasn't your first kiss. Heck, you've kissed two girls during this contest."

"Two girls?"

"That girl in the cafeteria—"

"I pecked Bailey."

"And Marita at the party."

"I did not kiss her. She kissed me. Totally different."

"You kissed her before. When y'all were dating."

He lifted his gaze to the ceiling, then returned it to me. "So last night wasn't my first kiss. But I think it might have been yours, and if so, I let your first kiss happen on camera in the middle of pig slop."

I took his hand in mine, stroked the inside of his palm, and leaned into him. "It was perfect."

"Perfect?" He chuckled. "I don't understand girls, but I'm not dumb enough to buy that."

"Fine." I smirked up at him. "You'll just have to kiss me as many times as it takes to deliver the perfect kiss."

He tossed back his head and laughed. "Challenge accepted," he said and settled his lips onto mine, kissing me breathless.

When we finally pulled apart, I tilted my head to the side. "I'd give that an eight-point-five."

"Damn." He curled up one side of his mouth into the sexiest smile. "I'll have to work on it. But I did promise you dinner and a movie."

We grabbed our plates from the kitchen, and I followed him upstairs into a slanted room furnished with two rows of couches, each reclining seat with its own cup holder. The screen in the front was bigger than Godzilla, and the sound system as room-filling as his roar.

We took the middle seats, dove into our food, and watched the first movie he'd picked—*Labyrinth*.

As the credits rolled, Logan turned to me with wide eyes. "Well?"

"Well, it's not every day a classic rock star pulls off the role of Goblin King."

He grinned. "See? I told you it was good."

Puppets? David Bowie? An actual labyrinth? And musical numbers? It deserved high marks for putting that all in one movie.

Not to mention pretty great costuming. "I give it three and a half stars."

"You're rating everything today, aren't you?" He held my hand and stroked my skin with his soft, guitar-callused thumb. "By the way, I'd give your kisses a solid ten."

I moved forward into another teriyaki-flavored kiss. But it was the underlying taste of him—his lips, mouth, and tongue—that saturated my senses. I pulled back, my heart beating at full throttle, and murmured, "Ten. Definitely a ten."

He cleared his throat. "Um, it's your turn to pick the movie. Unless you'd rather keep kissing. Which I'm totally on board with, by the way."

I scooted back. I'd only recently had my first kiss and didn't want to move too fast, too far. "I should dump you right into the deep waters with *An American in Paris*, but I'm going to spare you and go with *Grease*."

He narrowed his eyes. "Spare me, huh?"

"You'll like it." I stood and gently slapped his knee. "While you cue it up, I need a bathroom. Where should I go?"

"Left into the hall, last door on the right."

I followed his instructions and landed in a bathroom that was not a bathroom. It was a showplace. After taking care of business, I toured the space and noted its features. A walk-in shower with double shower heads, two marbled sinks and ornately framed mirrors, and monogrammed towels hanging from bronze bars.

As I reached for the doorknob, voices appeared in the hallway. I stilled. Their volume rose.

"—never trust me!" *Deedra*.

"Why should I? When you choose to make a mockery of me!" That tone was lower and sharper than I'd heard before, but still the distinct voice of KHAL News's Jenna O'Farrell-Fine.

"Make a mockery of you? This isn't about you!"

I took my hand off the doorknob. Not the best time to leave.

"You have a YouTube channel with a boy mooning the camera. And my coworkers saw it. Do you think your choices don't reflect on me?"

"Oh please. You did a whole news report on the safety of sex toys. Did you even consider how that might embarrass me?"

"Grow up, Deedra." Her mom's voice went from scolding to sardonic. "People use sex toys."

"Aarrrrhhh." Deedra's scream pierced the sound barrier. "I don't want to know about your sex life."

"And I don't want to my daughter hosting an ass parade on social media!"

Something slammed in the hallway, and I shrank back against the wall.

"You're just mad because that reporter wants to do a story about my contest."

"That newbie reporter was only sucking up because you're my daughter. Your side show isn't the least bit newsworthy."

"If I get more followers than you, you have to stand by your promise." Deedra's words were lined with determination or desperation—I couldn't tell which.

Her mother cackled. Literally cackled. "I can stand by that promise, because it won't happen. What will happen is you going to college, joining every club I tell you to, and getting everything you want the right way."

"The right way?" Deedra scoffed. "You mean your way."

"I want the best for my daughter, and I've worked too hard and too long not to pass on what I've learned. So if you fail—or rather, when you fail—you'll stand by your promise and Do. It. My. Way." The words dropped like a string of bombs, *plop, plop, plop*. Ready to explode when they reached their target.

Footsteps stomped away.

"Everything I could ever want?" Deedra mumbled. "You mean everything *you* could ever want. As if you even care what I want."

I held my breath, clenched my stomach, and waited. The argument was over, finally, so this was when Deedra would also stomp away. And I could finally leave.

The doorknob rattled.

I jumped back and stared at the jiggling knob.

"C'mon, Logan." Deedra knocked. "What are you doing in this bathroom? Were you eavesdropping?"

I stepped back, sat on the toilet, and wrung my hands. It was bad enough hearing the fight she'd had with her mom, but her knowing I'd heard it? If I said nothing, surely she'd go away.

Deedra knocked again. "Logan."

Where was he anyway? Hadn't he heard that whole verbal battle?

The knock became a pounding. "Logan!"

My nerves kicked like a chorus line under my skin.

"What?" Logan's voice entered the hallway.

"If you're there, then who's—"

My stomach tumbled to my ankles. Steeling myself, I turned the knob and cracked the door open, keeping my eyes on the floor. "I'm sorry. I didn't mean to overhear. I was just using your—"

"Logan Barrett." The pissed-off in Deedra's voice was beyond what I'd heard when I'd run into her car. More controlled, but scarier. "Why is she...?"

"I invited her." Logan stepped forward and grabbed my hand. "And this is as much my house as yours."

I lifted my eyes, my gaze grazing over silver high heels, a royal blue cocktail dress, and a diamond pendant necklace. When I reached Deedra's face, I felt a punch in my throat.

She was pale and glassy-eyed. Her chin twitched, and her head trembled. "How could you?" she whispered.

Was she speaking to me or Logan?

She jogged down the hallway, opened a door at the very end, and slammed it closed behind her. Sobs seeped through the door into the hallway.

"What happened?" Logan asked.

"Didn't you hear the argument with her mom?"

He shook his head. "I had my headphones on. When I took them off, I heard her yell my name."

"You and your headphones." I shook my head. "Let's just say it was bad, like Worst Moment Ever bad. And then she discovered that it all happened in front of me."

My chest burned with a strange, new desire to waltz into Deedra's room, hug her, and tell her everything would be okay. Because if anyone understood how horrible an audience was at your worst moment, it was me.

27
SPOTLIGHT

Monday morning, I fell into an alternate universe. In this universe, Charlotte Romero was recognized at school, had a popular boyfriend, and was hailed by a fan club. My inner loner screamed for refuge.

I beelined to the band hall to meet Kat after morning marching practice. I wanted her to walk with me to class as my personal buffer, a protective barrier, between me and all this new attention.

As soon as she saw me, she took the sticks in her hand and drummed the wall. "Ladies and gentlemen," she announced, "I give you the contest queen."

A half-hearted *whoop* erupted in the band hallway, and I waved my thanks.

So much for a harbor in the storm.

"I was trying to avoid people," I murmured to her.

"As your campaign manager—"

"Self-appointed," I murmured.

"I must remind you that every vote counts. Any support we can pluck away from your opponents and drop into your column is worth a little extra effort."

Logan appeared at my side and slid his hand into mine.

My heart leaped.

"Hey," he said, "I've been looking for you everywhere."

"Really? You were?"

I needed a crash course on relationships. Were we supposed to find each other in the mornings now? Was that what boyfriends and girlfriends did?

My musical-based education only set up an expectation that one of us would soon break into a ballad to declare our undying love. Appealing, but unlikely.

Kat cocked her head at Logan. "It was a spider?"

He blinked and refocused on her. "What?"

"On the trampoline. I thought you were mounting my bestie when you were scurrying away from a creepy crawler. Why didn't you just say so?"

He opened his mouth to speak, but two large hands landed on his shoulders from behind. Walker arrived with a posse, surrounding him like supporting actors encircling their lead. "The itsy-bitsy spider..." He sang off key. "Climbed up the pig pen."

The other guys joined. "Down came Logan, shaking in his skin."

Logan's hand fell from mine, and his face turned pink. "Yeah, yeah," he muttered.

More hands slapped his arms, shoulders, and back. "Out came a girl to save poor Logan's hide. But nothing can save Sir Barrett's wounded pride."

Logan smirked and nodded, accepting the tease, while they shook him and ruffled his hair.

My mouth went dry. Should I be upset at the way they were teasing him?

Then again, their lyrics were pretty good. Not Lin Manuel Miranda good, but not half-bad.

Suddenly, they turned to me. A couple of guys squeezed my shoulders, and a few more lifted their hands for high-fives.

"Way to go, Charlotte!"

"Thanks for saving our bro!"

Heat rushed to my cheeks, and I darted my eyes to Logan, unsure of protocol.

He grinned. "Go ahead. You deserve the kudos."

I lifted my hand tentatively and got slapped heartily.

Once done, the group of guys laughed and high-fived each other, apparently not done slapping people. As they wandered away, someone dropped a fake spider onto Logan's arm, and he flinched.

I palmed the spider and shoved it into my bag. "I'll get rid of this."

Logan gave a grateful sigh, then faced Kat. "This mocking here and a lot more? Among the reasons I didn't fess up before about my fear of spiders."

Kat folded her arms. "You can't make choices based on the idiots of the world."

I tilted my head at her. "You think the 'idiots of the world' are all but about ten people."

"Shh." She leaned her head in, then glanced around the hallway. "We need their votes."

I just stared at her.

Where was the Kat Jamison I knew? And who was this cunning campaigner who'd taken her place?

Logan wrapped his arm around my waist. "Here's the thing, Kat," he said, touching me but looking at her. "When you have a phobia, it isn't about choice. Fear doesn't listen to reason."

I gazed up at him.

That was like a movie line—powerful and concise.

Kat shrugged. "Fair enough." She adjusted her backpack on her shoulder and tucked her drumsticks in her back pocket. "Romance is also entirely unreasonable. So I'm getting out of here before you two start tangling yourselves together like a web. Later."

She took off, weaving through the students now filling the hallways.

"See you at lunch!" I yelled at her back.

She flicked a wave but kept going.

Logan took my hand. "I'd say something about your friend being odd, but after that serenade from Walker and Company, I have no room to talk."

I laughed, and we set off together down the hall, heading toward my first class.

He shot me little smiles every few seconds, which I tucked in my heart like second-grade valentines in a decorated paper bag.

"How's Deedra?" I asked.

He shrugged a shoulder. "Home's tense."

I swallowed all the follow-up questions I wanted to ask.

We'd cut our date short after Deedra's breakdown, even sneaking down a back staircase to get out of his house unnoticed by her mom. Once I'd explained to him what had happened, Logan had shifted his focus to consoling Deedra—a development I hadn't expected.

We turned a corner, and he swept me forward.

I scrambled to keep up. "What's the hurry?"

"I have something to show you."

We passed through the center of our school, a hexagon hub of crossing hallways, and made our way to the large hall in front of the lobby.

He raised his chin. "Look!"

I followed his eyes to a banner hanging just below the ceiling. It was bright pink with black marker and read "Deedra's Dares Favorite Couple: Logan + Charlotte." At the far end was a blurry, heart-framed photo of me and Logan snuggled together in the pig stall.

My heart fell to my feet. "Did you put that up there?"

I couldn't keep the annoyance out of my voice. Even I knew this was too soon for our first fight, but wasn't it enough for the whole video to be on YouTube? Did my face really need to be plastered on the school wall?

"Nope." Logan shook his head, but his grin displayed supreme satisfaction. Like he was happy to claim that moment in front of God and everybody.

A squeal came from down the hall. "There they are!" yelled one girl.

More squeals followed, and the mob came running.

My eyes popped from my head, and I instinctively grasped Logan's arm with my other hand, drawing closer for protection.

"Charlotte! Logan!"

"I voted for you."

"You're our favorites."

"I wish I could vote for both of you."

"What an amazing kiss."

I agreed with that last one, but this was too much. Too, too much.

Georgia stood at the front like the leader of the goose flock, but pleased as a peacock. The rest of them, eight more girls, were practically swooning.

"Don't worry about me, ladies." Logan let go of my hand and wrapped his arm around my shoulder, tugging me close. "Charlotte's the one who should get your votes."

"Thanks," I mumbled. "D-d-did y'all make that sign?"

Georgia nodded so hard and fast, I thought her head might topple off. "Charlotte's Angels wanted to show support and get other people to support y'all too."

Logan cocked his head at me. "Charlotte's Angels?"

"That's what we call ourselves," Georgia answered. "We're supporting Charlotte. But we wish we could support you too."

"Y'all are the cutest couple," another girl said, saccharin oozing through her words.

This was all so surreal.

"Ugh." Deedra strolled up behind us. "Do you know how gross it was to watch my brother slither his tongue down the throat of his latest girlfriend?"

And with that, I was back to reality.

I'd spent the whole prior day feeling awful for her, about her mother screaming and Deedra bawling. I couldn't shake what she'd said—that her mother didn't care at all what she wanted—while my own mother was tucking away nickels and dimes for an NYC trip because it's what I wanted. It was crazy to think she had to host a silly contest and give away five thousand dollars to earn the possibility of living her own life.

And in one fell swoop, Deedra crushed my compassion.

I glared at her, hoping my harsh expression let her know the disdain flowed both ways.

"No one forced you to put a camera in the stall." Logan stroked the back of my neck, reassuring me, while staring down Deedra. "And she's not my latest girlfriend. She's my girlfriend, period."

"Aaawww," Charlotte's Angels crooned in unison.

Deedra pressed her lips together and circled her index finger in the air. "Whatever. You're still not going to win my contest. I'd put my money on Walker or Shay."

Something crackled in my gut, rose through my chest, and surfaced in my mouth. "Gamble where you want, but plan on putting your money in my hand. When I take first prize."

Huh. Apparently, that *something* I'd felt was courage.

Logan pulsed a gentle squeeze on my shoulder.

Deedra's nostrils flared, like a bull ready to charge.

I tensed. Maybe I'd blown past courage to stupidity. In my defense, the two could be hard to distinguish. Just ask Walker and his butt show.

Deedra snapped her focus to Logan. "Tell your *girlfriend* that her days in my contest are numbered. Even if she makes it through this round, the next dare will be right up her alley. The kind of alley where you get knocked out."

Logan eyes popped wide.

Gasps hissed around the circle of girls, while I imagined my feet cementing to the floor.

I would not let her intimidate me. I would not...let her...

First bell rang.

Georgia leaned in and whispered, "We have to go to class, but remember, we love you!"

Love? A freaked-out flutter made its way down my spine.

The girls scuttled away like a flock of flamingos.

I called out, "Thanks!" not sure what other response was appropriate. Should I start working on my autograph?

Logan let go of me and stepped closer to Deedra. "What is wrong with you, Dee?"

She looked taken aback at first, as if it was a good question that she didn't have an answer to. Like she recognized something had gone awry in her and didn't know what to do about it. But the reaction didn't last.

"What's wrong with me?" she spit back. "You seem to have forgotten who this contest belongs to. It's not Logan and Charlotte." Deedra thrust out her arm toward the neon banner hung by Charlotte's Angels. "It's Deedra's Dares." She marched away, stomping the tile floor with her strappy sandals, punctuating her anger.

My muscles stilled. No wonder she didn't like me. If Deedra didn't get her way, she'd have to go her mom's way. And she genuinely believed I was in her way—stealing her spotlight.

A spotlight I didn't even want.

Or did I? I needed that spotlight if I was going to get votes.

Logan slid his hand into mine. "Don't worry about her."

I smiled back up at him, but I was much less worried about Deedra's antics than what I was going to have to do to win her contest. It was already going to take every fiber of courage I had to be comfortable with a spotlight, and she'd promised the next dare would make me feel like a deer in headlights.

28
Audition

While Dizzy helped Kat adjust the drummer seat, I sat on one end of the garage's worn couch, ready to hear her audition. One that would hopefully end with Logan's face intact and Kat becoming the fourth member. "Did y'all choose a band name?"

Logan said, "Red Earth."

Dizzy said, "Fire Eater."

Jeremy said, "Unknown Territory."

They traded annoyed looks.

I laughed. "Still working on it then. But I like Fire Eater."

Dizzy beamed a triumphant grin.

Across the room, Hendrix's furry legs hung over the lip of the keyboard. The cat blinked slowly, as if miffed that we'd invaded his space.

"Speaking of Fire Eater"—Logan went back to fiddling with an amp—"you're not just swallowing fire in this contest, Charlotte. You're on fire."

I scoffed. "I don't know about that."

Kat pumped the pedal that made the bass drum boom. "Don't be modest. About your dares or my deals. You moved to fourth place."

"Fourth of six," I reminded her. Although, when I'd found out, I'd done a happy dance worthy of Fred Astaire.

"And I'm back to number one," Logan boasted.

"Spiders." Jeremy sprawled on the other end of the couch, plucked guitar strings, and nodded once. "Sympathy vote."

Logan shot his own Hendrix look at Jeremy. For days, he'd been teased. He even opened the sound board one night at theater rehearsal only to have silicone spiders jump out at him. His scream had nearly split the rafters.

Dizzy grinned ear to ear. "I voted for you, man." Then he turned to me. "Sorry, Charlotte."

"Of course you did," I answered with a smile. "He's your friend." Kat had voted for me every round.

"Voted Charlotte," Jeremy mumbled.

"Of course you did," Logan answered with a headshake.

Jeremy shrugged. "Contest's less boring with both of you."

Kat pointed her drumstick at Jeremy. "True. People love to root for couples. We should use that to our advantage."

I shuddered. "What—like another banner?" The banner had only stayed up a couple of hours before getting torn down, but the chatter about it had kept rolling all week. "No. Just no."

Kat turned to me. "You have superfans now, Charlotte. Hard-core followers. Like those people who wait in line overnight to buy concert tickets the second they go on sale. Superfans don't just support you, they get other people to support you."

My stomach twisted. "Superfans? Who am I—Patti Lupone?"

"Who?" Jeremy asked.

Kat rolled her eyes at him. "Patti in her world is like Bono in ours." She turned back to me. "Point is, they like the couple angle. And we should keep them happy."

Logan leaned forward. "What are you proposing?"

"Well, if we could get you two kissing on camera every week..."

"I didn't kiss her for votes." Logan's voice went steel-hard. "Anyone who thinks I'd do that is dead wrong."

Kat tipped her head. "Calm down, Romeo. I know some people have said that—"

Blood rushed from my head. People had said that? How many people?

"—but I'm not those people. What I think we should do is join forces. Work together on future dares to play up the couple angle and keep you both in the contest as long as we can."

Logan lifted his chin. "So Charlotte and I would coordinate?"

"No." I stood, walked the length of the garage, and turned back to the foursome. "Logan's already been at the top multiple times without any help from me, so the only reason to work together would be to get me votes. I don't want the pity vote."

"It's not a pity vote." Logan turned his focus entirely to me. "You're doing way better in this contest than anyone expected, including yourself." He winked.

I blushed.

"But you and Kat have already coordinated, right? And Marita did my makeup. We did the dares, but we got help from others with planning."

Dizzy beamed his white smile. "So we can get involved? Sweet."

Hendrix stood and swished his tail, as if he agreed.

Logan spread out his hands and smiled. "If two heads are better than one, how about five?"

"Nope," Jeremy said, his tone a flat line.

Kat narrowed her eyes at him. "What do you mean 'nope'?"

"Already did my part." Jeremy leaned back. "First dare."

I laughed. "You mean when I pecked you?"

He barely bobbed his head in a nod.

"Oh, please." Kat threw her head back. "Can't you put out a little effort? You barely move. Are you even alive?"

He didn't even turn his head toward her. Just his eyes. "I'm conserving energy. You should try it."

"Anyway," Logan continued, "I think it's a good idea." He turned to me. "Are you in?"

I felt the others' eyes on me, waiting for an answer.

But something felt...off. Not about them, but me.

I bit my lip and waved Logan over. "Can we talk privately?"

He nodded and lifted the garage door.

"No trampoline," Kat called after us.

We ignored her, let the door fall, and walked to the street's curb. Within moments, a drum groove came from the garage followed by Jeremy's guitar and Dizzy's keyboards.

Logan glanced at my hands, then tucked his hands into his pockets, as if stopping himself from touching me. Waiting to see where this was going. "What's up?"

I heaved a big sigh. "I didn't know people were saying you kissed me for votes."

He flinched. "I didn't."

"Most of me believes that. But the thing is...you're you, and I'm me."

"What's that supposed to mean?"

"I didn't hear those rumors, but I see people looking at us like I'm your charity case."

"Charity case?" He looked genuinely confused, but how could he not understand why people would say that?

I was the wallflower, the underdog, the girl who sat in the cinders. He was Prince Charming. And I had no fairy godmother. Unless you counted Kat, who was more devilish sprite than fairy godmother.

"If we work together, people will think you're doing it to be nice to the girl who couldn't make it on her own. And I'll look like, well, the girl who can't make it on her own."

He gave a Kat-worthy eye roll. "Stop worrying what they think. I live in that world, and it sucks. My parents, Deedra, Deedra's parents—they're all so concerned with how they look to everyone else. I'm with you because you're not like that. You're just...you."

"You have the luxury of not worrying about what others think because you're already popular." And likely to win the contest, unless something drastically changed.

Our eyes locked as the music faded. Voices came from the garage, all sounding positive, like Kat's audition was already going well.

Logan reached out, took my hand. "Look, if I come out of this contest with no money, few friends, and no chance at prom king but I get to hang out with you and my band"—he nodded at the garage—"and I've been a decent guy, I'm good with that. But if you come out of this contest being the kind of person who cares a lot what others think, then that's a loss. That's who Deedra is, and you see how it's ruining her."

"I don't care what everyone thinks. That should be obvious with how much I know about show tunes, and how little I know about this music"—I pointed at the garage, where a new song had started, heavy on bass and drums—"or what's on the radio these days."

Logan snorted a laugh. "They think we're talking about the contest, and they chose to play 'Another One Bites the Dust.' I bet Jeremy picked it."

I grinned. "I wouldn't put it past Kat."

"You care what *she* thinks."

"Yes. And my mom, and my grandmother, and other people I care about. But also myself. I don't want to coordinate with you if it means losing myself."

"I would never be that boyfriend. And if anyone thinks I am or thinks you can't stand on your own, then Kat's right: they're idiots. And we shouldn't make choices based on them."

I smirked. "Don't tell Kat she's right. This contest has given her delusions of grandeur."

He laughed. "Well, for once, she's right and Shakespeare's wrong. The world isn't a stage. We're not always performing, or shouldn't be."

"And yet she wants us to perform as a couple." To share the spotlight.

"We'd perform *as* a couple, not *that* we're a couple."

My chest warmed. He'd said all the right things. I felt all the right things.

"So the world isn't a stage, and we're not always performing, but we are going to plan out our dares together? From now on?"

"Until one of us goes out and supports the other."

I narrowed my eyes. "You just want my superfans, don't you?"

He leaned in, brushed his mouth against my ear, and whispered, "Patti Lupone was the original lead in *Evita*."

My heart skipped. *Suave, suavecito*, this boy.

I pulled back, looked up at him, and smiled. "Well, how can I say no to someone who knows that?"

29
CHOREOGRAPHY

The bleachers weren't standing room only, but close. We could see the full crowd from the top, back row. I had no idea so many students attended pep rallies.

"I can't, I can't, I can't..." I punctuated each *can't* with a backward head bang against the gym wall. Deedra's spiders-in-the-stall trick had taken direct aim at Logan, but this dare was pitch-perfect for playing on my fears:

Freshen your flash mob! Flash Mobs are outdated. Unless you can make it awesome. How you'll do that, I don't know. But that's your challenge: A flash mob that wows us.

"People. Faces. Watching." A flash mob of nerves danced in my stomach.

Logan stroked the back of my hair. "It's just lip-syncing."

My palms went slick, my mouth dry. "Kat's right. This place is the Vortex of Doom. I need to get outta here."

I stood to leave.

Logan tugged me back down. "You can't give up now." He took both my hands into his and gave me a soft smile. "We spent hours planning and preparing. We recruited about a hundred people and made them practice. Kat leaked rumors about what you're doing to Charlotte's Angels all week. I know you're scared, but I'll be right there with you. You can do this."

My stomach and heart battled for room in my throat. But I focused on his green-eyed gaze, let out a jerky sigh, and nodded.

Jeremy arrived, we scooched over, and he sat. "Ready."

"You sure we won't get in trouble?" I bit my lip.

"Shouldn't." Jeremy conserved words as much as energy, as if he had a small quota each day and couldn't waste them.

I breathed a little easier. Dizzy was apparently some kind of genius with amazing grades and high principal approval. He'd used his pet status to line up our performance.

Our dual performance. Featuring *Logan + Charlotte.*

The fight song began, cheerleaders tumbled in, football players jogged in and lined up—all accompanied by ear-splitting applause.

Given how Kat was always ranting about the unfair, preferential treatment athletes got, I didn't know how she stood going to these rallies. But there she sat in the front row banging away on her tom-toms.

The closer our moment drew, the more my nerves felt less like a flash mob and more like a flesh-hungry zombie mob. Eating my insides alive.

When the coach took the microphone, it was *go time.* Logan kissed my cheek and murmured, "They'll be focused on me, not you."

"At first," I mumbled.

Logan didn't seem to hear. Just jogged down the steps to the gym floor.

I pressed my hand to my gut, trying to quell the rebellion. Logan's efforts to calm me were sweet, but not entirely effective.

Jeremy gave my shoulder a quick squeeze.

Logan didn't hesitate but swiped the microphone from the coach's hands. The coach drew back, dropped his jaw, furrowed his brow, feigning shock and aggravation. But as smooth notes sounded from the speakers, the student body went wild—knowing it was another flash mob.

Logan handed the mic off to a cheerleader and started the lip-sync, mouthing the lyrics to Foreigner's "Waiting for a Girl Like You." I'd been hearing this song in my head all week long as we practiced to the *Rock of Ages* Broadway soundtrack, our compromise between my love of musicals and everyone else's lust for hard rock.

Several drill team members joined Logan and started their ballet-like dance moves. Logan moved in time with them, having learned a routine they'd performed at competition the prior year.

Amid the chaos of my anxiety, I still felt a thrill in my heart, watching him move on the gym floor like Gene Kelly.

Behind him, two cheerleaders rolled out a large white banner with block print that read LOGAN BARRETT.

My part was fast-approaching. My pulse quickened. My nerves trembled.

The female singing part came over the speakers.

Logan looked up to me in the stands, and all eyes followed.

I froze. All but my stomach, which was a bubbling cauldron of *hell no.*

Jeremy leaned in and muttered, "Up. Now." Then added, "You got this."

I stood and stumbled.

A few snickers erupted.

I took a deep breath and focused on Logan, and somehow all the hours of practice took over. My lips started moving in time with the lyrics.

He smiled and gestured his hand to me, beckoning, though it felt more like pointing. The female line went away, and it moved back to male. Instead of only him this time, several guys in the stands stood and sang to the girl they were with.

Logan ran up the bleacher steps to me.

The people around me parted, like I had repellent magnet powers, leaving me the center of attention.

I wanted to drop through the cracks of the bleachers, curl up underneath, and wait for all of them to go away.

He reached me and must have seen it in my face, because he tucked his arms under my knees and lifted me to his chest.

Not a move we'd practiced.

Cradling me against him, he carried me down the bleacher steps, still lip-syncing the whole way. The roars around us were deafening. But they didn't drown out the boom of my heart pounding against my ribs.

By the time we reached the bottom, the gym floor was like a main stage performance, with drill team girls joined by basketball players lifting them in artistic poses. Theater friends mouthed lyrics and did choreography.

Logan set me down, grabbed my hand, and twirled me in place. My head went as dizzy as my nerves, but once our feet hit the floor, my body seemed to remember the moves. I instinctively stepped forward, then back, and bent backward over Logan's outstretched arm. We finished the final words in a close embrace, with couples all around us doing the same.

A brief pause gave my breath time to quiver, my knees time to buckle, and my stomach time to roil.

But Logan held me up, and the music shifted.

Auto-pilot engaged.

I spun toward the audience, moved my eyes up to the wall above all the staring eyeballs, and lip-synced the first words of my song, Journey's "Any Way You Want It." The marching band stood and, one by one, ran out onto the gym floor.

As they took their places, the previous mob strode away.

My flash mob began executing our moves like a Beyoncé video, despite the song being a classic rock hit.

After the first verse, faculty joined in. And not just my drama teacher.

Somehow, Kat and Dizzy had recruited two English teachers, a calculus teacher, several other teachers, a school counselor, and our principal. The same principal who'd tried to shut down my fire eating.

My breath was fast disappearing, but at this point, I wasn't sure whether it was the exercise or my panic. As I spun toward the back wall, I caught a glimpse of the new banner held up by two basketball players: VOTE FOR CHARLOTTE.

I clenched my jaw tight. I had to push through. Votes were why I was up here, dancing my *culo* off. Even though I'd sworn I'd never perform before an audience again.

As the song ended, Logan skated across on his knees in front of me and spread out his arms.

I looked up at the audience, yelling, cheering, applauding.

My heart stopped.

My breath heaved.

My stomach bubbled.

Clamping my hand over my mouth, I ran toward the door. Somewhere between twenty and two million people stood between me and the exit. I waved my other arm in a get-out-the-way gesture. A teacher caught my drift and began to part the crowd.

Too late. It was coming.

I caught sight of a massive garbage can, planted where people could throw away their stuff before returning to class. I bent over the rim, and my stomach retched.

Suddenly, Logan was behind me. He gathered my hair up in his hand and held it back. And that's when the first wave came. Then the second. And a third.

Yep, Kat had nailed it: Vortex of Doom.

And yet, the crowd was still applauding.

30
Preview

Vomiting gets you sent home from school. But fear-based vomiting didn't mean I couldn't go out with Logan later.

Though what could a girl possibly wear to erase the image of her puking in a public trash can from her date's mind? I gave it a shot by pulling on a pair of leggings I'd only worn twice before, sliding on a purple tunic sweater, and adding a scarf borrowed from my mom.

Though even before my flash mob perform-and-purge, I'd been making extra effort to look like someone worth Logan's second glance. My plain gray tee hadn't left the closet for a week.

While I was finishing up my outfit with high-tops, a knock came on our front door. I tied my shoelaces, checked myself in the mirror, and headed to the bathroom to brush my teeth and swish some mouthwash. Minutes later, I emerged minty-fresh and hopeful that Logan wouldn't remember what had been in my mouth earlier that day. Not convinced, but hopeful.

Logan and my mom sat at our dining table, chatting casually, as if this was an everyday occurrence. She hadn't even bothered to move the stack of books and papers she had out to study for an upcoming exam. As if Logan belonged here as much as her friends or Kat.

I still wanted to pinch myself.

Not so much anymore because Logan Barrett was popular—I was fast becoming well-known myself—but because he was just, well, *him*.

He glanced up at me and smiled, a full-faced smile that creased his eyes. "You look nice."

My heartbeat sputtered.

Mom furrowed her brow. "You do look nice."

"Don't look so surprised." I smirked and slipped into the chair beside her.

"You should wear colorful clothing more often." She brushed my hair off my shoulder. "It contrasts well with your beautiful brown eyes."

I kept my eye roll to a minimum while Mom gave the kind of safety instructions parents love to dole out before you can have any fun. Then she shooed us out the door with yet another *my baby* smile on her face.

Would she think I was all that precious if she knew what I'd been up to with the contest? Thankfully, work and school kept her busy, and she was never one to gossip with other moms.

"She's right, you know." Logan took my hand in his. "Your eyes are a beautiful brown."

"I didn't think we were allowed to have our own eye colors," I teased. "Shouldn't Logan and Charlotte match?"

He laughed, opened my car door, and waited while I slid into my seat. "Restaurant and movie theater? Dancing at a club? Or we could swing by the football game."

I sucked air through my teeth at each suggestion. "Any chance we could avoid people tonight?"

He *hmm*ed. "Had enough attention?"

Dropping my head back, I sighed loudly. "To last till graduation."

"We could head back to my house. Plenty of elbow room there."

"Are you kidding?" My head popped off the headrest. "Deedra doesn't want me anywhere near her house."

He got in on his side, started the engine, and pulled away. "Dee's at the game. Her mom's at the station."

"They came home early last time."

"Deedra won't leave a game early. She's using every minute of every school event to get more followers."

Of course she was.

"Dad's the only one who could be home."

"And he'll be okay with us there?"

"Yeah. My bigger issue is that I didn't know you were coming and left out my stuffed bear collection."

I laughed.

He narrowed his eyes at me. Was he serious?

I stopped laughing, eased back, and enjoyed the smooth ride of the Mercedes he'd once again borrowed from his father, with another promise of wash and wax. My mom's old Volkswagen Jetta had been on its last legs for over a year, and Kat's Kia Sportage sounded angry all the time—thus, the name Jezebel. But this luxury car was like riding on a cloud.

When we pulled into his driveway, I was still daunted by his house. Even though I'd been here twice before, I couldn't help but picture my entire apartment fitting into his living room.

Logan walked into the house yelling, "Dad! Dad!"

No answer.

He shrugged, called for pizza delivery, and led me upstairs. "How about a little music before our pizza arrives?"

"Music?"

"Homemade." He stopped at a room I hadn't been in before, opened the door, and waved me inside.

I stepped into what was obviously his bedroom.

One entire wall had built-in bookcases with a desk in the middle, and the shelves held souvenirs, spine-cracked novels, and vinyl albums. A queen-sized bed jutted out from the opposite wall, with rumpled navy covers, and an electric guitar hung on the wall above the headboard. In the corner was an extra wide chair with decorative pillows, which looked like a model home addition more than Logan's style. Yet on it were several stuffed bears, all dressed in superhero costumes.

I beelined to the Batman bear and held him up. "Oh my gosh. You weren't kidding."

He shrugged. "I was nuts about superheroes when I was a kid. Not so much now. But I think Dad would take it personally if I got rid of those since they were gifts from him."

I chuckled. "Why wasn't this your secret?"

"Because even though I joked about it, it's no big deal?"

I humphed.

How did we decide what was a big deal and wasn't? Teddy bears: acceptable. Arachnophobia: unacceptable. Puking when you're sick: acceptable. Puking from stage fright: unacceptable. Was it just how we felt about it?

He shut the bedroom door, opened a door across the room, and walked in.

I peered around him and let my jaw drop. That wasn't a closet, it was a cavern. How much wardrobe space did a boy need?

He came back out holding an acoustic guitar, sat in the desk chair, and gestured for me to sit on the bed across from him.

With a glance at the closed bedroom door, I pushed down my worry, sank into his mattress, and pulled a pillow onto my lap. I caught a whiff of laundry soap mixed with Logan's scent and fought the desire to raise the pillow to my nose and memorize the smell. Because *that* would be unacceptable.

Even if it would be nice.

The guitar looked natural in Logan's hands, like an extension of his arm. He strummed a few chords, then sat back. "I'd play something from a musical, but I don't really know any of those tunes. Got any classic rock favorites?"

I twisted the corner of the pillow between my thumb and forefinger. "The ones I remember best are by women. Maybe because I can sing along in my head?"

"Like who?"

"Pat Benatar, Heart, Janis Joplin—"

"Joplin." He pointed a trigger finger at me. "I know one of hers."

He started playing "Me and Bobby McGee," stumbling over the lyrics but nailing the chords.

I watched his fingers stroke the strings and his head bob in rhythm. His playing was excellent, and his singing was good. Although...

He stopped. "What?"

My chest tightened. "Nothing."

"If it sucks, just tell me."

"What? No, it doesn't suck." I pushed off the bed.

"But...?" He appeared much more relaxed than I did.

"Well..."

He raised his brows, as if listening hard, wanting my feedback.

Just say it, Charlotte. I steeled myself. "Your jaw's clenched, so the sound doesn't have a lot of space to resonate. Opening your mouth would improve your vocal quality."

His mouth turned up at the corners. "What else?"

I bit my lip, moved closer, and placed my finger under his chin. "If you lift your chin a little, that will open your throat some so you can get a good breath." Moving my hand down, I pressed right above his abs. "And breathe from here, your diaphragm. If you don't know where that is, make yourself yawn and feel how deep that breath goes. That's where you want to pull from."

With a grin, he set the guitar aside and pulled me onto his lap. "You sound like a vocal coach."

I laughed. "Well, I had one once."

"You did?" His tone was half-surprised, half-impressed.

"Not me exactly. She coached everyone in the show."

"What show?"

I tugged on my bottom lip with my teeth, until he gently swiped his thumb over my lips, as if protecting them from my own nervous bite. "*Sound of Music.*"

"Never saw that one. What role did you play?"

"I was Marta Von Trapp, the eleven-year-old daughter of a strict naval captain. Anyway, I was fine all through the musical, when the theater was dark and the spotlight blinded me, but as soon as they turned up the house lights and I saw all those people..."

"What happened?"

I dropped my head into my hands. "Puked right on the captain's shoes."

"You know you're not alone, right?" Logan's palm made circles on my back. "Adele admitted to throwing up from stage fright."

I glanced up. "Streisand had bad stage fright too."

Logan's expression told me he had no idea who Barbra Streisand was. I needed to put *Funny Girl* on our movie list. "It's one thing to say the fear is normal, and another thing to experience it."

"Agreed." He sighed. "What other singing tips do you have?"

I winced. "You really want more tips?"

"Hell yeah," he said. "I've heard you sing. I know you're better than I am."

Nervousness swirled in my stomach.

He reached up and caressed my cheek. "Charlotte, I mean it. Help me sing better."

I bounced off his lap, shook out my hands. "Okay, stand up. And then put your hands on my stomach here and my back here."

He stood, slipped his hands in place, one palm below my rib cage and the other just above my waistband, and smiled. "Do all your tips involve you touching me or me touching you?"

My cheeks warmed, and my belly stirred. "For the next few minutes, you are not my boyfriend but my student."

"All right, Teach. Let me know what I need to do to get an A."

I demonstrated deep breathing, letting him feel the swell and contraction of my diaphragm, then made him try. I'd moved to explaining tone and projection when the pizza arrived.

As he shoved half a slice into his mouth, he mumbled, "You're really helping me."

"It would be better if I could show you." I picked off a pepperoni and ate it.

Logan wiped his hands with a napkin. "Why don't you?"

I scoffed. "You know why I don't."

"I'm not a whole audience. I'm just one guy."

"Is that how you feel about a single spider? It's just one?"

"Good point." He grabbed another pizza slice. "But you know what they say about overcoming phobias, right?"

"That it's pointless?" I gave a sarcastic smile.

He chuckled. "Flooding is one option. Like putting me in a room filled with spiders, and if I don't die, I emerge less afraid."

"And my stage fright version would be performing in Carnegie Hall with a barf bag in hand?" I shuddered at the thought. "No, thank you."

"The other, and much better option, is systematic desensitization. Meaning you sing in front of one, then two, then so on, until you can perform"—he flipped his hand out—"wherever you just named."

"Carnegie Hall? You really don't know Carnegie Hall?"

He lifted his brows and stared me down. "Are you going to fight your fear and sing to me or not?"

I straightened. "What's your phobia equivalent? Do I get to bring a daddy long-legs to our next date?"

His face paled. "Fine. I can negotiate with one spider, if and only if it's in a closed container." He tossed his pizza slice back into the back and added, "As all spiders should be."

I froze, my current slice halfway to my mouth. He really expected me to sing for him.

He waited, chin raised, challenging me.

"You have to turn the other way. No looking at me."

"Okay." He turned and faced his wall. "Anything else?"

Fear zoomed through my chest. "Don't say anything until I'm done, or you'll remind me you're here."

"You don't want to know I'm here?"

"I know you're here, but I can't think about it while I'm singing. I'm going to tell myself that I'm alone and see if that helps."

"If you feel like throwing up, the trash can is by my desk."

I dropped my pizza, grabbed the trash can, just in case, then returned to my spot and rolled my shoulders back. He hadn't asked me to sing anything particular, so my mind floated to my current obsession—the *Wolff* Original Broadway Cast soundtrack.

I took a deep breath and began, "If he could see..." The first notes wavered and then died. I pressed a fist to my chest and took slow deep breaths, counting to three as I inhaled and exhaled.

He's not here, he's not here, he's not—

Logan sat, attention on the wall, head cocked backward. Waiting.

I stepped silently around him to see his face.

He didn't move, and his eyes were closed.

Anxiety hummed in my chest. But I shut my own eyes and threaded "Dust and Destiny" through my brain, stitching its notes and words together.

And then...I sang.

"If he could see beyond my skin
Would he begin
To understand my heart
And show sympathy for what I feel
The depth of my grief?

If I could see beyond his mask,
But I won't ask
What's hiding in his heart
What misery makes him behave
Like a beast."

The notes floated into the small space, filling the distance between us. My head floated with it. When the last note came, I opened my eyes.

He was staring up at me, jaw open. "Thank you," he whispered.

I bent over. "I feel nauseous."

He grabbed the trash can, led me to the bed, and held the can in place while I waited. Nothing came.

After a few moments, he lowered the can, sat beside me, and leaned close. "Does this mean you're safe to kiss?"

I sucked air through my teeth. "You still want to kiss me?"

"More than ever." He tucked a tress of my hair behind my ear. "You keep surprising me. Impressing me." He paused and scanned my face. "Inspiring me."

Tingles ran down my neck and shoulders. "Inspiring you? I think you've got it backward. I'm the one who—"

His kiss cut me off. I leaned into it, grateful for every second. Now *this* was inspiring.

As we drove back to my house, he played an Eagles tunes and sang along. "Better?" he asked.

"Yes." I really could hear a difference in his voice as he tried to put my singing tips into practice. The tone was clearer, stronger.

He pulled the Mercedes into the only available spot in my apartment parking lot. "I think the gentlemanly thing to do now is walk you to the door."

We walked to my apartment, his hand threaded in mine. It felt natural for our fingers to be woven together, sparks of attraction and trust flowing each way.

My front porch was small, but big enough for one last goodnight kiss. I wrapped my arms around his neck.

"Charlotte?" Mom's voice came through the window. Her tone had an urgency to it.

"Something wrong?" Logan asked.

"I don't know." I peered through a crack in the curtain and saw her sitting on the living room couch, her expression somewhere between stone and fire. "I'd better go inside and see."

"Text me to let me know if things are okay." He squeezed my hand and walked away.

Inside, my mom was curled up on a couch cushion, an open bottle of wine and an empty glass on the end table.

I shut the door behind me.

"Do you want to explain this?" She tossed her tablet onto the coffee table. It slid a few inches before stopping.

The tablet was a hand-me-down from a coworker, several versions old with a cracked screen, but past the fissures in the glass was an open email. I leaned down and read.

Isn't this your daughter?

Below was a YouTube link to my latest contest video.

phic## 31
DIALOGUE

My feet rooted to the apartment floor, not because I wanted to be standing here attempting an explanation to my mother. I just couldn't move. My gaze was stuck on the screen where the link to my flash mob appearance seemed to taunt me.

My cheeks burned. "Who sent this?"

"Coworker." Mom pointed at the tablet. "Go ahead. Open the link." Her tension was thick and oppressive, a heavy fog hanging over the room.

Slowly, I sat on the nearby chair, pulled the tablet toward me, and—hands shaking—clicked the link. A news video popped up, titled "Teenage Flash Mob," and a KHAL reporter stood in front of our school.

"Is it a game show?" he said. "A reality show? Or simply a contest? At this local high school, it's a combination of all three. A contest hosted by senior Deedra Fine, daughter of our own Jenna O'Farrell-Fine, is stirring up student body interest and catching fire on the internet." He smiled like this was news gold.

The reporter didn't have the name recognition of Deedra's mom, and a ticker at the bottom let me know this was KHAL Online, meaning it probably hadn't shown on the local newscast—just their website. But still, I could barely breathe.

The reporter showed clips of our flash mob performances that ended with me back-bending over Logan's arm, my hair dangling behind me. I wrung my hands in my lap, matching the sensations in my chest, my gut, and pretty much everywhere else I had working parts.

When it finished, I kept my gaze on the coffee table, wondering how long the crushing silence would last.

Mom sighed. "That email came in about a half hour after you left. I spent the rest of the night researching this contest, watching videos of my daughter." Her voice was an ice block, cold and hard. "Dressed in spandex and kissing one guy, then a few weeks later kissing that boy who just dropped you off." He'd been *Logan* when he'd picked me up, but now he was *that boy*. "You went to a big party in an angel costume and then put a stick of fire down your throat."

I tucked my hands under my arms, protectively curling into myself. She'd watched all of them.

"And I saw you making out with that boy in some place that looked like a barn. On the very same night you were supposedly at Kat's house for a sleepover." She shifted forward on the couch, perching like a bird of prey ready to dive. "*Dios mío*, Charlotte. *Qué está pasando?*"

The chill in her voice was gone, replaced by hot fury that seared my nerves.

I shut my eyes against her anger. "The prize is five thousand dollars, and then I could go to New York without having to spend any of our money."

I looked up to see her shaking her head wildly. "We'd find the money. We always do. So why would you do this? Kat said you even threw up after this dare."

My heartbeat faltered. Kat had ratted me out? Although who knew how Mom had drawn that detail. She could be persistent.

"It was nothing." I waved it off, as if I routinely hurled in public trash cans. "And I don't *want* you to spend your money."

"It's my money. Don't tell me how to spend it!"

"Mom, you already—"

"Don't you dare pull that martyr speech on me. *Pobre mamá, she works her fingers to the bone, and I want to spare her.* I'm your mother, and we're doing just fine. We have a car, a roof over our heads, and food in the pantry. You've never lacked for anything you needed, and I am pulling together the money for you to go to Broadway." She stood and began pacing in front of the couch. "Or I was. But now that I know how comfortable you are lying to me—"

"I didn't lie." Not much. *And please, please don't take away Broadway.*

"You lied about sleeping over at Kat's."

"Okay, that part but—"

"You lied about being in this contest."

"I didn't lie. I just didn't tell you."

"You hid it. That makes a lie."

Ay. Why did parents equate omitting with lying? "I didn't want you to worry. Or freak out." I raised my voice. "Like you're doing right now."

Her gaze darted to me. "Just tell me this. Are you sleeping with that boy?"

I flinched. I'd never considered her mind would go there. "No." I shook my head. "No, no. Why would you think that?"

She huffed. "I've seen what you're willing to do in front of a camera. Who knows what you're doing in private?"

The verbal smack hurt. Not to mention the reminder that my mother had watched me make out. I shuddered. "Nothing happened. He's been a total gentleman."

"What about the other boy?"

I had to think for a moment. "Jeremy?"

"Is that the name of the boy you kissed while dressed like Spider-Man?"

"Spider-Girl," I muttered. "And yes. But that was just the dare. It was a quick peck. It didn't mean anything."

She sat back down. "Exactly how many boys have you kissed?"

I glared at her. "Just the two."

"Is there anything else I should know?" Her jaw tightened. "And this is the moment you'd better fess up to everything."

I'd never seen my mother so angry with me.

I tugged at the hem of my sweater, buying time to figure out what else I had to confess. The contest? Check. My specific dares? Check. How far I'd gone with Logan? *Shudder.* Check. The secret I'd told Deedra about her? No, she definitely didn't need to know that. It wasn't an issue as long as I stayed in the contest.

But there was one more thing I needed to cop to. I sucked in a breath and gathered a bit more courage. "I kinda hit a car."

"Hit a car? What does that have to do with the contest? And how could you hit a car? You don't have a car."

And yet I'd still managed it.

"I was driving Kat's car in the school parking lot. I sorta whipped around a corner and hit Deedra's car."

"Deedra? The girl who hosts this contest?"

"That's the one." Also the girl responsible for me throwing up today, because she just *had* to go for a performance dare. "I owe her for the damages. The five thousand bucks was to cover New York *and* the amount I owe her."

Mom crossed her arms. "How much?"

"Doesn't matter." Neither one of us had that money right now. "How. Much?"

Resigned, I opened up Deedra's email with the invoice on my phone and passed it over to my mom.

Her half-groan, half-sigh could be translated *Charlotte, you idiot!*

But where exactly had my idiot moment happened? Was it running into Deedra's car? Entering the contest? Or thinking somehow I could keep my mom permanently in the dark?

Yeah, that last one had *idiot* written all over it.

"How could you keep this from me?" Her voice shook. "I thought we had a good relationship."

I glanced up to see tears hovering in her eyes. She wasn't just angry, but disappointed in me. "Mom, I kept it from you *because* of our good relationship. I didn't want you to be upset."

She snorted then stood and wiped her wet cheeks. "You'll quit the contest."

A gasp rose into my throat. "But—"

"You'll quit the contest." This time, she said *quit* with the full ramming force of a semi. "You'll get a job and earn the money to pay this girl back for her car damages."

She couldn't be serious. "I wouldn't be able to do theater!"

"Then you'll quit theater." She pointed to the tablet on the coffee table, its screen as cracked as I felt. "But you will not be plastered across the internet lip-locking some random boy."

"He's not 'random'!"

"I didn't know he existed until two seconds ago. And I don't trust him with my daughter."

I shot up from my seat. "It's not your choice whether to trust him. *I* trust him."

"Ha!" she barked.

The way she looked right now, I barely recognized her. Mom had never been strict before. Then again, I'd never done anything to make her even sweat. But we'd always talked. Always. And she'd listened.

Tears welled in my eyes. "I know I messed up, but maybe you could try being a little happy for me. I beat out over fifty people to be in this contest. I learned to swallow fire. I went out there today and danced in front of the whole school, even though it nearly killed me. And I have a boyfriend—yes, *un novio*—who nearly every girl would be thrilled to have, but he wants to be with me." I jabbed my breastbone with my finger. "*Me.*"

My mother's teeth clenched. "Of course, he does. That's what charming men do—make you think you're the only woman in the world so you'll throw caution to the wind." Her voice had fallen to a lower volume, a lower pitch, but instead of calm, it felt more intense.

My heart puddled in my chest. This wasn't about me. It was about *her*. Her decision to sleep with a stripper she'd met at a friend's bachelorette party. Her throwing caution to the wind. Her getting pregnant.

I'd always seen my conception story as embarrassing, but not awful. I'd believed my mom when she'd said she'd do it all over again, if only to get me.

I sniffed back the tears. "I'm not you, Mom. And Logan is nothing like my biological father, whoever he is. Whether you believe in me or not, plenty of others do. They're voting for me. Supporting me. And I'm not quitting this contest."

I spun on my heel, walked to my room, and slammed the door. The *wham* echoed like a soundtrack to my rebellion.

32
Understudy

A news station satellite truck in the school parking lot wasn't usually a good sign.

Kat and I stepped out of her SUV and traded *what's up* glances over the hood.

"Maybe it's D.A.R.E. day again," she said. "Local news loves to cover every time a police officer gives one of those speeches. We get it. Don't do drugs. Haven't, won't, wouldn't."

My stomach clenched. "School shooting?" We hadn't had one of those, not in my district, but there'd been far too many. One was too many.

"We'd see extra security guards," Kat pointed out.

Relief hit me like a cool breeze.

"And those guards would be old, sweaty guys instead of young, hunky uniforms that I'd actually invite to pat me down."

I smirked at her. "No, you wouldn't."

Kat sighed. "We'll never know."

"Bomb threat?"

"Ooh, a bomb threat means we get to go home." She waggled her eyebrows, like a bomb threat would be a special treat.

But as we walked toward the entrance, my pulse was ticking like a bomb. I had a pretty good idea why a news truck was here, but after a tense weekend with Mom, I didn't need more exposure.

Behind the satellite truck stood Jenna O'Farrell-Fine. She wore a satin, royal blue blouse that made her orange-red hair pop off her fair skin. Black pencil skirt and heels completed the camera-worthy ensemble. A nearby technician was double-checking equipment while Mrs. Fine stared at, or stared *down*, her daughter Deedra. "They wanted me to cover it," Mrs. Fine said. "And with over two hundred thousands hits, I have to admit your little contest qualifies as local news."

I could only see the back of Deedra, matching hair cascading down her back, but her posture conveyed a truckload of tension. "Local? Try worldwide. I'm edging up on your followers."

"Don't overdo it, Deedra. It's a slow news day." Mrs. Fine's words syruped off her tongue with all the sweetness of vinegar. "Local news, human interest, fluff piece."

Kat grabbed my arm, cocked her head, and widened her eyes in a *can you believe them?*

Yeah, I got the memo. But this was nothing compared to the shout-out I'd overheard at their house. Or at mine.

"Still," Deedra said, "you have to interview me. It's my contest, my dares."

"Actually, I don't." Mrs. Fine's smile was slight and her tone bored, but they spoke volumes—speakers-all-the-way-up volumes.

I felt another odd wave of sympathy for Deedra.

"If I interview my own daughter," her mom continued, "I'll appear biased. I think the best angle is that girl in the gym. She's the underdog, right?"

My chest split in two, right down the middle.

"You can't be serious!" Deedra yelled, her voice sounding like a preschooler whining *but, mommy!*

"Whoa," Kat muttered beside me.

Mrs. Fine spun back to a twenty-something guy with a clipboard. "Grant!" she snipped. "What was that girl's name?"

"Uhhh..." He flipped a sheet or two, scanned his finger down. "Charlotte. Romero."

My skin crawled. They had my name. Of course they had my name. But hearing it aloud upped my anxiety.

Deedra stepped in front of the clipboard guy and faced her mother. "Did Logan put you up to this? He did, didn't he?"

I yanked Kat toward the school's entrance, drumming the sidewalk with my feet, hurrying to get out of sight as quickly as possible. Before this new bomb exploded.

We got as far as the stairwell when Kat yanked me back, making us both stop. "She wants to interview *you*."

"Yes, I have ears." And feet, that wanted to keep moving.

"Even after the flash mob, you were still fourth. We need something to push you to the top. You have to do the interview."

"No way. I cannot be on TV." On a good day, this was a bad idea. After the blowup with my mom, this was a terrible idea.

"Charlotte. You're viral." She pulled out her phone and clicked the screen a few times. "Or getting there. Since Friday, two hundred twenty-three thousand, one hundred fifty-six views."

I stared at the number on the YouTube screen, feeling lightheaded and lost. "That can't be right. I'm not—"

"When you entered this contest, you gave up anonymity." Kat sighed heavily. "You asked for the spotlight, because that's what it's going to take to win. And now you've got it. The spotlight is on you, and you need these votes."

Her words lit a fuse that sizzled its way into my gut. My hands trembled at my sides. I'd entered the contest, done more than I ever thought I could, and even burned a bridge with my mom to reach this standing. If I wasn't going for the grand prize, what was the point? "If my mom sees me on the news…"

"I told you, she'll get over it. She's just mad you kept stuff from her. Parents are like that. They don't want to know what you think, but they want to know everything you do."

I hadn't told Kat about the underlying reason for our argument. But remembering the secret I'd given Deedra reminded me once again of the stakes. If I was risking my mother's secret, I couldn't do this contest halfway. Even if my mom didn't understand, staying in—and winning—was for her too.

I nodded. "What should I say?"

"Just answer Jenna's questions. Smile a lot." Kat leaned back, took a long look at my face, and then dug into her bag. "And wear lipstick."

I huffed out a laugh. "Really?"

She moved close, dragged pink-tinted gloss over my lips, and fiddled with my hair.

"This could be a disaster."

"Or it could seal your rise to the top." Kat stood back and surveyed her work. "If you think you're going to throw up, signal me."

I raised my hand.

She slapped it down. "Not now. You're not going to throw up now."

At least I still had my sense of humor.

I peered down the near-empty hallway toward the theater part of the school. "I wonder where Logan is. If Deedra's here early, so is he."

Kat waved her hand in front of my face. "Remember, we're cooperating with him as long as it helps us. But Jenna wants to interview *you*. Don't give Logan your spotlight."

"You think he'd upstage me?" Exactly what I thought. Who wouldn't want to vote for Mr. Cool-and-Gorgeous? And he'd be as relaxed as Hendrix the Unflappable Feline in front of a camera.

Kat gave me a mild eye roll. "Stop worrying. Everyone's going to love you."

"Love me?"

She cocked her head, looked past me, and laughed. "Don't take my word for it. Ask your fan club."

I spun around to see Georgia and her Charlotte's Angels clan pointing at us. "There she is!" Georgia yelled.

Behind her, I caught a glimpse of that royal blue blouse. Panic rippled through me. Why were Georgia and her friends here early? Had they gotten a heads-up about the news truck?

Kat patted my shoulder. "Just answer. Smile. And thank her."

I swallowed and nodded. Watched my groupies speed-walk toward us. Focused on Mrs. Fine's heels clicking the tile. Tried to ignore the massive camera hoisted on the shoulder of the man trailing her.

When they reached us, Mrs. Fine gave me her prime-time news grin. "Charlotte Romero?"

Why couldn't it have been a bomb threat?

"That's me," I croaked, then cleared my throat.

"I'm Jenna Fine of KHAL News."

Duh.

"I'd like to interview you about Deedra's Dares. Would you be willing to answer a few questions?"

Willing? No.

Giving in? Yes.

"Um, sure."

Georgia and the Angels squealed.

Mrs. Fine beamed a patient smile at them. "Why don't you girls get behind Charlotte? Of course, I'll need you to stay quiet while we speak."

They gasped, like they'd been asked to go backstage at a rock concert, and then huddled behind me.

Kat moved behind the camera man, where she could direct. She wiped a finger in the air before her mouth, an upturned semicircle, reminding me to smile.

I blew out a gust of air while Mrs. Fine and her cameraman coordinated the particulars. Then I drew my face into as natural a grin as I could manage. A minute later, the camera began recording and the KHAL microphone was shoved into my face.

Mrs. Fine introduced herself, explained who I was, then turned to me. "Tell me, Charlotte, what made you enter the Deedra's Dares contest?"

Some part of me wanted to say "no comment," run away, and find Logan. Hanging out with him had to be a better way to spend the morning.

Instead, I looked down at the microphone, then back into the camera lens, and began to speak. "Our drama department is taking a trip to New York, and I want to go..."

Tick, tick, boom.

33
GREENROOM

Standing outside my apartment, I leaned back into Kat's SUV, said, "Wait for me," and got nods from each of the four people inside. Plus a wink from Logan in the back seat.

My front door loomed in front of me. It had never loomed before. After the marathon day I had—with the news interview, school and the contest buzz there, and a dress rehearsal for *A Christmas Carol*—home should have been a welcome beacon. But I wasn't looking forward to the conversation I needed to have with Mom.

Determination hardened my posture, and I walked into the house.

She sat in her favorite spot on the couch reading a book. Looking up, she gave me the same blank, yet somehow disappointed, expression she'd worn all weekend. "How was rehearsal?"

"Fine." Small talk. I didn't want to have small talk. "If I don't win the money, I'll quit theater"—my heart skipped—"and get a part-time job after school. But I don't want to quit the contest until I know."

She stilled, and I waited. Hoping she'd understand.

After several seconds, she ran her hand through her hair. "I just keep seeing you in that pig stall."

I shuddered. "Please don't remind me. No parent should see their teenager kissing."

"I'll second that." She shifted. "But Charlotte, this boy, this contest—"

"I won't lie to you anymore, but I'm not quitting. And it's not just the money. It's rediscovering a part of me I'd lost."

She looked at me then. Really looked at me.

"My friends are outside," I said, "waiting for me to invite them in."

She glanced toward the front door. "Friends?"

"I made them come here. So you could meet everyone and see for yourself."

"Meet everyone?" Her gaze darted between me and the entry-way.

"Kat and Logan, you know. But Jeremy and Dizzy are Logan's friends, and they're helping us. Actually, Kat's in their band now too. They play classic rock."

"Kat's in a band? Other than marching?"

"The point is that the five of us need to work on the next dare, and I asked them to come here, let you meet them, and maybe we could brainstorm tonight for a little while. Then you'd see that everything's okay."

Her brow formed a hard *V*. "I'm not comfortable with this contest."

I snorted. "Neither am I. This whole contest is the opposite of comfortable."

She rubbed her hands over her face, as if massaging away her worry. "You really want to keep going?"

I nodded. "There's another thing."

"Another thing?"

I steeled my myself. "KHAL was at school today."

"The news station?"

"Jenna O'Farrell-Fine."

"Isn't that Logan's stepmother?"

"And Deedra's mother. But she decided to interview one contestant—me."

"Why you?"

I shrugged. "Because I'm the underdog. And maybe to annoy Deedra. I don't know."

"She wants to annoy her own daughter?"

"They're kind of arguing. But it doesn't matter. What matters is that I did the interview, and it's coming on in a few minutes. Ten o'clock news."

Mom gasped. "You let yourself be interviewed?"

"Kat more or less demanded. I need the votes."

"Kat?" Every question she asked seemed to have more shock in its tone.

"She's like my campaign manager." I grinned. "Actually reminds me of a stage mom."

"Kathleen Jamison?"

"That's the one."

She sighed. Mom had a soft spot for Kat, so having her on my side had to help my case.

"Can I invite them in to watch?" I tilted my head toward the front of our house, where my friends were patiently waiting for a *come in* or *go home*.

Her head bobbled in an *I can't believe I'm doing this* head shake. "I don't have much in the fridge, but you should let your friends in. We can at least be hospitable."

I jumped off my chair and kissed her cheek. "Thanks, Mom."

She grabbed my hand and squeezed my fingers. "No more lies."

I gave her a reassuring smile. "No more lies."

Omission? Maybe. Lies? Definitely not.

She grabbed the TV remote. "What channel is this interview on? And do I need to pour a glass of wine before it starts?"

"Couldn't hurt." I could barely remember what I'd said, my nerves being on fire.

Within minutes, six people had crowded onto our couch, chair, and floor, and I'd made the necessary introductions.

Dizzy had given his extra-wattage smile as he shook my mother's hand, and even Jeremy had called her "ma'am." Logan had been his usual charming self. And Kat? Well, she was an acquired taste that my mom had already come to savor.

The newsy part of the ten o'clock program covered the same ground as always—trouble boiling in the Middle East, someone murdered in a gang fight in Houston, politicians promising things they couldn't deliver... We talked over the reports, and the three guys in my living room demolished our supply of tortilla chips and salsa. Any future visits from the male species would require more food.

When Jenna's flawless face came on the screen, I felt like one of those chips had lodged in my throat, even though I hadn't eaten any. Earlier-in-the-day me stood behind her, flushed and waiting, while Charlotte's Angels bounced excitedly in the background. Seeing myself on TV felt finger-pinch close to being on a stage.

"Yes!" Kat yelled at the screen. "Great smile, Charlotte. Makes you look very relatable."

"Ssh." I whispered. "Notes after."

Kat hushed herself, and we watched the interview.

I picked up on the tremble in my voice, but I didn't think it would be noticeable to everyone, and I didn't stumble over words. Maybe my theater training really had helped me with presentation skills, even though they'd collected cobwebs the last several years. Mrs. Fine dominated the scene, but I wasn't bad as a supporting character.

Even so, my nerves stabbed like a Shakespeare sword fight. I sat between my mom and Logan on the couch, and he squeezed my hand about halfway through, as if sensing I needed it. I felt a pat on my thigh from my mother's hand. My jaw started to hurt, and I realized I should pry my teeth apart. I took deep breaths through my nose and waited for the final moment. I could almost hear it as the camera pulled away from me—"*and scene.*"

My tiny audience whooped and clapped.

"Go, Charlotte!"

"Well done!"

My mother leaned close to my ear and muttered, "You did well, sweetheart."

I gave her a slight nod. I couldn't completely relax, because now it wasn't just an interview in the hallways of our school but on everyone's TV. How many people had watched? How many eyes had scrutinized me? My head started to sway, so I pushed myself against the back cushion.

"Wait, wait." Dizzy pointed at the screen. "Principal."

The room fell quiet.

Jenna Fine shoved her microphone into our school principal's face, the same way she'd done with mine. "Has this contest disrupted instructional time?"

Principal Dixon looked way more confident than I did, like he'd perfected his screen persona. "No, no." He shook his head. "We've coordinated with Deedra, the senior hosting this contest, and set proper parameters. No dares can occur during class time, and anyone attempting to do so will be disqualified."

I shot a glance at Kat.

She murmured, "Fine print."

Mrs. Fine returned the microphone to herself. "But isn't this a problem for the school? A contest hosted by a student?"

He beamed a broad smile. "Actually, since Deedra's Dares began, we've had better school attendance and participation. Maybe it's because the students are showing up to see what will happen next, but the result is more learning in the classroom and greater school spirit. As long as an activity doesn't interfere with the school's objectives or rules, we support students' creative endeavors, whether it's an extracurricular club or an unusual contest."

The camera refocused to Mrs. Fine alone. She concluded her report with the typical wrap-up language and a "back to you" at the news anchor.

Mom clicked off the TV.

Jeremy was the first to speak. "So as long as we don't start a fire, he's cool with the contest."

Kat laughed. "We already did fire."

I cringed, and my mother groaned.

"Sorry, Ms. Romero," Kat added.

Logan pointed at the screen. "Word is that ticket sales for all school events have increased, so he's getting more money to fund pet projects. That's probably why he's okay with it all."

"For money?" my mother asked.

Kat smiled at me. "You'd be surprised what people will do for money."

"Anyway…" I stood from the couch, hopefully leaving my jitters behind. "We need to work on the next dare."

Everyone started to rise, but Mom stopped us short. "What's the dare?"

I glanced back at her. "You didn't look?"

"If I did, I don't remember. I was too caught up in the videos." She shot a glare at Logan, like *I know what you did last summer…with my daughter.*

"Um, about that…" he started. "I didn't—"

I held up my hands, cutting them both off. "We're not having that conversation." I couldn't. Wouldn't. I turned to Mom. "But I will tell you the next dare."

"Here it is." Dizzy held up his phone and then read. "*Prank Up the Volume. Some senior classes do senior pranks. Our school has done exactly nothing. We have a few years to make up for. Plan and execute a prank that's big, fun, and buzz-worthy.*"

Mom shook her head—not the no head shake, but the super-worried head shake. "I still can't see how this ends well."

"What can I say, Mom?" I had an ace in the hole with my next statement, because she was a huge *South Pacific* fan who knew the lyrics to every song in that musical. "I'm a cockeyed optimist."

34
Run-through

High school is where optimism goes to die.

My positivity was gasping its last breaths when I walked into school Friday morning. With school, homework, theater rehearsals, dare preparations, and everyone talking to me and about me nonstop, I'd passed exhausted around Wednesday and was solidly in begging-for-a-weekend territory.

Not that the weekend would be any respite. *A Christmas Carol* had its first performance that night and a second on Saturday night.

"Hey." Logan met me at the front entrance, dangling his bootleg key and a weary smile. "I got all of my signs in the bathrooms."

I squinted my bloodshot eyes at him, wondering how he still looked so fresh and delicious. "You still haven't explained how you got that all-access pass. My key only opens the theater."

He pulled me into his arms, and Kat made a disapproving noise in her throat that translated to *hello, I'm here.* Logan ignored her and kissed me. "Would you believe I'm a spy? Bond, James Bond. I got Q to work up this skeleton key."

I snickered. "Does that make me a Bond girl?"

"The hottest one."

"Seriously?" I could hear the eye roll in Kat's voice. "Would you two focus on what's important right now? I did not stay up until one-thirty a.m. taping boxes and get up at the crack of dawn to watch you two make out. This is my one morning of the week off from band, and I could have slept in. But noooo, I'm here to make sure Charlotte stays in this stupid contest. Because that's the kind of friend I—"

"Do you ever stop talking?" Jeremy strode up behind her. "Save a few words for the rest of us, will ya?"

She tilted her head. "As if you use more words then 'yep' and 'nope.'"

"I just did."

I separated myself from Logan and yanked on Kat's arm, before this became another go-nowhere standoff between her and Jeremy. For whatever reason, they acted like two cats pacing and growling, pissed off for no other reason than being in the same alley.

"C'mon," I said. "We need to check on the maze. Wonder if anyone's gone through yet."

We marched together, the four of us, heading for the place we'd left several hours before.

Our school was built like the Pentagon, but with six long hallways spiking out from a central hub—a walled but open-aired courtyard. There were other connections between hallways, but at some point in the day everyone passed through the spacious hub to get from one wing to another.

When we reached the center, we stopped and stared at our gorgeous creation. Boxes and boxes and more boxes that we'd secured together with enough duct tape to wrap around our school ten times.

We'd collected every box we could get our hands on in the past week, from refrigerator size to shoe box, by asking for donations from grocery stores, collecting flattened boxes at the backs of discount stores, and running by liquor stores that left leaving empty boxes on their porch for anyone to take. The night before, we'd pieced them all together into a labyrinth like the one in that movie Logan and I had watched—only made of cardboard.

"Go big or go home," Jeremy muttered.

Kat shook her head. "Tell me you did not just say that."

"Hey!" A hand rose in the middle of the box maze, waving at us. Dizzy's thin-fingered, constantly fidgeting hand. "Some people have already gone through, and they think it's cool."

The worry I'd been holding in my gut eased just a bit. "It does look pretty good, right?"

Jeremy crossed his arms over his neon green shirt. "Yep."

Logan stroked my hand. "The Goblin King would be proud."

Kat surged forward. "Let's go through it."

"Again?" We'd been through the maze a couple of times the night before, but I followed her in anyway.

We met Dizzy in the middle, marveling at the fun of walking through a maze at school. It was like being a kid again, heading into the carnival fun house. Only instead of funky mirrors throughout, we'd added graffiti along the walls with magic markers—wordplay messages like "Be A-Maze-d" and "Go Out in a Maze of Glory." Jeremy had even added a picture of Jimi Hendrix with the words "Purple Haze Maze" beneath, which got a nod of approval from Kat. In between were reminders to VOTE FOR CHARLOTTE.

All of five of us huddled in the center and shared back pats and smiles.

Kat nudged me. "With the Logan and Charlotte angle, the viral video, and this prank? You're definitely making the next round."

My cock-eyedness grew as the morning wore on. Students gave me *attagirl* thumbs-ups and fist bumps and shouted at me across hallways.

"Great maze!"

"That must have taken hours!"

"Voting for you, Charlotte!"

I swung by the bathroom between classes and was greeted with a Please Wait To Be Seated sign—courtesy of Logan, who'd borrowed them from a restaurant supply company.

A straw-haired girl stopped, seemed confused.

I murmured over her shoulder. "It's a joke. Pee at your own leisure."

She turned around, red-faced with embarrassment, and muttered, "Thanks" before entering a stall.

But a new group into the bathroom simply laughed, snapped pictures, and noted the VOTE FOR LOGAN message on the other side. We'd done the bulk of work on my dare and elected for a simpler approach for Mr. Doing Just Fine.

I arrived to third-period English, settled into my desk, and cracked open my lit book to our current story, "Metamorphosis" by Franz Kafka.

The class intercom clicked. "Mrs. Salinas, would you please send Charlotte Romero to the office?"

I looked up, and heads turned my way.

Mrs. Salinas asked the intercom voice, "Is she leaving class or school?"

A pause, and the Louisiana drawl began again. "Just class. The principal needs to see her."

A collective "ooooh" went through the room.

I swallowed and gathered my things, trying to ignore the stares of my classmates and the scuffle of nerves in my stomach. There could be a number of positive reasons why I got called to the principal's office—an award or maybe another news interview.

But something about the wary tone in the school secretary's voice doused me with dread.

A few steps into the hallway, I caught sight of Shay setting up what looked like a lemonade stand—a cardboard booth propped in a wide part of the hallway with a cut-out rectangle on top. I strolled toward her, wondering what the prank was. She reached into a large garbage bag and pulled out a doll, a full-sized inflatable doll. Dressed in a Falcon cheerleader uniform.

My eyes popped open as I reached the front and saw it labeled Kissing Booth.

Shay turned and winked at me. "I got five of these booths around the school. But I'll be lucky if I make it home with even one of these dolls."

"Um—"

Her giggle cut me off, not that I had any idea what I was going to say.

Before I could come up with something, pounding feet caught my attention.

Shay and I both spun around to see Walker jogging toward us. "Oh yeah." He reached us and grabbed the doll. "You definitely have my vote, Shay. My. Kind. Of. Prank." With every staccato word, he shoved the doll against himself in a disgusting display I expected to be repeated many times throughout the day with the guys.

Gross.

"Give me that." Shay yanked the doll from Walker. "You couldn't satisfy a woman if you grew octopus hands and an actual heart."

"Good luck," I murmured, leaving Shay to wrangle with Walker.

The office was located past the main corridor, meaning I'd have to go through the maze again to reach it. As I neared, I heard rips and murmurs. I picked up speed and turned the corner into the hallway that led straight to our crafty creation.

One step into the new hallway, I stopped. My chest caved.

Half the walls were gone, and a pile of flat boxes lay off to the side. Three custodians were disassembling my maze, piece by piece.

I started running, my heartbeat setting the pace. "Stop it! Stop!"

The three men turned and gazed at me with confused expressions.

I reached the maze, bent over with sharp breaths, and pleaded, "That's my maze. You can't take it down. It's my dare. Please, please leave it up. I have to—"

"Principal's orders." The one who spoke jerked his head toward the office, like *take it up with the authorities.*

A sob swelled in my chest, but I shoved my crying back down. Still, the tears crept into my eyes. As I stumbled past the workers, I tried again. "Just wait. Let me talk to the principal. I'm begging you not to take any more down. Please."

In minutes, they were tearing apart what had taken us days to plan, hours to construct.

They exchanged wary glances. It seemed fifty-fifty that they'd stop working until I got back. Or eighty-twenty, against me. But I had to try.

Scurrying into the office, I wiped away my tears, approached the front counter, and leaned over to address Mrs. List, the Louisiana-native secretary who'd summoned me. "I'm Charlotte Romero. Here for the principal."

She took one look at my face, grabbed her Kleenex box, and hustled toward me. "Oh, darlin'. I'm so sorry. Here you go." She plucked out a tissue and handed it over.

I dabbed at my eyes. "They can't take down my maze."

Mrs. List had sympathy written all over her eyes, but *not my choice* written all over her face. She could do nothing more than follow the principal's orders either. "He's got someone in his office and someone waiting, but you should be up next."

I followed her into the back hallway. When we reached the waiting area, surprise swallowed my breath again.

Seated in one of three chairs outside the principal's door was Deedra, looking as furious as I was flustered.

35
Director

Outside the principal's office, I sat in the chair at the end of the short row, leaving one chair between me and Deedra. Not that I'd had any choice with her Michael Kors handbag resting on the seat.

"What is wrong with you people?" She huffed and straightened her slim skirt.

I turned away and sniffed back the last of my crying jag.

"Can't you read the fine print?" She kept her voice low but needle sharp. "No damage to school property, no disruption of instructional time. Why are you making my life soooo hard?"

"What are you talking about?" If I didn't challenge her, she'd probably consume with me with an hours-long rant that centered around Deedra, Deedra, Deedra. Since that's all she seemed to understand.

She shook a thin finger at the principal's office. "Kirk's in there right now, getting in trouble. And you're next in line."

Pinpricks danced around my scalp. "What did Kirk do?"

She shook out her hair, which remained perfectly styled, and her perfume rolled through the air like a floral-tinged stink bomb aimed at my nose. "At least this will finally get you out of my contest."

"What?" I bit my lip, leaned forward, and looked past Deedra to the principal's office.

As if on cue, the door flung open and Kirk stepped out.

I jerked back.

"Again, I'm sorry." Kirk cleared his throat. "Really sorry, sir. If there's anything I can do…"

The principal came up behind him. "You can think long and hard about your choices. You can use your head, son. That's what you can do."

Kirk bounced his head in a frenzied nod. "Yes, sir. Of course, sir."

My sympathy for him was immediately followed by dread for me. What had he done? What was his punishment? And what was coming for me?

The principal nodded once at Deedra, then gestured to me to enter his office.

I watched with my breath in my throat as Kirk hung his head, murmured "sorry" to Deedra, and walked out.

Deedra responded with a disgusted grumble, like she couldn't bear to put up with such lowly beings.

I held on tight to my stuff, my courage, and my glare as I walked past her. If I was going to get tossed out of the contest anyway, I might as well go down wearing a defiant scowl.

Principal Dixon lifted his chin. "Shut the door."

I closed the door and took the seat nearest the exit across from his desk.

"Miss Romero." He clicked the end of a pen over and over with his thumb. "I understand you are responsible for the maze in the middle of our school?"

"Yes, sir." I sat on my hands to keep from wringing them in my lap.

"Well…" He finally quit with the pen-clicking. "It created a bottleneck, and students were unable to reach classes on time. We received complaints from teachers and students."

I sat straighter. "I'm sorry. I had no idea. I didn't think—"

He cut me off with a raised hand. "I understand it wasn't your intent. But we have to take the maze down. We cannot allow these pranks to disrupt class time."

"I understand." All that effort, wasted. All my excitement this morning, gone. My maze was live for less than three hours.

"Unless you have someplace to put all these boxes right now, they'll go in the dumpster."

"Dumpster's fine." My voice cracked. It had taken several trips with Kat's, Jeremy's, and Dizzy's vehicles to collect all that cardboard. And we were going to recycle it all in the end anyway. But I hadn't imagined the end would be so soon.

He nodded once and returned to clicking his pen.

I sat, waiting for the next part, the part where he delivered my consequence and I took it like a champ. Or at least didn't fall into a heap of shame on his over-worn carpet.

"You have something to say?" he asked.

Was this my opportunity to throw myself at the mercy of my judge? I swallowed. "I'm sorry. We didn't think about the number of people who'd be going through and how that might affect the school schedule and—"

"I'm still assessing whether any real damage was done. So far, the worst I've heard is a freshman who cried when she was late to a pop quiz." He smiled and shook his head. "Most students would do anything to skip a pop quiz. Let's hope that's all there is."

"Yes, sir." I would not only hope, but pray. Fervently.

"That's it for now." He jerked his chin toward the door. "Get back to class."

I jumped up and headed for the door. "I promise to be super careful from now on." Assuming I had a from-now-on.

I walked out of his office, and a millisecond later, Deedra was on her feet and in my face. "How busted are you?"

The hopeful glee in her expression hit all wrong. Deedra wanted to dance on my grave. In a pair of blue suede booties.

Why did she dislike me so much? Because I was in her contest? Because I was dating her stepbrother? Because I unintentionally overheard her argument with her mom? That wasn't my fault.

"Who really stands to lose if several of us get ousted?" My voice took on a plead-my-case tone. "What would you do with the remaining rounds? You'd have to call the contest early. And you'd never get all the attention you want."

Her eyes narrowed like lasers. "I don't need the likes of you. I already have national attention."

A stab of guilt hit me even before I spoke. But I already felt ragged, and her haughty tone scraped me raw. "You have national attention because of *me*. Your mom didn't even want to interview you, but she was happy to stick a mic in my face."

Direct hit. Not just for Deedra. My guilt grew spikes and burrowed into my gut.

She pressed her lips together and rolled them into her mouth, as if she needed a bit of warm-up before she unleashed on me. "How dare—"

"Deedra!" Principal Dixon called out from his office. "Step on in, young lady."

"This is not over," she murmured to me. Then she grabbed her designer bag and pushed past, making sure to shove my shoulder.

I stumbled back a few steps. The principal's door slammed behind her. Righting myself, I leaned against the wall and tried to regain my composure. Not wanting to be there when Deedra re-emerged, I left the back office.

As I walked past Mrs. List, she asked, "Not in too big o' trouble, I hope?"

I gave our receptionist a fake smile and shook my head.

She smiled back with the reassurance of a grandmother. "All's well that ends well."

"Yeah, I guess so."

But as I walked back toward my classroom, I couldn't help it—tears rose to my eyes. I had read the fine print that the administration taking action against a student for a dare's consequences could be disqualified. Or *would* be disqualified. I didn't remember which.

Was my chance at Broadway over? Would I have to get a part-time job? Were my theater days numbered? Had I let the whole gang down?

If so, it had not ended well.

36
Ensemble

Distractions can be a good thing. With winter break hitting right after our pranks, I'd gotten no information out of Deedra on whether I was disqualified. But the performances of *A Christmas Carol* had gone well, my *abuela* had visited and made her delicious tamales for Christmas, and now I was heading into a nightclub with friends.

Not that these events kept my mind completely off my contest fate. That would require a distraction of apocalyptic proportions.

The sign above the door read "Fins" and had a drawing of a single shark fin sticking up from a three-pronged wave. Neon tubes formed the words, the picture buzzed and blinked, and the massive wooden door creaked as Kat pushed it open.

My nose twitched at the stale mixture of salty air and fried food that poured out.

"Nice club fashion." Kat nodded approvingly, her voice raised to combat the music pouring from the open doorway. "Leggings look good on you. Although a rock band shirt would have been better."

I stuck out my tongue playfully. "I like my outfit." She'd offered to loan me her T-shirt with Tom Petty & the Heartbreakers, a band I could name only one song from, but I'd opted to show off my Christmas loot. Mom had gifted me with black leggings and a *Wolff* musical T-shirt, which I'd paired with a secondhand denim jacket and my pink Converse.

We were barely through the door, and I was pulled back against Logan's chest, his arms wrapping tightly around me. "I missed you."

I giggled. "It's been four days. And we texted the whole time."

He pushed my hair off my neck and kissed my collarbone to my ear, sending sparks through my skin and heat into my bones. "Can't do that on the phone."

"Seriously?" Jeremy stood a few feet away, arms crossed over his chest. "Get a room."

Kat's eye roll was so quick I barely knew it was there. "For once, I agree with Jeremy. We're not here to make out. We need to check this place out."

Logan released me from the hug and slipped his hand into mine. "Why don't *you two* get a room?"

"What?" they both screamed.

Dizzy laughed and walked away, a bounce in his gait and his fingers thrumming his thigh to the beat of the music.

I glanced at Logan, wondering what I'd missed.

"C'mon." He pulled me forward, following Dizzy's path.

Kat and Jeremy brought up the rear.

The word *club* had made me think splashy room with sleek bar, shiny lights, and slick dance floor. Instead, something crackled under my shoes, and one downward glance revealed nutshells and grains of sand littering the peeling concrete floor. The bar and tables in the large room were weathered wood, decorated with graffiti written in ink and etched with knives. Walls were covered with rock band posters, some secured but others torn or hanging by one or two remaining staples. Over the laminate dance floor in the middle hung a disco ball, missing about a third of its tiny square mirrors.

Kat muttered behind us, "Everyone's gotta start somewhere."

We ordered drinks that all came with the word *virgin* in front of them, although I was sure plenty of the teens in the club weren't going alcohol-free. We spotted an empty bar-height table for two and squeezed around it. I shrugged off my jacket, pulled out my phone for the millionth time today, and opened Deedra's website.

No further damage had been reported from my maze. However, the juiced-up grapevine had revealed Kirk's prank infraction—putting detergent in the school's fountain that ended up killing the koi fish. Unintentional result, but he might face greater consequences when we returned in January.

Logan leaned closer. "Nothing when I checked five minutes ago."

"Doesn't she usually post by eight?" I pushed a slow sigh past the six-foot-thick wall of tension in my body. Kirk wasn't necessarily out, since the contest fine print had said *could* be disqualified, leaving Deedra options.

"Give it a few more minutes. Results will be up soon."

A four-member band stood on the small stage up front and played a song heavy on drums, reasonably dance-worthy, and completely unfamiliar.

"So..." I slapped my phone onto the table, face down, trying to refocus. "What is this music?"

"Sounds eighties," Logan answered.

"Clash?" Jeremy asked.

Kat rubbed her eyes, as if hiding the eye roll underneath. "Ramones. And we could play it better."

The four of them descended into a long discussion about which songs they'd include in their sets, how they'd arrange themselves and their instruments on the stage, and whether the manager's statement that their music samples were "pretty good" was enough to secure a future gig.

I *yoo-hooed* with my hands. "Don't you need a name if you're going to perform?"

"Rented Radicals," Logan said.

"Flaming Bees," Dizzy said.

"Butter Stick," Jeremy said.

They traded annoyed looks.

"Butter Stick?" I grimaced.

Logan shrugged. "Inside joke."

Kat slurped the last of her slushie. "We are not naming our band Butter Stick."

"Fine." Jeremy jabbed his finger at Kat. "What do you suggest we name the band, new member?"

She grinned, cockily. "How about Psycho Kitty?"

He snorted. "If you're referring to Hendrix, try Lazy Cat."

Kat scowled. "Well, you should know lazy. And psycho, for that matter."

"I'm not—"

"Let's dance." Logan pulled me to the dance floor. He wrapped his arms around my waist and swayed us in rhythm to the slower song. "I can't take another minute of those two arguing."

I glanced back at Kat and Jeremy talking and glaring at one another. "Did I miss something?"

"They won't shut up in practice."

"Trouble already?"

"Nah, just sexual tension."

I froze, pushed away from him. "Sexual tension?"

He laughed, then drew me back in and spoke in my ear. "Can't you feel it? It's like they're in heat."

"Kat and Jeremy?" Kat had never said one word about liking Jeremy. Actually, she was always complaining about him being a smart-ass.

"Don't worry about them." Logan dragged his palm up my back, slowed on the bare skin of my neck, and curled his fingers into my hair. "What you really missed is me."

"Did I?" I couldn't ignore the high kicks of my heartbeat, but I could act the part of unaffected.

"Remember this?" He kissed the corner of my mouth, gave me a soft peck, then teased my lips open with his tongue.

The room seemed to close in on me—all the people around, possibly watching us. I flinched away from him. "We're making out *here*?"

He leaned his forehead against mine. "Just giving you a taste of what's coming later."

My breath staggered, stalled.

I'd missed kissing Logan over the holidays, but the memory of my mom seeing our pig stall video... What if someone videoed us? Posted it online? Shared it with my mom? I didn't want a repeat of her panic and our conflict.

I bit my lip. "As much as I enjoy—"

Someone tapped my shoulder and squealed.

I spun around to see a familiar face, but I couldn't come up with a name. Still, she was one of Charlotte's Angels.

"Hey." She beamed at me, darted a glance at Logan, then back to me. "Your maze was awesome. I can't believe they made you take it down."

I grinned. "Yeah, well. It was making some students late."

"Still." She squeezed my arm. "You'll be higher next time."

Tremors rippled through my chest. I broke contact with Logan and started to grab for my phone. Then realized it was on the other side of the club. I turned back to the girl. "Um, thanks." In seconds I was back at the table with my phone in my hands.

Logan called after me, "Charlotte!"

Ignoring his voice, as well as Kat, Jeremy, and Dizzy all asking what was up, I clicked on the website. My stomach uncoiled as I scrolled down and read the news I'd been waiting for.

Kirk, disqualified due to school suspension for last dare.

Me, still in the contest.

"You in?" Logan peered over my shoulder.

I slowed my finger on the screen and read again, this time pausing on the vote totals and contestant placement. My brain fumbled. "Um, yeah."

Kat bumped shoulders with Jeremy. "Told ya. You owe me ten."

It should have bothered me that Jeremy had bet against me, but my mind was far too stuck on contest results.

Logan's hand covered mine, and he lifted the phone to read himself. The muscles in his chest and arms tensed where they touched my back and shoulders.

Dizzy had his own phone out. "Whoa. Charlotte came out ahead of you."

"What?" Kat grabbed the phone from Dizzy's hand then scoffed. "Of course she did. She's a great contestant and has a kick-ass manager."

"Whatever," Jeremy said. "We all helped with both dares, remember?"

Logan's hand dropped from mine, and he stepped back. "Congratulations."

I wanted to jump into his arms, scream at the top of my lungs, and celebrate my second-place finish. But the disappointment in his tone, the slack in his shoulders, the half-hearted smile on his face made me feel guilty.

"Thanks," I managed to mutter.

The sad look in his eyes said so much more than the grin he attempted or the hug he pulled me into. He was the one who was supposed to be at the top, while my best showing had been middle of the pack. But I was second, and he was fourth—the final one listed.

"Hey," Jeremy shouted. "I got it!"

We all turned toward him, expecting who-knows-what.

"Band name." He lifted his half-empty glass like a toast. "Last Place. In honor of Logan's finish."

Logan's hands fisted, and his face flashed annoyance. But just as quickly, he let out a breath, released his hands, and reset to his usual cool expression. "It's all good. We're in for another round."

37
TAKE FIVE

We all sat on the worn garage couch, hovering around Logan's laptop and looking through the Deedra's Dares website. Everyone but Kat, who sat on the drummer stool and rubbed Hendrix under his furry chin.

This dare wasn't the doozy we'd been expecting, but it wouldn't be a cinch either.

Jeremy slumped on the couch's armrest. "Charlotte second. Logan fourth." He grinned, clearly amused that he could rib Logan about slipping in the ranks.

"I know, I know," Logan answered with a you-got-me tone, but his shoulders and jaw clenched.

He'd been outwardly cool about everything the last couple of weeks—having me over to watch movies, finally introducing me to his father, and delivering kisses so delicious they rivaled McGregor-Kidman in *Moulin Rouge,* my guilty pleasure musical. But any reminder of his last-place finish was like a pebble plunked in the middle of his mood, creating ripples that disturbed his trademark calm.

I was equally sympathetic and annoyed. Why wasn't I allowed to bask in my success without it messing with his ego?

Dizzy raised his fist for a bump. "You got fans, baby."

I gave him a quick tap of my knuckles.

"And a fabulous manager." Kat leaned into the cat's face. "Idn't dat right, Hendrix? Idn't dat right?"

Well, now everything was upended. Not only had Kat become frighteningly invested in me winning this contest, she was baby-talking the furball sprawled on an amp.

"Can we get back to this, guys?" Logan pointed at the laptop.

Dizzy jerked his head toward the screen. "Read it again."

I lifted my chin and projected my voice, as if reading for a play. *"You're on camera now, and some of you could use a makeover. This week, ALL of you are getting one. Change your appearance—drastically. Think cover model. We'll vote for the Best Extreme Makeover."*

"Recap." Logan rubbed his hands together, as if he couldn't wait to get this dare done and get back on top. "Kirk's out. The principal's watching. Deedra could get suspended if another dare messes up class or school property. This dare seems like dialing back a bit."

"I don't know." Kat dragged the lazy cat onto her lap. "Click that new button on Deedra's site."

I clicked at the top right corner of the screen, where a button read *Support Deedra's Designs*. It opened a crowdfunding page with Deedra's face on the sidebar and a description of her invest-in-me campaign.

Logan leaned in. "Told you she had something else up her sleeve. Now that the contest is getting national attention, she's sending people through to finance her startup."

"What startup?" At Kat's raised voice, Hendrix jumped onto the floor and wandered away.

I hadn't told Kat about it before, Deedra's idea seeming somehow private—something she should reveal. But she was definitely
revealing it now. I read from the web page. "Fine Nine Fashion.
Slim Feet, Stylish Shoes."

Logan nodded. "Dee's got super-thin feet and wants to make
shoes for people like her."

Kat snorted. "Snooty rich girls with money to throw away at a
ridiculous collection of shoes? Whatever." She grabbed her drumsticks and twirled them in the air. "About the makeover, you can
borrow anything in my closet."

"She said 'cover model,'" Jeremy said, "not undercover cop."

"What, like a drug dealer?" Kat *pfft*ed. "I'm not a thug! I'm a
beautiful, confident woman whose already good enough for the
cover of any magazine I'd want to be on."

"Hey, hey." I waved my hands. "Could you two maybe call a
truce long enough for us to deal with this dare?" Or maybe Logan
was right and they needed more than a truce. She'd said *nada*
about feelings for Jeremy, but were the sparks between them from
annoyance or attraction?

"Undercover Cop," Dizzy murmured. "Band name?"

Kat turned her glare to Dizzy. "We are not naming our band
Undercover—"

Logan stood, shoved two fingers in his mouth, and whistled.

We froze.

Hendrix yowled.

"Enough," Logan said. "We need to take this seriously." He
seemed tighter than a guitar string, ready to burst at one too-hard
pluck.

Jeremy spoke. "Chill, dude."

"I am chill," Logan said with plenty of heat in his voice.

The rest of us stayed silent, as if waiting to see if that pluck would come.

Jeremy folded his arms. "No. You're not."

"Fine, I'm not." Logan's face reddened, his voice rose. "But I'm the one doing these dares to get your equipment a decent ride!" Pluck. *Snap.*

I shoved the laptop away, stood, and pointed at him. "You and I need to talk. Now."

I'd never used my *I mean business* tone with him. Or anyone. I didn't even know I had an *I mean business tone*, but my words came out with the force of a battering ram.

He winced.

Out of the corner of my eye, I caught the others trading con-fused glances. But I walked out of Dizzy's garage and headed to-ward the trampoline.

Logan followed, his heavier feet crunching the grass behind me.

I lifted myself onto the trampoline and walked the perimeter. "No spiders, no webs. It's safe."

He climbed up and took a seat in the middle.

I sank down across from him, close enough to chat, but not close enough to touch. I didn't want distractions. "This isn't working."

His face fell, and his shoulders and chest crumpled. "What?"

"This." I swirled my hands in the air, indicating *the whole thing.* "It's not working."

His lips parted, but no words came. The color seemed to drain from his face. Finally, he shook his head. "No, no, no. You can't break up with me. I—"

"What?" I winced. "I'm not breaking up."

"You're not?"

"Do you want to break up?" My stomach trembled.

"Why would I want to break up?" He ran a hand through his hair, messing it up more. Then shimmied closer and covered my hands with his own. "But if you're not breaking up, what do you mean 'it's not working'?"

"I meant the contest."

"The contest?"

His thumbs circled on my hands, reminding me how much I enjoyed his touch. But whenever the contest came up, his touch, words, and expressions were all tinged with tension.

I let go and leaned back on the trampoline. "I don't want to work together anymore."

His eyes widened while his brow narrowed. "Why not?"

"That." I pointed back at the house. "You've been a bit of a, well, *pendejo* about me beating you in the last round."

"What's a *pendejo*?"

"Let's just say it means jerk." He didn't need to know that it was a bit spicier. "But you've treated me coming out ahead like I was trying to unseat you."

"I never said—"

"You didn't have to." Actions spoke louder than words. "It shows in how you treat me and that little outburst in the garage."

He brought back that kick-back smile. "I didn't have an outburst. And what do you mean—how I treat you?"

I stood, and the trampoline wiggled. I reset my feet to keep from falling. "You're so peeved about your last-place finish that I feel like I shouldn't be celebrating that I got second place. And that's a big deal for me."

"I know. I'm happy for you." His smile had faded.

"Yeah, well. Maybe you need to deal with the fact that I'm not Charlotte Nobody anymore, that I have just as good a chance as you at winning this contest."

He flinched, then set his jaw hard. His gaze pierced me through. "I never—*never*—said you were a nobody. I didn't think that then, and I don't think it now."

"So you're not bothered that I beat you?"

His nostrils flared and he stood, jiggling the trampoline more. "You know what I never did in any other round?"

With him weighing more, my feet fought to stay solidly in place.

He didn't seem to waver in the least. "I never said, 'I beat you.' That's not how I looked at it. And the fact that you do says a lot."

"You didn't answer the question." I pressed my soles down and hunkered further down into my anger. "Are you bothered that I edged you out in the prank? Because our group came up with two dares, and you're the one who told me to take the box maze."

He shook his head. "Unbelievable." He crossed the trampoline and jumped down.

I planted my fists on my hips. "Are you going to answer?"

"You want my answer? Fine." He spun around, and a new level of showed on his face. "I'm not upset with you. I'm not jealous of you. I'm not anything but on your side." Somewhere in there, his voice had risen in volume and finally reached yelling. "But since the feeling's not mutual, we definitely shouldn't work together."

"Logan, I'm on your side. I just don't want things to be bad between us."

He scoffed. "Yeah, like this conversation hasn't hurt anything."

I opened my mouth to speak.

But he held up a palm. "Look, I'm not breaking up. But maybe we should take five."

His words were like a needle threading my gut, then weaving knots into my belly. *Take five?*

"Logan." My voice was shaky, breathless, repentant. "I didn't mean for anything to change about us—just the contest."

He stared at the ground and tucked his hands into his jean pockets. "Yeah. I'll come up with my dare. You come up with yours."

"So we're okay?" *Please say yes, please say yes, please say yes.*

He shut his eyes briefly. When he opened them, he was different—harder, darker, farther. "I'm going home. May the best contestant win."

38
DRESSING ROOM

Logan was avoiding me, and I was avoiding the inevitable—coming up with a makeover plan that would impress people enough to make them vote for me. Even with Kat working behind the scenes and Charlotte's Angels cooing over everything I did—*so weird*—I couldn't rest on previous success. I had to earn my spot. Every. Single. Round.

I turned a corner at school, heading to my next class and nearly ran over Deedra. I backed up. "Sorry."

She jutted out her hip and tongued her cheek. "Why are you always in my territory?"

I hadn't been for the last week. Not a single visit to Logan's house. "Why do you always ram into people?"

She glanced down at my feet, then back up to my eyes. "Do you even own another pair of shoes?"

"I like these shoes."

"Don't take it personally, but I cannot have you be the face of my contest." Once again, she acted like I'd invaded her contest, rather than entered it like everyone else.

And I was tired—tired of her, tired of the contest, tired of the stress seeping through my life. "I'm not trying to be the face of your contest. I just want the money."

She narrowed her eyes. "So you can pay me back for the damage to my car with my own money?"

"So I can go to New York for a trip to Broadway. Which I don't have the money for. Believe it or not, that's the main reason I entered this thing."

She shrugged a cashmere-sweatered shoulder. "Been there. Done that. *Phantom of the Opera* sucked. Creepy guy in the basement, opera singer—what's the point?"

I ground my teeth together to keep my tongue from lashing out. The fact that she'd been to Broadway and I hadn't proved just how cruel life could be.

"Good luck with the dare." She smirked and walked past.

I spun around. "Rather than treating me like gum on the bottom of your overpriced shoe, you could be nice to me. I am helping you get followers."

Shaking her head, she turned and sneered. "You know, Logan's an even bigger jerk because of you."

The switch in subject blindsided me. "What are you talking about?"

She rolled her eyes up to her fiery red hairline. "I can barely do my homework with him doing those vocal exercises you taught him. And he can't shut up about you. Not to mention the last week of *Charlotte's breaking my heart* songs he's composing. It's pathetic."

Heat traveled up my arms, strangled my neck, seared my scalp. "He's composing songs about me?"

"Don't get excited. As soon as Logan starts landing gigs, do you really believe he won't toss you over for some hot chick he meets at a club?"

My chest pinched. "Screw you." I marched away, wishing I'd had a better retort. But at least I'd said something. And Deedra thinking I wasn't worthy of her stepbrother? Just made me more determined to stay in her contest.

And win.

I walked into theater tech and strode right to my safe space, the costume closet. If Logan had arrived to class, I hadn't seen him. Hadn't looked. As much as I hoped Deedra was right about him missing me, he'd been the one to ask for the break. He should be the one to mend it. I wasn't going to beg.

Ignoring the static of *will we or won't we* buzzing in the back of my mind, I kicked around the closet and focused on wardrobe for various spring musicals we might do. We had costumes from previous performances of *Guys and Dolls*, *Little Shop of Horrors*, *Annie*, and *Mary Poppins*—that "British nanny bitch," as Kat had called her. Popular productions now were *The Addams Family*, *Beauty and the Beast*, and *Mamma Mia*. I still had my fingers crossed for *Wolff*.

I slammed my backpack into the corner, took a deep breath, and opened the cabinet where we stored accessories, not sure what I was even looking for. We had swords, hats, belts, fake jewelry, wigs...

A wig we'd used for a children's theater production of *Little Mermaid* caught my eye. I pulled out the long red Ariel hair, gathered up my own hair, and tucked it under the wig.

Opening the cabinet door further, I looked in the mirror tacked there. My body stilled. The hairpiece was close to the color of Deedra's. Darker, but close.

I yanked off the wig and practically ran back to the stage. Logan was helping to move some furniture, but Marita was standing off to the side swiping an iPad screen.

I grabbed her arm. "C'mon, I need you."

"Me?" She fumbled, startled by my sudden tug on her arm. But I kept pulling, and she handed the tablet off to someone else and let me lead her away. "Where are you taking me?"

"Dressing room."

We reached her favorite place, where Marita was the master of makeovers. I dropped the red wig and pulled out my phone. Clicking through, I found what I was looking for, enlarged the picture, and shoved it forward for Marita to see. "This. Can you make me look like this?"

Her jaw fell. "You want to look like that?"

I lowered my phone. "If she wants a makeover, I want to give her a makeover."

I watched Marita closely, trying to decide whether she was an enemy, a bystander, or an ally. At different times, I'd felt like she was each.

Her shock gave way to a broad smile. "This is effin' brilliant. It'll be hard, but yeah, I think I can do it. I can at least try."

My chest puffed up like popped corn. "Let's give it a shot. What will I owe you?"

"Oh no." She folded her arms. "The look on her face will be payment enough. But does Logan know?"

Logan. Maybe he was composing songs about me, but I didn't know for sure what that meant. And regardless, we'd agreed to work apart.

"No." I shook my head to punctuate the point. "And he can't find out."

This dare would be all mine.

39
ADAPTATION

Yep, this dare was all mine. And I'd gone for broke.

For two hours, I sat with my back to the mirror while Marita worked on me. She refused to let me peek, but the expressions on her face told a story. One in which she played Dr. Frankenstein and couldn't decide whether to be happy or horrified by her creative skill.

With a big huff, she finally set down an eyeliner pencil and grabbed a lighter red wig that she'd borrowed from somewhere.

I kept still as the angel statue I'd been while she settled it onto my head, pinned it securely, and tucked away any stray strands of my own hair. "Well?" I hadn't a clue whether she'd actually pulled it off. Or whether this was even a good idea. But it was my idea, and I was sticking with it. Even if Kat thought it was supremely strange. "How do I look?"

Her eyes spread bigger than her bra cups. "*Mierda.* That's scary."

"Scary?"

"Yeah, all that contouring was a bitch, but the result is worth it."

I popped out of the chair and turned toward the mirror.

Dios mío.

Gone were my brunette hair, dark eyebrows, brown eyes, rounded cheekbones, thicker lips and, well, everything that was me. The girl who looked back at me had red hair, strawberry eyebrows, smoke-gray eyes—thanks to a pair of colored contact lenses—angular cheekbones, and thinner lips.

I barely found my voice. "Five stars and then some."

Marita preened. "Thank you."

Based on her talent, next year's musical should be something like *Cats.* "Well, here goes nothing. Time to get dressed."

Several minutes later, I emerged wearing a new face and a completely-unlike-me outfit. Acid-washed skinny jeans purchased from Goodwill for couch change, a shimmery silver top Marita loaned me that cut lower than any of my T-shirts, heeled boots I'd snagged from my mom's closet, and massive earrings I'd found in the costume jewelry section of our drama wardrobe. I couldn't have felt more uncomfortable if I'd been wearing a Disney character costume.

Teetering on my heels, I walked behind Marita into the school gym.

Football and marching band were over, but basketball season had begun. Since our basketball team was way better than our football team, it was a well-attended event. And even more crowded since rumor had it that all four remaining contestants would be making an appearance.

The second the door opened, I was assaulted by the squeak of cleats on the gym floor, the screams of fans, the screech of a whistle. All that noise couldn't compare to the thunderous heartbeat pulsing in my ears. This makeover would make or break me.

Marita squeezed my arm. "Good luck." She took a few steps forward, turned back, and shuddered again. "Freaky. Just freaky."

She left me alone. I bowed my head, trying to gather my courage. I couldn't hide in the narrow space beside the risers forever. I had to be seen.

I can do this. I can do this.

Lifting my head and imagining Deedra's gait, I strode forward. If I could pull off this lookalike, I'd deserve a Tony.

At first, most people didn't seem to notice as I passed the stands. A few did a double-take, as if trying to reconcile two things at once. Which they were.

Kat sat on the front row looking around and beyond me. How long would it take for her to notice the doppelganger coming right at her? I'd nearly reached her when her face went slack, horrified, and a little impressed. Maybe a lot impressed. She popped up and grabbed both of my shoulders, holding me back away from her.

A guy yelled for her to move out of the way.

"Oh. My..." She stalled, as if searching for words—something Kat had never had a problem with before. "Move over, Marilyn Manson. This is so much creepier."

"Good enough for votes?" And to get under Deedra's skin?

Para, Charlotte! This craving for revenge needed to stop. Even if she deserved it, did I want to be the kind of person who reveled in her discomfort? No, but it was ever-so-tempting to revel.

The same guy yelled at us again.

Kat flicked him a *shut-up* look. "They're in a time-out." Then returned her gaze to me. "Though we should move anyway, because we have got to work this room. I want eyeballs on you, phones snapping pics, Insta and TikTok blowing up. Charlotte's Angels will be all over this. I saw Georgia at the concession stand."

Shifting back into her take-charge self, she strode forward a few steps.

I stopped and scanned the gym. "Have you seen Logan?" He'd texted that he would be here. Wanted to make sure I was coming too. The conversation after that had been sparse.

Kat shook her head. "Are you coming?"

I heaved a sigh and nodded. "Yeah, but we have to go slow because I'm not used to these heels."

We stopped off at a section of marching band members and chatted for a while, carefully watching people's reactions. There were plenty of *wows* and *how did you do that*s?

A few minutes in, Jeremy sauntered in holding a bag of popcorn and a drink. He took one look at me, jolted, and spilled both. "What did you—" He cringed. "That is so...wrong."

Kat tilted her head at him. "Deedra said extreme makeover. This is extreme."

"And disturbing," he added. "What about Logan?"

"What about him?" I asked, hoping for hints that he was nearby and wanted to end our "take five" already.

"I'd be pretty rattled if the girl I wanted to nail looked like my sister."

"Wanted to nail?" Kat looked like she had swallowed a cock-roach...or thought Jeremy *was* a cockroach.

He shrugged. "I'm just saying he likes her. You like a girl a lot, you at least think about nailing her."

"What is she, a two-by-four?"

I could tell this was going to quickly descend into another chemistry-charged showdown between Jeremy and Kat. I sighed and swished past them. When I looked back, they were still arguing, but sitting together with Kat's hand in Jeremy's bag of popcorn.

I located Georgia in the hallway and began a round of selfies with each and every person in the Charlotte's Angels fan club. After which I obliged everyone else who swung by and wanted their picture taken with *faux* Deedra. Kat had insisted on me practicing my Deedra pose, and I had it down—chin lifted, lips puckered, and a smile underneath that pushed up my cheekbones and conveyed "I love being me."

The next hour involved me being flagged down in the gym, the hallways, and the women's restroom for people to *ooh* and *aah*, ask questions, and take pictures. I found myself slipping into Kat's role as I made sure to say, "Would love your vote," before they wandered away.

I was reapplying lipstick on my talked-out lips when I heard another buzz down the hallway.

"Whoa, look at Shay," someone said beside me.

Even with my high heels, I had to get on my tippy-toes to see past the people gathering in front of me.

The crowd parted as she made her way toward the gym.

Shay had become a caricature—like Bratz or some anime character. She still had her tell-tale blond hair, but it was slick straight. Her eyes looked huge with black eyeliner and fake eyelashes giving her doll-like proportions. Her face was pale with pink cheeks. And the plaid mini-skirt and white blouse combo screamed University of Barbie.

Marita sidled up to me from somewhere. "You were a living statue. Guess she's a living doll. The makeup's good, but I like your idea better."

I wasn't so sure. Sex still sizzled off Shay, but in a naughty schoolgirl fantasy way. If Jeremy was right about guys and "nailing"—though in Jeremy's case, I thought that was mostly talk—Shay's look had to get some votes.

"Did you see Alec?" Marita whispered. The way she spoke, it sounded like she'd had a celebrity sighting.

"No. Where is he?" I darted my eyes around the hallways and peered into the gym, looking for him.

"You won't recognize him. You know that geek-turned-god cliché?"

I nodded.

"Turns out it's true. I had no idea he was such an Adonis."

I couldn't imagine Alec—brainiac boy with a lean build, messy hair and glasses, and a collection of science-based T-shirts—being *GQ* worthy. "You have to show me."

I followed Marita, wondering if we were becoming more than allies against Deedra. She hadn't just done my makeover but really supported me. We might be friends. Who knew I could have so many?

Once we reached the gym, Marita didn't point to Alec but someone else. "Well, there's Logan."

He leaned against the wall, hands in black jean pockets, looking up at the audience in the stands. Gone were his loose curls, replaced by a 1950s ducktail with a single curl dipping onto his forehead. He wore a black tee, black loafers, and one costume piece I'd recognize anywhere—a Rydell High letter sweater, exactly like the one Danny Zuko wore in *Grease*.

My heart fell to my stick-thin heels. I shook my head. "Why?"

He was all kinds of cute in that getup, but it was a barely-there makeover. Not the extreme one the dare called for. Why hadn't he done more?

As if sensing my gaze, Logan glanced in our direction. Turned away, then turned back. Pushing off the wall, he stared and let his jaw drop.

Marita bumped my shoulder. "Seems like you two need to talk. I'm going to find Alec and see if I can snag a date. I know that makes me seem shallow, but if he kisses like he looks, I think I can live with myself."

Logan began walking toward me, but I couldn't keep my eyes on him. I kept getting interrupted by people talking to me about my makeover, congratulating me, promising to vote for me. Or just looking at me, shuddering, and walking away.

I felt his hand on my arm before I saw him up close.

His normally stubbly jaw was smooth, and he smelled like aftershave. "This is..."

"I'm sorry if it's weird for you." I bobbed my head toward the stands. "Jeremy said it might be. But I'm not trying to make you uncomfortable."

"It's amazing." He knotted his brows. "How did you do that?"

I gave him a slight smile. "Marita."

He nodded slowly, still scanning my face and taking in the particulars with a perturbed look on his face.

"Why this?" I pointed at his sweater. "Not many people our age even know who Danny Zuko is."

He gave a mild shrug. "It's thematic. We finally watched that movie over winter break, and I paid attention. Danny also did a personal makeover because 'I'm gonna do anything I can to get her.'"

"That line's from the movie." From one of my favorite musicals.

"Yep."

My smile broadened. "Are you expecting me to go all Sandy for you? My own makeover with hot pants and heels?"

"That would be better than pretending to be my stepsister. Which is...something."

"I've heard scary, creepy, eerie, freaky, bizarre, wrong, and effed-up." I smiled. "Take your pick."

He laughed. "I was going to take you in my arms and say what I'd rehearsed...but I'm not sure I can do that right now." *He rehearsed something?*

"What did you want to say?"

"I wasn't upset that you beat me, but I was upset that I didn't do better and I didn't handle it well. We don't have to work together in the contest, but I don't want to be apart. I had my break, and it sucked. I want to be with you. You're the one that I want."

I had to force down a squeal. "That's from the movie too."

He swiped a hand through his hair, and it oddly stayed put. He must have used a jar of gel and a can of hair spray. "Pretty cheesy, huh. It sounded better in my head."

I leaned forward, then paused. "Can I at least kiss your cheek, or would that be too weird?"

"Hold on." He closed his eyes. "Go ahead. I'm imagining the real you in my head."

I brushed my lips against his cheek, then moved to his mouth.

His arms slid around my waist and pulled me close.

I clamped my hands together behind his neck and savored this incredible moment. My guy had gone all Danny Zuko for me. For *me*.

"Oh. My. God!" Deedra's voice sliced through.

We broke off, dropped our arms, and turned toward her.

Logan looked irritated, and I looked—well, I assumed shocked. Not that I hadn't expected to see Deedra, but I didn't think I'd be kissing Logan when it happened.

"How dare you!" She got in my face, nose to nose. If it felt awkward to be looking back at herself, she didn't show it. "You have a supreme amount of nerve. I don't know what made you believe you could pretend to be me, but it is *not* okay."

I swallowed a thick knot of fear. I couldn't let her get to me. "I can totally understand why you would be upset."

"Upset?" she screamed. "I should shred you where you stand."

Several heads turned our way.

Logan tapped her on the shoulder. "Dee, c'mon…"

She jerked her shoulder away. "Leave me alone, you traitorous prick."

"I'm not—"

"I got this, Logan." This was between me and Deedra. I turned back to her, leaned closer, and lowered my voice. "I'm just doing my best to get as many votes as I can. Honestly, Deedra, this will help you get more followers. We could even take a picture together for you to post on—"

"No," she snarled at me. "Don't you even try to make us equals."

Any residual guilt I had crumbled like a crushed cookie. Every time I tried to be a little nicer, she made clear that there was no point. "You don't want me as the face of your contest? Fine, I'm giving you the face you want."

"You can't have *my face*."

"You can't push me out of your contest. I didn't break any of your rules. It's up to the votes now."

If she had any reaction to what I'd said, I couldn't see it. Either she was too angry to respond or mesmerized by looking at someone who wasn't her but, with a whole lot of makeup, came close.

I took Logan's hand and led us both away. He turned back once, but then looked forward, kept pace with me, and said nothing more about our interaction with his stepsister.

As we walked through the gym, heads turned and phones lifted. Curious observers were searing this image into my history with snapshots that would be uploaded to the internet in seconds. My name would be underneath, but it would be Deedra's face they'd see.

And yet, I felt more like myself than ever.

40
Fade Out

I groupied up for the band's first-ever gig at Fins. Hopefully, not their last.

Sitting at the closest table to the stage, I'd worn a denim miniskirt, borrowed from Marita, and a bright pink tee I'd bought on Walmart clearance then studded with rhinestones to spell out "Feral Sound."

Needing a band name for this appearance, the guys and Kat had thrown ideas in a jar and pulled out one. Feral Sound had won, but there was still grumbling in the ranks.

Once at Fins, I'd been shooed away while they painstakingly unloaded their instruments and equipment from Kat's SUV and Dizzy's old hatchback.

Logan came in carrying two amps to the front. Much as I'd adored the Rydell sweater, his muscles were admirably on display in his short-sleeve Choose Your Weapon T-shirt with four illustrated guitars. "This is why I want to buy Deedra's old SUV."

"You should be happy." Kat trailed him into the club, toting cymbals on stands. "Without Jezebel, I don't know how you'd have gotten all your crap here."

He scowled. "Who's Jezebel?"

"Her SUV," I answered. "You sure I can't help?"

Logan dropped the amps, swaggered over to me, and landed a kiss on my lips. "Nah. Your job is to hold this table and be my biggest fan."

"Can do." I ran my hand down his arm, enjoying the backstage pass I had for touching him this way.

He glanced at my shirt. "Still can't believe you made that for us. Although you could have worn a shirt that said 'I'm with the Lead Singer.'"

I grinned. "And you could wear one that says 'I'm with the Hot Chick on the Front Row.'"

He tugged gently on a strand of my hair and smiled.

"Seriously?" Kat slapped him on the shoulder. "She sits and get ogled by you while I lug stuff? I'm done." She pulled up the other stool and sat. Firmly. Decisively.

Logan furrowed his brow but walked away without protest.

Kat smiled as he ducked out, and Dizzy and Jeremy ducked in carrying more stuff. "Anyway," she said. "You've got your alarm set, right?"

I chuckled. "Yes, but this is your night. Stop worrying about my contest."

"As soon as you get results, you hold up the exact number of fingers for what place you got. I bet Jeremy you'd be first, and he bet second."

"What if I'm third?" Or ousted. My stomach kinked.

She played with the earring dangling from her right ear. "We all bet on Logan being third. I said you first, then Shay, then Logan. All Alec did was clean himself up."

"True." But he cleaned up good. Like that moment when we all realized the kid who played Neville Longbottom had grown up to be a hottie.

Kat glanced up to the stage. "Whoa! Be careful." Jumping from her seat, she rushed over to Jeremy and directed him how to set up the keyboards.

For almost an hour, the band focused on setting up, warming up, and run-throughs. It was another hour-plus before the club started to fill, during which they played their B-list of songs. When things got hopping, they pulled out their faves.

I had to smile when the ZZ Top song they played was "Gimme All Your Lovin'" instead of "Tush." The guys had dropped their original choice after Kat's fifteen-minute rant on the shallowness of men singing about butts. Easier to switch songs than argue.

Marita showed up with a few theater friends and Alec on her arm. He stood with our group at the small table looking extremely uncomfortable and periodically darting guilty glances at Marita's boobs. Conversation was near impossible with the music booming in my ears, so I kept my responses to smiles and nods as my friends—*friends?*—yelled back and forth.

When they started up Journey's "Any Way You Want It," Marita grabbed my arm and pulled. "I know you can dance to this one. Let's go!" She dragged us to where the disco ball trickled light onto people swaying and bouncing to the beat.

Alec joined us a moment later.

Catching my eye, Logan gave me a smile and a wink. It felt like an invitation to loosen up and let go. And so I danced. Four songs in a row.

When so-called Feral Sound finished "All Day and All of the Night"—which I could swear was recorded from some band named the Kinks—I was breathless and laughing.

"This is fun!" I yelled.

A swash of red hair passed, and I dropped my laughter and watched Deedra walk to the front of the club. What was she doing here?

She stepped onto the stage, as if all spaces were open to her invasion.

Logan glared at her.

I moved to an angle where I hoped to read their lips.

She shook her head and mouthed what looked like "out."

The break between songs became an awkward silence with all eyes turned toward the stage. Their heads moved closer, and the conversation became private.

The band shuffled. People murmured. And then, Logan brows creased, and he darted a glance at me.

My stomach dropped to the wood floor, and I looked at Marita. "What time is it?" Not waiting for her answer, I pulled my phone from my pocket and saw that I'd missed the alarm four minutes ago.

Logan spoke into the microphone. "Thanks to everyone for coming out tonight." The music started up again.

I didn't recognize the song. Not that I could think about that anyway. I was too busy opening Deedra's website and reading results. Where was my name? Oh, there it was. First place...Charlotte.

A thrill ran up my torso and tickled my face. A squeal bubbled up inside me and came out in a strained, secret celebration. Charlotte Nobody had cleared first place in this round.

I hadn't won the contest, but winning was possible. Not a pipe dream, but truly possible.

Marita leaned closer. "Well?"

Her voice pulled me back to reality. I stared at the results again and felt a twang of guilt. Third place, Shay. Second place, Alec. Logan wasn't listed.

I showed the screen to Marita, then turned back to the stage where Logan sang as if nothing had happened.

Kat shot a quick wave in my direction. I remembered our deal and held up a single finger. She beamed a big smile, a personal victory. She'd helped me reach the top of the heap and won her wager with Jeremy, whatever they'd bet.

Logan glanced at me, a wary look on his face.

I rolled my lips into my mouth and shook my head. As in *no, you're not in the contest.*

He turned back to the microphone, sang the next lyric, and didn't look back again. What did that mean? Had he understood my message? Had Deedra already told him?

Alec strode up holding his own phone and pumping a fist. "Yes! I'm still in." Then he smiled at me. "Congratulations. Your makeover was incredible."

"Thanks," I yelled.

A thin, manicured hand tapped my shoulder, and then Deedra herself appeared. "I bet you think you're clever." If she could spear me with her sharp fingernail, I suspected she would. And twist a little to make the wound really burn.

But I was done. So. Very. Done. "Why do you hate me so much?"

"Hate you?" She scoffed. "As if I'd expend enough energy on you to hate you."

"Fine." I gave her a Kat-worthy eye roll. "Why do you dislike me? Or dismiss me? Or don't want me in your contest?"

I felt the stares of the people around us, growing more and more uncomfortable. But I simply waited for her answer, ready to bury the hatchet—in her chest if necessary.

She pressed her lips together, then leaned close where only I could hear. "He sacrificed his spot for you. Do you get that? Do you really get that?"

Shock rolled through my body. Of all the things she could have said, I never imagined it would be about Logan. Actual concern for Logan. But her tone was pleading, caring, sisterly.

"I—I didn't—"

"Of course you didn't." She moved back and resumed the Deedra face I recognized, confident and callous. "The next dare is with you in mind. Let's see how bold you really are."

Blood drained from my face as she strode away. *She was right.* Logan could have done anything he wanted with the makeover dare, and he'd done something meaningful to me. But not something that would get him votes. And he knew it.

Alec interrupted my thoughts. "Did you read the next dare?"

"Is it bad?" I winced. Deedra had said it was personal, with me in mind. No telling what that meant.

He swallowed the lump in his throat, visibly. "Um..."

"Gimme that." Marita grabbed his phone from his hands and read, "'*Underwear Bare.*'"

Just the title made my ears burn. What fresh hell...

"Plenty of people say swimsuits cover as much as underwear," Marita continued. *"So why not show off your barely theres? Appear in a public place—not school—wearing nothing but your underwear. Dare ya!"*

Panic churned my insides to butter. "Is that even legal?"

Alec nodded once. "Looked it up already. It's legal. Disconcerting, but legal."

Marita edged closer to him, a seductive smile lifting the corners of her mouth. "Boxers, briefs"—she paused—"or commando?"

His face went blank, then pink.

She laughed, clearly amused by the effect she had on him. From what Logan had said, she was far more yipping bark than tenacious bite. Flirtatious and up for kissing, but not the she-wolf she came across as.

Still, Alec was bitten and smitten.

Meanwhile, all I could think was *undies undies undies.* "Of course, it's personal." I gestured to Alec. "You can wear boxers and call it a day. Half of Shay's wardrobe already looks like it should be on a Victoria's Secret poster. But me? My mom will die if I go out in my undies. *I* will die if I go out in my undies."

Marita finally moved her roaming eyes off Alec and grabbed my hand. "Honestly, half this contest, I was rooting for Logan. I voted for Logan. But he's out. And you, girlfriend, are still in. If Deedra's making it personal—"

"I made it personal." I had to admit that. "I made myself over to look like her. If that's not personal, what is?"

"Fine. Forfeit." She grabbed Alec's hand. "But not tonight. Tonight, Alec and I are going to forget this contest and dance our asses off. Maybe you should do the same."

They left, and I turned my eyes to the stage, where Logan was singing "Hold On Loosely." His voice was smooth and strong, improved since he'd been practicing my singing tips. As if sensing me watching him, he homed in on me.

He gave a half-hearted smile as if he was happy for me. But the smile didn't reach his eyes. Was it sadness or regret?

41
BALCONY

"Deedra's going to kill you." I stood in Logan's kitchen nibbling a potato chip I'd grabbed from a huge bowl on the counter. "Probably spear you with a bobby pin in your sleep."

"I'm not apologizing." He finished arranging the drinks in the massive cooler below the island. "She's got eighty percent of the followers she needs to overtake her mom, and she can just deal with me being on your side. Although you might not want to date a guy who is officially car-free, sings lead in a band that cannot choose a name, and got kicked out of his stepsister's contest." He blew out a gust of air.

I frowned at him. "You did not get kicked out. You just didn't—"

"Get as many votes as you." He forced a smile. "Or Shay or Alec. It's okay."

"I was going to say 'you just didn't do this dare to win.' Logan, you gave up your spot so that I could—"

"We've talked about this," he said with a sigh, "and you'd have advanced no matter what. I have no regrets. It's okay."

It's okay. He'd said that many times over the last week, and each time, I didn't believe him one bit. Deedra's dad had sold her old SUV the prior weekend, and Logan was wading through the teen stages of grief—denial, anger, comparison, and self-deprecation. But he was moving toward acceptance. He'd get there.

"Thank you," I added.

"Forget me. Let's talk about you." He grazed my body with his eyes. "What *are* you wearing under there?" His real smile returned, with a splash of mischief. "Briefs? Bikini? Thong?" He pulled me closer and whispered in my ear, "Please say thong."

There was a tinge of humor in his voice, but my breath caught and blood rushed into my cheeks. I pushed him gently away. "Not a thong. And you'll see."

He laughed and shrugged a shoulder. "Anytime now. You're going to have to reveal."

I glanced down at his shorts. "So are you."

The doorbell rang, and Dizzy called out from the living room, "Time to show off our skivvies!"

My heart slammed into my ribs. "Is this crazy? Am I crazy? What if only a few people show up? What if no one comes in their undies? What if they do and it turns into an orgy?" With each question, my pitch rose and my panic increased.

My mom had barely approved this idea, with preconditions about what I would wear and guidelines in the invite about what others wore—something you could wear on Christmas morning or to the beach. And not the French Riviera topless beach. We'd even promised that anyone with TMI would get covered or sent home. Though what counted as TMI hadn't been clarified, leaving a pretty large loophole.

Logan flicked my hair off my shoulder. "You heard the buzz at school. People will show. And we'll monitor to make sure it stays in the Can Be Seen on YouTube category."

"Still." I sucked a breath through my teeth. "My mom's been pretty great about everything lately, but this is underwear we're talking about. *Someone*'s going to show up in a thong."

"Breathe, Charlotte, breathe." He ran a thumb down my cheek, trying to smooth out my worry.

"And what about your parents? If this gets out of hand, Deedra might not be the one to kill you. It could be your dad." His father and Deedra's mom had gone on a date, leaving the house up for grabs to host the party—the party I'd suggested.

He shrugged a shoulder. "Worst case scenario, I get grounded. Since I don't have a car to go anywhere anyway—"

The doorbell rang again.

Kat popped her head in. "Strip down already. People are here."

Logan nodded and yanked his shirt over his head, revealing bare skin that rippled with muscles.

A shiver darted across my shoulders. "How does a guy who plays guitar all the time look like that?"

A blush rushed to his cheeks. "Workout equipment in the garage. I keep in shape so I can play Ultimate Frisbee. Which is way cooler than it sounds."

The front door opened and closed in the other room.

Logan slid off his shorts, revealing a pair of baggy boxers. He smiled and turned around, showing off the back with musical instruments and the caption "Rock Bottom" written across his butt. "Get it?"

I laughed. "Of course you'd wear something like that."

He turned around and nodded at me. "Your turn."

Jeremy peeked into the room, wearing a pair of plaid boxers and a white T-shirt that looked more like lounge wear than undies.

Which was how I'd hoped this night would go. "People here. More coming. Starting music." Without waiting for an answer, he disappeared.

Several shirtless guys entered the kitchen, high-fived Logan, and grabbed snacks.

Walker was among them in a pair of underwear I couldn't entirely look away from, despite the terrible image it seared into my brain. Elephant boxers with a trunk—his junk in the trunk. He scanned the kitchen. "Where's the keg?"

Logan gave his charming host smile. "Sodas in the cooler. Get plastered and vomit elsewhere. And no complaints—you're seeing girls in lingerie tonight."

Walker glanced around him. "Deedra here? Wouldn't mind seeing her. I'm thinking lace corset and—"

"Dude, that's my sister." Logan cringed.

Walker shrugged and lifted his chin at me. "Isn't this your party? Why aren't you in your underwear?"

"I'm...um...getting there."

"Excuse us." Logan pulled me into the nearby utility room. "Look, I know you're nervous, but if it's too revealing, I won't let you go out there. I don't want guys like that"—he tilted his head back toward the kitchen—"seeing too much of my girl."

I took a deep breath. "Have you ever seen *Cabaret?* The musical?"

"Heard of it. Haven't seen it."

"It's set in the 1930s, and there's a song, "Mein Herr," where these women sing and dance basically in their lingerie."

He raised his eyebrows. "Why don't they show guys scenes like that to convince us to like musicals?"

"Very funny." I ran my hand along the seam of my T-shirt, feeling supremely awkward that I was about to undress in front of Logan. "Just know that was my inspiration."

He didn't answer. Just fisted his hands and clenched his jaw tighter than Kat's tom-tom. Logan was one of the good guys, but he was still a guy.

I slid my sweatpants down to my ankles, revealing my legs and black, thigh-high stockings.

His gaze lingered where one was topped off by a ruffled garter. "Well, this explains the shoes."

I glanced down at my black character shoes, borrowed from the school's costume closet. "They're a little big, but they're comfortable."

Logan crossed his arms over his bare chest, tightening his body even more. "We need to get out there."

Noise seeped into the room, the pounding of music coming from the speakers in the living room and talking and laughter just beyond the closed door.

I nodded. He was right. But *need* didn't translate to *ready*. I kicked the pants off my ankles and slowly drew my tunic shirt up over my butt, my stomach, my chest, and finally my head. Not like a slow tease, more like I had to argue with myself over every inch revealed until I squashed my nerves into submission.

Logan dropped his arms and stared with lips parted and eyes wide. "Whoa. You are...you're..."

"Should I change?" My voice screeched at the end.

At Kat's insistence, I'd taken the money she'd loaned me for New York and splurged on my outfit—a full-coverage corset bra and a pair of waist-high tap pants, both in black. It covered way more than most swimsuits, but I was still freaking out inside.

Especially with the breathless way he was looking at me.

"It's fine." He swiped a hand across his mouth. "But it's also all kinds of sexy. I don't think I've seen you bare your shoulders, much less your..." He pointed at my stomach, bare between my boobs and my belly button.

I resisted the urge to grab one of the towels from the laundry basket behind him and wrap it around me. "Well, it's not a thong."

He chuckled then circled an arm around my waist. "Damn, girl. You make me crazy."

My heartbeat did a heel-kick. The air conditioning in the small room whirred, and the breeze ruffled my loose undies—under which I'd worn another pair of undies. But a swath of warmth curled around my torso and heated my face.

His jaw tensed once again. "If anyone messes with you, you tell me. Any of those guys out there. Okay?"

I bit my lip and nodded. Surely I didn't need his protection. But it was nice knowing it was there, just in case.

"Don't let Deedra mess with you either," he added.

I tipped my head back and sighed up to the ceiling. "I am crazy. I'm hosting an underwear party under her nose at her own house."

Logan turned the doorknob to lead us out. "Like you said, it's not about being in your underwear so much as being the *only* one in your underwear. Now we all are. And you'll be the contestant who threw the most-talked-about party of the year."

"Let's hope you're right."

We walked out of the utility room into a kitchen filled with teenagers in their "barely theres." Most of the guys were in boxers, a few in boxer briefs. The girls primarily wore bras and panties with more coverage than their summer bikinis. But it was still odd to be in a room with people I went to school with wearing underwear in public.

Logan and I greeted people, thanked them for coming, and commented on their outfits.

"Funny." To the novelty boxers.

"Nice polka dots." To the matching bra-and-panties set.

"I'd pegged you a whitey-tighty." To Dizzy.

A couple of cases of beer now sat on the kitchen table, half-empty. Logan sighed and walked us past. "I knew that was coming. At least we didn't pay for it."

Our pooled money covered sodas and dirt-cheap snacks from the warehouse grocery store, but we were relying on music and undies to make the party memorable.

Moving into the living room, my mind was completely blown. Not by someone's undies, but Jeremy in his boxers and Kat in her sports bra and what looked like bike shorts dancing, laughing, and definitely flirting.

I pointed at them. "She's never acted like that with a guy before. So hot and cold."

"Sometimes that means you feel more." He pulled me closer to him. "Trust me."

His bare hand on my bare waist startled me yet again. But in the best way. The roar of the party around us dulled to a hum in my ears. A thrill pulsed through my chest, or maybe that was my heart doing *42nd Street* musical numbers. I wanted this feeling to get repeat curtain calls.

A crack exploded into the air.

Everyone stopped and turned toward the front door, where the Contestant Mostly Likely to Become a Playboy Model stood, wearing black panties and a leather corset and holding a bull whip. Shay broke the dominatrix exterior with a big, sappy grin. "Who's ready for some fun?"

Walker raised his hand, and possibly his trunk. "Me. I'm ready."

I flinched at the thought, but the silence only lasted a second, immediately replaced by people fawning over Shay's undies choice. Once again, how could I compete with a girl who played to the horny guy vote so overtly?

Logan murmured in my ear, "You're hotter."

I gave him an appreciative smile. At least I had my boyfriend's vote.

Moments later, Alec made his own appearance, appealing to the horny girls—not a small voting bloc. He donned a pair of Superman briefs, a billowing red cape, and matching socks with the distinct *S* on them. A fair number of female hands ran across his pecs and abs, with Marita barely able to keep her own claws dug into him as she escorted him inside.

Soon enough, though, it was just another party. Or what I guessed parties were like. Given my vast experience of the *one* before I'd attended here at Halloween. People were eating, drinking, dancing, talking, laughing, and yeah, some kissing and groping. But probably no more than usual.

Just when I thought there'd be no more surprises, the music clicked off and the room blacked out. The party goers groaned.

When the lights flickered back on, all eyes rose to the second-story landing where Deedra stood. Wearing a red satin bodysuit with the words "Dare Ya" scripted across her slender waist. Fishnet stockings and insanely high heels completed the look.

She took up only a sliver of space above us but seemed to own the room. A cameo appearance. "We have three contestants left," she announced. "Shay."

Shay strode forward and posed, and applause erupted.

Deedra gestured toward the back of the room. "Alec."

Alec waved, and a posse of girls screamed like it was a boy-band concert.

I caught Kat's eye roll from across the room.

"And Charlotte." Deedra smirked in my direction.

I stepped forward, not sure what else to do, and heard some shouts and clapping. My stomach belly-flopped at the thought of me standing there showing off my lingerie.

Logan cupped his hands over his mouth and yelled out, "Who had this idea for a party and hosted it for you!"

The applause turned into an ovation, with claps and cheers echoing off the walls. A small surge of relief hit me. I could accept praise for a party far more than recognition of my corset and tap pants. At least, I hoped that's what it was.

After what seemed like a million years, I waved and mouthed, "Thank you!"

The clamor finally died down.

Looking back at Deedra, I noted the familiar press of her lips, pointed right at me. As if she wanted to eat me alive. "Anyway," she continued. "I thought we deserved a real celebration. So I had kegs delivered to the backyard!"

The room exploded. The noise was deafening, and people started toward the backyard.

Logan held my hand while they rushed past. His face twisted. He combed his free hand through his hair. "Unbelievable."

Once the room had emptied, except for a few stragglers, Logan let of me and moved to stand directly under Deedra. "You're trying to get the cops called. Get me busted with my dad."

She gave a haughty smile. "Your party sucks, bro. I'm helping you out."

He shook his head, angrier than I'd ever seen him. "You can't stand someone stealing your show."

"You're not in the show anymore." She pointed at me. "Thanks to her."

I pressed my back against the wall.

Kat came over and placed a firm hand on my shoulder.

Logan kept his focus on Deedra. "She has nothing to do with me getting out. And you didn't even want me there. Just face it, Dee. Your mom is like every other mom in the world—she doesn't get you and isn't going to. You acting like a bitch isn't going to make her understand."

Deedra's high-and-mighty expression withered. Her eyes darkened.

He'd hit her where it hurt.

I felt the stab. Understanding, supportive moms did exist. Hers just wasn't one of them. I strode forward and grabbed Logan's arm. "Don't."

He didn't even look at me, just glared at his stepsister, who'd turned quieter than an empty theater.

Behind us, the party had moved outdoors, and the noise with it.

"You of all people should have some sympathy." I spoke low to Logan, hoping only he could hear. "Deedra wants to do something with her life that her mom doesn't want her to do. But why shouldn't she do it? Even if this contest is a crazy way to go about it. When this whole thing is over, y'all still have to share this house and car rides. Don't make things worse."

He finally looked at me, then back to Deedra. I felt the muscles in his arm relax, saw his chest rise and fall. "I'm sorry. It's your house too. Do what you want."

Shirking off my touch, he walked away toward the kitchen.

Deedra wandered away to the bedrooms upstairs, and Kat and our other allies headed to the backyard.

And I glanced around the house—wondering if I should head to the kitchen and talk to Logan again, find Kat outside and get solace for myself, or even seek out Deedra upstairs and try to shake some sense into her.

Instead, I played hostess, greeting people who wandered in and out for almost an hour. Right up until we heard the sirens.

42
INTERMISSION

On the silent ride home with Mom, I pressed my head against the passenger window, wondering how long it would take for her to calm down enough to speak.

I'd left Logan standing between Deedra and their parents on the front lawn, just as the cops finally drove away. My offer to help clean up had been batted away by Logan's dad, who'd promised that Logan would take care of every drink spill, chip crumb, and beer can by himself. Deedra's mom hadn't offered what punishment her own daughter would get.

We arrived home, but Mom still didn't say a word until I emerged from my bedroom, having exchanged my 1930s *Cabaret* costume for a tank top and pajama pants.

She wore a T-shirt, yoga pants, and three layers of anger. "Time to talk."

I swallowed and settled on the couch, expecting a tongue-lashing like I'd never heard before. She'd probably make Miss Hannigan, the horrible woman who ran the orphanage in *Annie*, look like a saint. Or she might actually send me to an orphanage—my own hard-knock life.

Her cheeks puckered, and her nostrils flared. "We had a deal." She wasn't yelling. Instead her words were tight, controlled, a scalpel instead of a hammer. "You would wear something I could imagine my daughter wearing on stage for a performance, and this party would be short, controlled, and alcohol-free."

"I kept the deal we—"

"Was there or was there not beer at that party?" Her arched eyebrow made another slice at me. "And what some of those teenagers were wearing—"

"Is no less than they wear at the swimming pool."

She seethed. "You have no idea what it's like to walk up to a house and see your daughter standing there with a boy in his boxers, drunk teenagers stumbling out in their underwear, and police all over the lawn."

"I wasn't drinking," I muttered. "And nothing happened with me and Logan. I've told you—he's a total gentleman."

Unless you counted the thong comment and a few sideways glances, but that was nowhere near what I'd heard Walker saying to girls. His elephant trunk was practically trumpeting all night long.

Mom shook her head, like she couldn't believe what our lives had turned into.

Join the club, Mom. Join. The. Club.

"What kind of mother am I?" she nearly yelled. "Letting you do this? Just think of the photos and videos of you on the internet for the rest of your life. What if that keeps you out of college? Out of a job? What if it hurts my job?"

"Your job?" I winced.

"I work for a faith-affiliated nonprofit, Charlotte. There's a character clause in my employment contract."

"But you didn't do anything. I did. They can't fire you for that."

"No, but it doesn't make me look good when my daughter is trouncing around in her undies at keg parties attended by minors!" Her voice crescendoed to a volume loud enough to make me flinch.

I turned my gaze back to my mom. "Things were going really well until...someone got kegs delivered. But that wasn't us, I promise." Best to leave Deedra out of my explanation. Implicating the contest queen might tempt my mom to, once again, call for me to back out.

Mom sat down and held out her hand. "Phone."

I lifted my head. "What?"

"I want your phone. In my hand. *Ahora.*"

I huffed. "I just said I wasn't to blame for anything."

She dropped her hand, cocked her head. "This isn't a punishment. It's a break. You and I need a break. Me from school, you from this contest, and both of us from the world. You know it's true."

Narrowing my eyes, I studied her. She seemed calm, now. But she wanted to take away my phone...

Mean mothers took away phones.

She walked to her purse in the kitchen, reached in, and took out her own phone. With a few taps, she turned it off and then dropped the phone into the key bowl on the counter. "Your turn."

"Mom, I can't—"

"Break, Charlotte." She pointed to the bowl. "We return to normal life on Monday, but for the rest of the weekend, it's you, me, junk food, and musicals." Her expression softened even more, the last of her hard edges melting away. "Give me this one. If nothing else, this whole experience has convinced me that you're growing up. Let me savor some time with my daughter."

Claro que sí,, she had to go all sentimental. I looked at the bowl, down at my phone, up at the bowl, down—

My phone buzzed. A text from Logan: *Can't talk. Dad's prisoner for the weekend. See you Monday.* ♥

With a resigned sigh, I looked back at my mom. "Can I at least text Logan and Kat to tell them?"

She gave a curt nod, and I fired off the same message to both of them: *No phone this weekend. Movie marathon with Mom.* Then stood, turned off my phone, and dropped it into the key bowl.

Twenty minutes later, Mom and I had settled into the couch with a bowl of popcorn on our laps and *Bye, Bye Birdie* on the screen.

43
STAGE MANAGER

I was one step into school on Monday morning when Charlotte's Angels came running toward me.

"Look, look!" Georgia pointed at her pink T-shirt, the same one all seven of them were wearing. "We got them made."

I stared, trying to process what I was seeing. The logo matched the original Charlie's Angels image, only different. *Was that—*

She touched the black silhouette on the left. "This is you with a fire torch." Then the one on the right. "Here's you dancing in the flash mob. And the middle one is your angel costume. Of course."

I slapped my hand over my mouth.

Georgia seemed to take my gesture as surprised appreciation. "We've got a shirt for you too. But I wanted to make sure we had the right size. Small or medium?"

"Um. Medium?" I choked out.

A girl behind her pulled a shirt out of a bag and handed it to me. "You're going to love it! There's a ton of buzz around these shirts already."

I'll bet, I wanted to say. Instead, I put on a happy face, tucked the shirt into my backpack, and said, "Thanks."

Georgia beamed. "You're going to win this. We've got your back."

And my front apparently as they expected me to put three silhouettes of my contest self on my chest. At least they'd gotten the shirts printed before Charlotte-in-her-undies had made the logo lineup.

I glanced down the hall to see Logan at the other end fast-walking toward me, dodging people, barely nodding at others.

Charlotte's Angels made a cooing sound, and someone whispered, "He's so into her."

Was he? I thought so, hoped so. But having it said that way...

Logan reached me, breathless, smiling. He glanced over at the group of girls near me, muttered "Ladies," and then turned to me. "I missed you."

Georgia cleared her throat. "We'll leave you two alone." The Angels scurried off with backward glances, puppy eyes, and giggles.

Once I was sure they were out of earshot, I turned back to Logan and smiled. "It was only a couple of days."

He touched his forehead to mine. "Fifty-seven hours. Much too long."

My body temperature rose a few degrees. Writing songs and counting hours away from each other? Okay, maybe he was that into me.

He pulled back but took my hands in his. "So, what do you think of the spring musical?"

I yanked back, breaking our connection. "What?"

"The musical. Miss Holt posted it over the weekend. I figured you heard about it."

I shoved his shoulder. Not hard. Well, maybe a little hard. "What did she pick?" My words came out hurried, tense, eager. "What is it?"

I held my breath while the corners of his mouth turned slowly up, up, up until he wore a wolfish grin. *Oh please, let that be a sign.*

Logan shook his head. "I wish you could sing for an audience. You'd be perfect as Scarlet Hood."

I shrieked, jumped up and down, pumped my fists.

People around us turned, chuckled, and one guy said as he passed, "Hell yeah, the party was awesome!" Then gave us a thumbs-up.

Logan and I both laughed, and I breathed a long sigh of relief. "I'm such a drama geek, aren't I?"

He pulled me close, wrapped his arms around me. "After this past weekend, you needed some good news."

"You know what?" I stared up at him, all messy hair, soft eyes, and easy smile. "Other than the cops, this weekend was really good. I had a great time at the party, it was kind of nice to have the movie marathon with my mom, and she's not blaming me anymore for the party going sideways. Though I'm still on shaky ground."

"Meanwhile, I am so busted."

Kat's head peeked over his shoulder. "How busted are you?"

He let go of me and stepped back to let Kat inside our circle.

She joined us with her arms crossed over yet another black tee peeking out through her jean jacket.

Logan sighed. "My dad was pissed about the police having to break up the party."

"I'm sorry," I muttered. "But didn't Deedra get any of the blame?"

He shook his head. "Not how it works in my family. My party, my fault."

"Or..." Kat smirked. "Your party, your praise." She dipped her head in a mini-bow. "You're welcome."

Logan's skin paled. "What do you mean 'you're welcome'?"

"Before you freak out, hear me out. I made a strategic choice." Kat paused, we waited. She took a quick breath. "I'm the one who called the cops."

My stomach dropped, and my jaw with it.

Logan growled. "I can't leave the house because of you. Maybe for the rest of my life."

Kat gave her full one-eighty eye roll. "It would have been worse if all those people had started hurling on your furniture and having sex on your living room carpet. They were drunk and in their underwear! And who has white furniture anyway? Is your stepmom a masochist? Or just so friggin' rich that she replaces the couch every time someone spills?"

Logan ran his hands through his hair and groaned like a wounded animal. "You. Are. Unbelievable."

"Hey, no one's more shocked than me. I'm hardly the type that rats on others." At least Kat realized she was not herself. "But I gamed this out and did it anyway. To help you and Charlotte."

I flinched. "For me? How does getting Logan grounded for the rest of his life help me?"

"You are now not only the girl who threw an amazing underwear party, you are the girl whose party was so off-the-charts that someone called the cops. We have to finish strong." Kat finally uncrossed her arms.

My jaw went from dropped to unhinged.

Paired with Kat's regularly ripped jeans and military boots was not a rock tee, but the Charlotte's Angels logo shirt. Not pink, but black.

A choked huff came from Logan. "What. Is. That?"

Kat opened her jacket to show it off. "This is a conversation piece, courtesy of Charlotte's Angels. Someone comments on the shirt, and I make the pitch to vote for Charlotte. I already got nine commitments this morning."

I whimpered. "You're going to make me wear mine, aren't you?"

Logan chuckled. "You have one too? Where do *I* get a shirt?"

"You'd wear one of these?" I pointed at Kat while she stood proudly showing off me-as-triplets on her chest.

He took my hand and squeezed. "Anything for my girl."

"Sweet," Kat mumbled, then reached into her backpack. "Because I already got you one. Special-order black, same as mine." She handed a shirt to Logan with zero fanfare, knowing all along we'd submit to her ad campaign.

I shook my head at her. "You look like Kat, you talk like Kat, you seem to be Kat...but I think a pageant mom has taken over your body."

She shifted and planted a fist on her hip. "Do you want the crown or Miss Hospitality?"

"Do I have to decide between the two?"

The bell rang, saving her from answering.

Logan held up his shirt, said "Thanks" to Kat, and then nodded at me. "Walk you to class?"

Kat poked Logan's shoulder. "Make sure you kiss her before she goes into the classroom. PDA polls well." *Polls*? She walked off before I could ask.

I blew out a gust of breath. "When Kat decides to do something, she goes all out."

Logan tilted his head. "She's a little like Deedra that way."

My eyes popped, and I glared at him. "Never, ever, ever tell Kat that."

Logan lifted one hand in a palm-up surrender. "No problem."

We started our stroll down the hallway, encountering hellos and waves as we went. My face heated with every step, unsure how to accept all the attention. I needed that level of recognition for votes, but would it go away when the contest ended?

I hoped so.

Mostly.

We turned a corner, reaching a less crowded hallway, and Logan leaned closer. "I'm grounded 'until further notice.'"

"I'm sorry."

"Stop apologizing. It's not your fault."

We stopped in front of my class. "I know. It's Kat's fault."

"There's something else." His pained expression told me something huge was about to come out.

A rough rope of worry coiled around my heart and knotted tight. "What?"

He slumped against the wall. "I can't go to New York."

The rope tightened, cutting off my breath. "No." The word came out as a strained whisper.

"It's fine. I've already been to New York."

"But I want you there with me." Ever since we'd gotten together, I'd imagined him standing next to me on Broadway Avenue. "Maybe I shouldn't go."

He pushed my hair back from my face. "You will go. Then you'll come back and tell me all about it."

My heart sank. Partly because he wasn't going, and partly because of course I'd go without him if I could.

I wanted to be Miss Hospitality too, but having come this far, we both knew I wanted the crown.

44
OFF BOOK

I surrendered to wearing my Charlotte's Angels T-shirt on Friday.

In my original universe, my best friend would've taken one look at me and ranted for twenty minutes on the ridiculousness of groupies creating shirts that featured a contestant competing for some rich girl's money by embarrassing herself in front of not only the entire student body but everyone with online access and a rubbernecking interest.

But when Kat picked me up in the morning, she simply said, "Why didn't you wear that before, while votes were being collected? It's too late now."

So much for Original Universe Kat.

After school, and approximately one million comments on my shirt throughout the day, we gathered at Logan's house.

Being grounded meant all band practices would be held there for a while where his dad could keep an eye on him. On top of that, Deedra's mom made them unplug their amps.

"How am I supposed to be quiet?" Dizzy twirled his drumsticks. "These are drums, man."

Kat ran her fingers over the keyboard. "Just tap them. Or I can take over and you can play the black and whites."

I sat on a couch in the extra den.

Logan lay across the cushions with his head on my lap, while I played with his casual curls. He smiled up at me, as if I was the best view he could possibly have.

Jeremy snickered from a nearby chair.

Logan turned to him. "What?"

"Those shirts are—"

"Awesome?" Logan grinned, daring him to insult our matching Charlotte's Angels shirts. Unlike me, Logan had worn his every day this week.

Jeremy shook his head. "You are so whipped."

Kat fired a wadded candy bar wrapper right into Jeremy's chest. "Hey, I'll have you know those Angels have moved votes our way like a bulldozer. Instead of mocking them, maybe you could've helped by wearing a shirt."

Jeremy gave her a flat look. "Maybe you could've helped by *not* wearing a shirt. We all have our boundaries."

Logan and Dizzy chuckled while Kat glared at Jeremy.

I rolled my lips into my mouth to keep from laughing too.

Deedra came in, and I lost my desire to laugh or even smile.

All heads turned toward her.

"Thought you'd want to know," she said in a sing-song voice, "I posted results."

Logan sat up. "And?"

She narrowed her eyes at him. "Are you unable to work the internet?"

He blew out a frustrated breath. "Just tell us, will you?"

"I'm almost there." Kat punched her phone.

As if sensing her show was about to be stolen, Deedra strode forward and looked me right in the eye. "You're still in."

I nodded. "Thanks."

Her expression changed from cocky to curious. "Aren't you glad? I thought you wanted my money."

Logan laid his arm across the back of the couch, spreading himself into my space. "Of course she wants your money. And you should get ready to fork over the cash."

But I was stuck on Deedra's question: *Aren't you glad?*

I'd expected my usual reaction—excitement, pride, relief. Instead, I felt calm, aloof, casual. In this universe, deep down, I'd been sure I'd keep going.

My breath caught. That, not the result, surprised me. Was my newfound confidence soaking in? I guessed it was, making this an even bigger makeover than I'd done before.

Dizzy tapped the rims of his drums. "Who's out? Alec?"

Deedra's sigh had a gravity of its own. "Shay."

"Shay?" Jeremy jolted in his seat. "That sexy getup didn't advance her?"

Kat's face flashed shock, or maybe hurt, but it was only a flash. "Not everyone is as shallow as you."

He shrugged.

"Apparently"—Deedra raised her voice to regain the floor—"some thought my outfit and hers were too much alike. Others thought her choice was too predictable."

Kat smiled, right at Jeremy. "And some thought Alec was lickably good in his Superundies."

Logan and I exchanged glances that said *jealous much*? Not that Jeremy or Kat would admit it.

I leaned forward, draping my arms on my knees. "What's the last dare?"

Deedra's eyes twinkled, like a fairy godmother or a mischievous villain. "You'll see soon enough. But trust me that it will be hard for both of you to complete this round."

She turned to leave, and I called out after, "How's your crowd-funding campaign? Are you getting investors?"

Rotating around, she studied me. "Why do you care?"

Another good question. I paused for a moment and came up with the honest answer. "Because I think it's a good idea."

From the breathless stares I got from everyone else, I might as well have sucked the oxygen out of the room.

Deedra peered at me closely. "You think Fine Nine Design is a good idea?"

"You're obviously a good planner to put this whole contest together. Lots of moving parts and details."

Logan tapped—or more like poked—my shoulder a few times. Like I was betraying him to side with her. Granted, she'd gotten him grounded for the foreseeable future.

But the last time her mother had mentioned the contest on KHAL News, she'd once again avoided her daughter's name, focusing instead on the list of pranks, including the shocking development of dead koi fish in the school pond.

I only had one parent—the other being a random stripper dude at a bachelorette party who didn't even know about a surprise-the-contraception-failed pregnancy. But I'd drawn a really good hand with Mom. We didn't agree all the time, but I knew that she was on my side, that she loved me.

I didn't think Deedra was so sure about her mother.

"So your fundraising?" I reminded Deedra.

Her eyes darted between me and Logan, as if gauging whether our relationship might turn out to be okay after all. "Halfway there," she answered. "But it's bare minimum stuff. I know you're aware of the bet with my mom, and the money I get there would seal the deal. Just a few thousand more followers, and I'll overtake her."

I stood and approached Deedra, the room seeming to close around us, as if we were the only ones left. "Maybe the last dare will cinch it. Assuming you gave us something worthwhile to do."

She shifted uncomfortably, like the temperature had suddenly plummeted, and lowered her eyes. "This whole contest has been about facing your fears. All dares are."

Her discomfort reached me. There was a hidden message in what she was saying, but I didn't know what it was. I folded my arms around myself. "I've faced plenty in this contest."

Her head tilted, like a brief *sorry*. An apology from Deedra? Was that right? She straightened and stood taller. "Not like this. Just remember, it's a dare contest."

She wheeled around and left the room, leaving me feeling dazed and confused.

Kat brought out her phone again. "The website says the dares are personal this time. Doesn't say what, just that you and Alec have to do something you'd rather not do."

I tugged nervously at the hem of my Charlotte's Angels shirt. "I've already done a bunch of stuff I'd rather not do. Like prancing around in my underwear in this house just last week. How much worse can it get?"

Logan scoffed. "Don't tempt her. She'll rise to that challenge."

The room fell silent.

Jeremy set down his guitar, walked straight over to Kat, and pulled her to standing. Her eyes flew wide as he planted his lips right on hers.

My pulse pounded in my eyes, an empathy quickening of my heartbeat.

Dizzy, Logan, and I stood frozen in the wings, watching the show.

It was several moments before Jeremy pulled back, still holding Kat in his arms who was now breathless and staring right into his eyes.

He didn't take his eyes off her either, just spoke over his shoulder. "If I can do that, Charlotte, you can do whatever dare Deedra's got for you. It's all about how much you want something."

Kat grinned up at Jeremy. "Maybe you're not an idiot after all." She grabbed him by his shirt and pulled him down for an encore.

45
TRAPDOOR

Deedra's email pinged my phone extra late that night. Mom was up studying, and I'd just finished an English essay due by midnight.

I opened the email and read:

"Fashion icon Sophia Amoruso said, 'Compete with yourself, not with others.' For the final dare, you're competing against yourself to see if you can overcome your deepest fears."

Deepest fears. No biggie, right? I took a deep breath before continuing.

"You shared a secret with me at the beginning, and I promised to reveal it only if you pulled out of the contest. I didn't and never planned to—no matter what. I just need that information for this final round."

Was Deedra saying that I could have pulled out at any time with no consequence? I couldn't let myself go down that woulda-coulda-shoulda trail of thought. At least I knew she wouldn't share my secret.

"But to win, you must expose your own secret—publicly, permanently, passionately. Do it in a memorable way that makes people vote for you, the real you. I'm counting on you to make it worth the win."

The words seemed to jump from the screen and stab me in the chest—deep gashes that struck my soul. My head swam, and I stared at the message barely able to breathe. Like someone had erected the *Les Misérables* barricade in my throat.

So she wouldn't share, but she wanted me to. The result was the same.

How could she? After everything I'd done, all the hoops I'd jumped through, all the publicity I'd gotten her, the support I'd given her business idea...and *this* was what Deedra had chosen for our last dare?

I threw the phone across the room, wincing when it slammed into my *Wicked* poster. Mom had bought me a nearly indestructible phone, but the poster wasn't so protected. Still, even if it got nicked, it felt right that the Deedra's Dares website had landed on a witch face.

Mom burst through the door. "What was that sound?"

I swallowed the barricade, gunpowder and all. "Nothing," I murmured. "Phone slipped, flew across the room."

Mom stared at me, like she wasn't quite certain.

I stood, retrieved the phone from the carpet—no cracks—and waved it at her. "See?"

She stayed in the doorway, narrowed her eyes, crossed her arms. "Whatever's going on, you can tell me."

No, I can't.

I hadn't given Deedra *my* deepest secret. I didn't care that my biological father had been a one-night-stand and a stripper, because he'd never been in my life. Even if he showed up tomorrow, he wouldn't be my dad, just the guy who donated the sperm.

But my mom cared. She felt like it said something about her, something she didn't like. I'd given Deedra *her* deepest secret, *her* darkest fear. How could Deedra? How could *I*?

"I'm really tired, Mom. I let go of my phone. No need to worry." Nothing I said was technically a lie.

Mom sighed, her eyes still narrowed, like she was contemplating my answer.

I pulled back my covers, sat on my bed, made it look like her staying even a moment longer was depriving me of much-needed sleep.

"Good night," she mumbled and started to close the door. Then she stepped in, walked over to me, and kissed my forehead. "*Te amo.*"

Ignoring the guilt in my gut, I smiled up at her. "Love you too."

After she left, I sat for several minutes, knowing what I had to do, but dreading having to do it. No one would understand, because explaining would mean revealing my mom's secret. Which I couldn't do.

To everyone else, it would look like I just gave up.

Gave up on winning the contest.

Gave up on going to New York.

Gave up on my supporters, my fans, my friends.

My stomach settled, and a hollowness took over. A sense of resignation. Maybe this moment was the real test of my courage. Could I let everyone else think what they wanted while I simply did the right thing?

My fingers trembled as I typed my reply to Deedra's email: "I forfeit." Before I could over-think it, I pressed send.

And then melted onto my bed for a good, long cry.

46
Cue

The next morning, I woke up to *bam! bam! bam!* It took me a few seconds to realize someone was pounding on our front door. I wiped my eyes, went out to the living room, and peered through the side window to see who was on our porch.

My best friend stared back.

I'd barely opened the door when Kat barged in. "What do you mean you forfeit? You can't come this far only to surrender. Whatever the dare is, we'll figure it out, like we have every other one."

I rubbed my temples, as if that would wake up my brain the rest of the way, then yawned. "Could you keep it down? My mom's still sleeping."

"No, she's not," Mom said.

Blood rushed to my face.

I turned to see her standing in her bedroom doorway, wearing lounge pants and a Charlotte's Angels tee.

Mom pointed to her chest and smiled at Kat. "Thanks for the souvenir."

"You're welcome." Kat grinned and gave me a *so there* nod.

"When did you—how did you—why did—" I shook my head. "Never mind." Kat had delivered a shirt to my mom, she was wearing it, and the Alternate Universe was alive and well.

Mom strolled to the coffee pot in the kitchen. "What brings you by, Kat? Y'all have plans today?"

"Yes," Kat answered. "I'm here to find out why—"

I yanked Kat's arm. "We're heading over to their band practice."

Kat gave me a confused look, glanced at my mom, and then back at me. With a sigh, she followed me to my bedroom.

I shut the door on the sound of mom's coffee brewing. "I haven't told her yet."

Kat sneered. "You haven't told *me* yet."

"How'd you even find out?"

"Deedra told Logan, Logan told Jeremy, Jeremy told me." Guess she and Jeremy were a full-on item now.

I retrieved my phone from the bedside table and saw a slew of missed calls and texts. Apparently, I'd slept hard after last night's sob fest. I sighed as I clicked through the texts, most of them peppered with question marks and exclamation points.

"What's going on?" Kat demanded. "What was so bad about the dare that you thought you had to pull out? Which you are not doing, by the way."

"Yes, I am." I set the phone down and turned to her. "You've been an amazing manager and a wonderful best friend. But ultimately, I'm the contestant, and I get to decide whether to continue or quit."

For once, she just stood there, speechless.

From her expression, I figured she was looking for a crack in my demeanor, hesitation in my resolve, an opening for her to change my mind. She wouldn't find it.

Alec would take the prize.

Mom's secret would stay safe.

And I'd go back to being not-so-special Charlotte.

I could live with that. I'd come out ahead with greater confidence, a drool-worthy boyfriend, and my silhouette on about forty T-shirts.

Kat scoffed, walked out of my room, and beelined to the kitchen.

I ran behind her, grabbed for her arm.

She eluded me and planted herself at the counter next to my mom. "You need to talk to your daughter."

Mom jerked to attention.

"Kat," I protested, my eyes wide. "No."

Mom looked between us. "What's going on?"

"She decided to—"

"Kat, stop. Please."

Kat huffed and glared at me, clearly on the edge of *shut up or spill the beans—that is the question.*

Mom's gaze seesawed between us and landed on me. "Charlotte...?"

The doorbell rang.

We all turned toward the sound.

"Expecting someone?" Mom asked.

"Reinforcements," Kat muttered and headed to the door.

My shoulders sank as Logan, Jeremy, and Dizzy entered. I should have been embarrassed to be seen wearing pajamas and sporting bedhead hair. But that's not what hit me. Nope. It was the way Logan looked at me with pure disappointment. That cracked my heart.

"What happened?" he asked. "What did Deedra ask you to do? She won't tell me."

Kat, Dizzy, and Jeremy all stood nearby with similar looks of disapproval, confusion, frustration.

I shut my eyes against the onslaught of guilt I felt. If only I'd given Deedra another secret, my own secret, I'd still be in this contest. But I'd screwed up, and it wasn't only me who had to deal with the consequences. I'd let my friends down too.

When I opened my eyes again, everyone was staring at me, silent, waiting.

My mother set her coffee cup down, slipped her hand into mine, and said, "Time for a little mother-daughter chat."

No one else moved.

I followed Mom to her bedroom, and we sat on the rumpled covers beside books and notepads spread out on the mattress. She kept her hand in mine. "My questions come before theirs," she said.

I kept my gaze on my knees but nodded.

"Why are your friends here? And why does Kat say I need to talk to my daughter?"

I was going to have to say...something. I took a deep breath and let it out with a long shudder. "I quit the contest last night. They found out this morning."

I felt her wince. "Do you want to tell me why?"

"No."

She gave a half-laugh. "It wasn't really a question. A decision this big, when I know what this contest meant to you, requires an explanation."

I finally looked up to see her peering down at me with the same look she gave me when I was sick. Tender, sympathetic, sad. How could I be honest but still spare her?

I thought through my next words carefully. "The last dare involved me breaking a confidence, and I can't do that. So I did the right thing and quit the contest instead."

Her brow furrowed at me. "Whose confidence?"

"Doesn't matter." I shrugged. "I'm not changing my mind."

She let go of my hand, leaned back against her headboard, and folded her arms. "Is it Kat, Logan, or me? Because none of us want you to quit."

"You wanted me to quit before."

"Yes. Then, but not now." She moved forward. "You could actually win this thing. You could pay off that debt, go to New York, maybe have a little spending money for once. It could even be good for your college résumé."

"What?" I shrank bank.

"My boss's wife works at the university, and she said that a well-written essay about your contest experience would stand out and show both your creativity and bravery."

I had to smile. My mom was wearing a Charlotte's Angels T-shirt and boasting that this crazy contest could get me into college. "I can still write about the experience, even if I don't finish."

"But not finishing says something about you."

"It says I do the right thing." No matter how hard it was.

Mom stood, sighed heavily, and glared at me with new intensity. "*Cielos*, what's the dare?" Her voice echoed in the small room, surely carried out to the living room.

My heart tripped.

It was awfully quiet in the other room. Were my friends listening? Ears against the door?

"What. Is. The. Dare?" Mom repeated.

My chest burned. Who was I kidding? With my mom in here, and four friends just outside the door, I was outnumbered, out-flanked, outgunned.

I *ughed*, stood, and marched back through the living room.

My friends scurried out of my way, alarmed by whatever they saw on my face. If I was showing half the dread I felt inside, I didn't blame them.

Without a word, I grabbed my phone, turned back, and re-turned to my mom's room, not bothering this time to close the door. "Fine." I tapped my screen, brought up the email, and dropped the phone on the bed. "Here's the dare."

She read the dare aloud and then looked up at me. "What was the secret?"

Heat swelled in my chest, tears in my eyes. I tilted my head, a plea on my face. Please...just let it go.

"Charlotte, I was reluctant at the beginning at this contest. Or opposed. But once I knew how much this meant to you, I have been there for you, supporting you however I can. All I've asked in return is that you be straight with me."

"I know." The words came out as half-mumble, half-whisper. "But this one is different."

She scoffed. "Different than spending a night with a boy in a barn? Dressing up in lingerie for a party? How much worse could it be?"

So much worse. "Mom, just trust me. I'm forfeiting for both of us, okay?"

"Both of us? What could you have possibly revealed that—" The color drained from her face. "*Tu papá*," she whispered. *Your dad.*

My heart fell, like a trap door had opened beneath it. "Mom, please."

Her expression went solid, immovable, determined not to let it go. "It's your dad, isn't it?"

Something broke inside me, and years-long frustration spilled out. "If you mean the sperm donor who left town and couldn't be found after you learned you were pregnant, then yes."

Kat gasped behind me. She knew the story about my dad—she was the only one who did—but now she knew I'd told Deedra too. And it was being held over me like a ransom.

But I couldn't blame Deedra. This was my fault.

Mom took a cleansing breath and turned to my friends. "So here's the deal. After my friend's bachelorette party, I hooked up with the male stripper they hired. That was very unlike me, and I turned up pregnant."

My limbs went numb, my mind blank. I'd blurted it out, but she'd confirmed it. What would my friends think?

They just stood there, brows raised, mouths open. Probably no clue what to say to that.

Mom pulled me into a hug. "But the stupidest thing I'd ever done gave me the best thing I've ever had."

Her embrace melted my anxiety and plugged the cracks of my heart. "I'm sorry," I murmured into her shoulder. "So sorry. But I quit, and no one else ever has to know any—"

She pulled us apart. "What are you talking about?" She turned her gaze to Logan. "Do you think your sister will let Charlotte back in the contest?"

Back in? What was happening?

"Stepsister," Logan corrected, "but yeah. She needs the publicity."

"Good." Mom walked past my friends and into the kitchen. She grabbed a pen and paper from our junk drawer and dropped it onto the dining table. "Charlotte, you text Deedra. I'll go get us some breakfast burritos, and then we'll all brainstorm for the next dare."

I swept up to her. "Mom, you can't do this. I can't do this. I should never have told Deedra anything. I was just desperate and stupid and—"

"Charlotte." Tears gathered in her eyes, but she sniffed back her emotion and cleared her throat. "You've faced your fears. It's time I faced mine."

Before I could thank her, she grabbed her purse and headed out the door.

I felt a strong urge to go after her and make sure she was okay. But something told me she would be. If my mom was anything, she was strong. Gentle, but strong.

A long moment of silence followed.

Finally, Logan cocked his head. "You okay?"

I nodded. "Yeah, I'm good."

He strode up and took my hand. "So, your bio dad was a party stripper? The surprises never end with you."

"Here's hoping," Kat said, "we can surprise everybody with this last dare." She sat in front of the paper and raised the pen. "Who's got any good ideas?"

47
LEAD

Not only did Deedra let me back into the contest, she thanked me.

Logan and I stood by the theater door, still early enough that the halls were empty, the silence welcome. The sign-up sheet for spring musical auditions hung on the outside bulletin board, along with a pencil dangling from the string tied to a push-pin.

It should have been a simple thing—adding my name. But my heavy heart seemed to weigh me down. I couldn't even lift my arm.

Logan curled his hand over my shoulder and leaned into my ear. "You can do it."

"I could barely sing with you in the room," I muttered.

"I'll make the spotlight so bright you won't be able to see anybody. Probably won't see your own feet."

I chuckled but didn't feel much better. Just knowing an audience was present was enough to make my stomach revolt.

"This was your idea," I told Logan. "You write my name."

"Nope. It's gotta be you. Your dare, your audition, your life."

I blew out a breath that made my lips sputter. "You're irritatingly supportive, you know?"

He *hmmed* into my hair and waited.

Waited.

Waited.

I forced my hand to take the pencil, placed the tip on the next open line, and—with my last ounce of determination—signed my name.

"Good girl," Logan said.

I laughed. "What am I, a puppy?" I spun around and caught him grinning.

"No, you're the future winner of Deedra's Dares, a contest you bested at every turn."

I gave him the *you are so sappy* eye roll I'd perfected around Kat and Jeremy's mushiness.

"And"—he nudged me with a soft elbow—"the future lead of our spring musical."

"Don't count on that." I pulled out my bootleg key and shoved it into the theater's door lock. "I have to be able to sing on stage first, and I only have a few days to practice getting through the song without hurling my breakfast."

He held the door open. "We'll keep the trash can nearby, just in case."

"Better than the captain's shoes," I murmured.

At the end of the day, we emerged to see a news van parked outside school. Again. But this time, it was in the lot beside the stadium.

"What now?" I asked.

Kat's head was on swivel, turning this direction and that. "Where's the camera? If we can get you in front of it again, that could translate to a hundred or more votes."

Logan pointed to the field house. "Over there."

No one checked with anyone else. We just barreled forward—the three of us, along with Dizzy and Jeremy—joining a stream of people headed toward the stadium.

We reached the edge of the large circle that had formed around the athletic field house.

Jenna stood in front with Alec beside her, a cameraman setting up equipment, and another guy who seemed to be calling the shots. "You have your facts for the lead-in, Jenna?"

She nodded to him and turned to the cameraman. "Just make sure you get me in good lighting. No shadows on my face this time. Got it?"

The cameraman grunted, which she seemed to take as a yes.

I let go of Logan's hand, turned back to him, and murmured, "Need to get closer."

He nodded and parted the people in front of us with his hands and a big smile. "Excuse us."

I squeezed past, expecting Logan to come up behind me. Instead, Kat slipped through, and the crowd fell back together, cutting Logan, Dizzy, and Jeremy off.

Kat grabbed my hand, and we went forward together, jostling, ducking, and squishing our way through until we reached the front.

"Hey," someone yelled.

I pulled Kat down to a squat, where we could see but not block others' views. No telling what devious scheme was going through Kat's mind, but I couldn't keep my eyes off Alec.

He bounced on the balls of his toes, shook out his hands, looked around at everything and nothing. Whatever he was about to do, this was his dare. His last entry into the contest, and he was getting it over with a few days early.

But why the newscast?

Alec's gaze paused for a moment, and his eyes widened. Then he looked away and seemed to swallow a large gulp of fear.

I peered up and over the crowd to see what had triggered him. But I couldn't see much.

And then I caught a flash of blue. I pulled out my phone, snapped a pic of what I could see through the gaps between people, and enlarged the image.

Tingles scurried up my shoulders, settled on the back of my neck.

It wasn't just blue. It was police officer blue. With the tell-tale shoes and utility belts to match.

I nudged Kat—"Look"—and showed her the photo.

She was still taking it in when the news staffer turned around and said, "Hey, hey. We need quiet. If you make noise, you'll be escorted out."

Kat gave me her *I call B.S.* eye roll.

KHAL had no authority on campus to escort anyone anywhere, so that was an empty threat. But an effective one.

The talking fell to a murmur, then a whisper, and finally silence.

Soon, the camera was rolling.

Alec went very still, serious, resigned.

Jenna began, "Five years ago, the practice field behind us caught on fire. The flames spread to this high school's field house. No one was inside, and no injuries were reported, but the building burned to the ground. Arson was suspected, but the investigation revealed no actionable information, and no one was ever charged."

The whole crowd around us seemed to breathe in at once, as if we took in air and clutched it in our lungs, waiting for the rest of the story. Knowing what was to come, but having to hear it to believe it.

Alec's secret.

Jenna turned toward Alec, who somehow maintained his cool and collected expression. "I'm here with Alec Lopez," Jenna said. "What can you tell us about the fire, Alec?"

He glanced once over at the police standing at the perimeter, then returned his focus to the camera's eye. "I was eleven at the time and had just gotten a science experiment kit for my birthday."

Jenna nodded. "Sounds like many eleven-year-olds."

"Yeah, but I was a bigger nerd than most." He turned to her with a smile, a natural for TV. "I was really into chemistry and decided to alter some of the experiments."

My stomach twisted.

"For that," he continued, "I needed a larger space, and we live just down the street, so I came out here late one night to the practice field."

"What happened then?" Jenna prompted.

Alec paused, and his smile dropped.

My heart cringed. This was the split-second when I should jump up and stop him. Tell him that neither of us would do this last dare, that we could share the prize, that Deedra could go stuff herself.

My body leaned forward, my legs tensed.

Kat wrapped her hand around my wrist. "Don't," she whispered. "It's *his* choice."

"The stuff I mixed together started a fire," Alec said.

I breathed in and out, nodded at Kat, and she loosened her grip.

"I tried to put it out," Alec continued, "but it just kept going. And then at some point, I got scared and ran off. I figured it was just grass, and it would peter out. I didn't know about the field house until the next day."

Jenna gave him a look of motherly sympathy, a look Deedra likely hadn't seen in a long time. "How difficult that must have been for you. Did you ever think of confessing? To your parents, a teacher, anyone?"

Alec's mouth contorted, and he wiped his eyes, probably pushing tears that threatened to come. "I'm sorry, y'all. I was so relieved no one was hurt, but then the news was talking about how you could go to jail for arson and I didn't want to go to jail. So I kept it to myself."

Jenna tilted her head. "It's been five years, Alec. What made you come forward now?"

Kat sighed beside me, but I didn't ask why. I was too caught up in Alec, in his emotional pain. In what would happen next.

Alec shook his head. "I'd like to say it was because I realized it was the right and moral thing to do. But I'm in Deedra's Dares contest, and revealing my biggest secret is the final dare. This is my biggest secret, but I also know I should have taken responsibility sooner. Again, I'm sorry for the damage I caused."

Jenna shook her head at him, pity oozing from her pores. "You were only a kid." Then she turned back to the camera, big smile plastered back on. "We'll have more on this story as it develops. I'm Jenna O'Farrell-Fine of KHAL News."

The second she stopped talking, conversation erupted around us and people started milling around. A few students started toward Alec, but he was blocked off by the news crew.

Kat and I stood, and Jeremy, Logan, and Dizzy showed up beside us.

Somewhere to the side, I heard Walker's voice. "I say he did us a favor. The new field house is much better than the old one."

We watched while the news crew huddled around Alec, and the cameraman turned his massive lens toward the outside edge of the crowd. The two police officers walked toward Alec, and the whole crowd shifted to watch. Alec turned and offered his wrists to the cops, who counseled him, cuffed him, and led him away.

"Oh, come on!" Kat threw out her arms. "He's getting arrested? We can't compete with that."

I turned and gazed at her like she'd lost her mind. Or maybe her heart.

But it was Logan who said, "Are you crazy?"

She jerked her head around and looked at each of us in turn, all staring at her like we didn't know who she was.

She sighed. "I'm not a terrible person. I think it's awful that Alec kept that inside for five whole years, that he's probably getting charged with arson, that he might have to pay for the damage done to the field house. But those of us who did background research into the contestants know that Alec is the son of two attorneys, one who practices criminal law. The likelihood of that guy"—she pointed to where Alec was getting into a patrol car—"serving any time for an accidental fire at age eleven is negligible."

"Yeah." Jeremy dropped his arm over Kat's shoulder and glared at us. "Stop judging my girlfriend."

She elbowed him. "Like you didn't think I was evil two seconds ago."

"Evil and sexy." He smiled. "That's how I like 'em."

She shook her head. "Anyway, I'll give Alec a Welcome Back from the Slammer party myself when this is all over. But so far, Charlotte's been the underdog, and this could give Alec the sympathy vote."

My head was spinning.

I stepped up, placed both hands on either side of Kat's face, and stared into her eyes. "Climate change. Corporate welfare. Boy bands. Homecoming queens. Is any of this awakening your old self?"

She reached up and pinched my cheek. "Aw, you miss my rants?" Her tone was half-sappy, half-sarcastic. "I feel so valued for who I am."

Jeremy stepped back from her. "What's *your* biggest secret?"

Kat snorted. "As if I'd tell you."

"I'll tell you mine."

Logan groaned. "Can we just not—"

"I was born with a tail."

My nerves jumped. Ten feet high.

"What?" Kat barked out as a half-laugh.

"It's called a vestigial tail." Jeremy shoved his hands in his pockets, rocked on his feet. "It's supposed to disappear during gestation, but mine stuck around. I came out with a small tail, just a couple centimeters long. They removed it surgically, but I have a scar where it was."

No one spoke. We were all too stunned.

It was Dizzy who broke our group silence. "Maybe that could be our band name. Vestigial Tail."

48
THEATER

I'd never seen so many people packed into our school theater.

Auditions had always been open to the public, but nobody cared enough to show up before. It was usually drama people milling around, waiting for their turn. But with word that the final dare would happen here, every seat was filled, the aisles were stuffed, and the crowd snaked around the perimeter, standing shoulder-to-shoulder. If the fire marshal stopped by, we'd be in trouble.

I was tempted to report the violation so they'd clear the place. But Kat would never forgive me for forgoing votes.

She stood on the far side of the stage, sheet music in hand. Auditionees on one side, accompanists on the other.

Logan stood close.

Nauseous and dizzy, I darted behind the curtain and shoved my back against the backstage wall. My slinky dress clung to my legs, and my feathered boa itched my shoulders.

Logan took my hands. "Remember the mental imagery we practiced. Stop and take a deep breath if it comes to that. Then just start singing again when you can."

I dragged a slow breath through my nose and let it sputter out my mouth. "Where's Deedra?"

His brow creased. "Why do you care?"

"I want to know where not to look."

"Look at your mom."

I gave him a parody of my smile, the real one buried beneath piles of stress. But it was a nice thought. Mom had not only given me the go-ahead, she'd listened to me sing all week, over and over and over. I'd always been able to sing in front of *her*, and she'd given me the feedback I needed to perfect this performance. As least in theory.

"You can do this, Charlotte." Logan gave my hands a supportive pump.

I can do this. I had friends supporting me, groupies rooting for me, and a mom who loved me, no matter what. She'd be my focal point.

"Is it hot in here?" I slid off my opera glove and wiped my forehead, expecting to find sweat, but I was dry as a bone.

Logan lowered my hand. "Stop it." He took the satin glove and wriggled it back onto my arm. "You look amazing. You sing amazing."

"I look like a stripper."

"You *are* a stripper."

I gave him a Kat-worthy glare.

He laughed. "Not you, the character."

"It's not a big deal, right?" My voice shook a little. "Strippers are just people, people who strip. And the guy who gave me half my genes happened to be one of them."

Logan closed his hand over mine. "I don't think it's a big deal. But even if you do, you're your own person, apart from whatever your parents did. I wouldn't want anyone judging me by my parents' choices. And I don't think they do."

I stared up at him, wishing I could siphon off his confidence and use it to fuel my own.

He grinned. "You know who you are? You're the girl about to win this contest. And maybe the lead role in our spring musical."

My chest burned. "Don't say that. Right now, performing an entire musical sounds awful."

"You introduced yourself to an empty theater as a Tony award winner. Some part of you still wants to perform in a musical."

"The stupid part."

"Next," Miss Holt called from the seats, and the next student took the stage.

I shut my eyes, squishing the lids together so hard I caught orange flares of light moving through the black. Then I opened my eyes and went through another three rounds of supposedly stress-relieving deep breaths.

Dizzy strode up holding a white sack. "Got the barf bag. Just signal if you're about to..." He imitated throwing up, along with a sick sound.

I held up a hand for him to stop talking. "Thanks. I'll try not to need it."

I turned and peeked through a crack in the curtains. As I looked out over the audience, heat rose up my neck to my cheeks.

But there were friendly faces in the crowd. My mom and Jeremy sat together, fifth row center, discussing who-knows-what. My fan club with their T-shirts took up a small section. And our drama tech peers sprawled out on the aisle carpet.

Marita even held a sign that read "Vote Charlotte." Had she changed loyalties? Alec was out on bail, and his new bad-boy persona had attracted plenty of female attention. Maybe Marita was over him. I'd get the story later. Because, against all odds, we were becoming friends.

"Next!" Miss Holt sat several rows back, clipboard in hand, clearly in charge. She'd be calling me soon.

Logan's hand pressed against my back. "You ready?"

My heart thundered inside my chest. "Does it matter?"

"Gotta go." He squeezed my hand. "I'd kiss you, but with all that stage makeup..."

"It's fine. You can show you care by giving me one big, blinding spotlight."

He gave me a smile and a wink, then jogged away to work the theater's lighting. Not that auditions typically involved spotlights, but I was a special case. Hopefully, Miss Holt wouldn't mind. As Kat had said, "Permission is the long way. Forgiveness is a shortcut."

Too soon Miss Holt yelled, "Next!"

Kat strode onto the stage, gave me a quick, reassuring nod, and sat on the piano bench.

That was it.

I strolled onto the stage, each step feeling heavier than the last. When I reached the middle of the stage, time stalled. I forced myself to turn toward the audience...and froze. I couldn't see my mom, or Charlotte's Angels, or anyone familiar. It was just a cacophony of noise and a blur of people. My heartbeat drilled my ribs. So. Many. People.

The crowd fell silent.

Miss Holt spoke. "Name and song, please."

Everything—this dare, the contest, my life—had all seemed to lead here. To this moment.

I took my three long, settling breaths. They seemed to echo in my head. I cleared my throat. "Charlotte Romero singing 'Let Me Entertain You' from *Gypsy*."

The crowd roared.

Most of them had probably never even heard of *Gypsy*, the musical about a woman who started performing vaudeville acts as a young girl and became one of the most popular strippers ever. But the audience knew that I'd reveal my secret, and that's what egged them on.

And *ay*, were they egging me on.

My stomach weaved and dipped like a roller coaster—a roller coaster in hell. I wrapped my arms around my torso and pushed my forearms against the myself, hoping to quell the diabolical twists and turns.

Miss Holt gave the go-ahead hand gesture. "When you're ready."

Kat was surely waiting for me. But I wasn't ready. So. Not. Ready.

Whomp. The spotlight hit me with the force of a lightning bolt. More hollers erupted, as if that was some fantastic special effect.

I rolled my shoulders back, looked right at the spotlight, and imagined the theater absolutely empty. Then I spread out my arms, feathered boa ends in gloved hands, and flicked one wrist.

Kat's cue. She started the intro.

When I opened my mouth, I expected heaves to come out. Instead, somehow, I began to sing. The notes were timid, but they were there, on pitch, decent. My heartbeat competed in volume with the sound of my voice, but I kept going. I just had to make it through twelve lines of singing before I reached the talking part. The part where I'd changed the lyrics to reveal The Secret instead.

My skin turned hot, and my hands went slick. No parts of my body seemed to connect to any other. And still I sang. Getting a little stronger as I went.

If no one knew better, they might think I was doing this on purpose. The character Gypsy had her own stage fright to overcome, which showed up in this song—tentative at the beginning, confident by the end.

A wave of relief struck me as I reached the last sung line—immediately followed by a new wave of worry. I was telling the secret, my secret, my mother's secret.

The piano part kept going, and I stepped forward, feeling the burn of the spotlight, inviting it to block out everything but me and this moment.

"Hello, everyone!" I yelled out.

"Hello!" people yelled back.

Shock made me flinch, but I remembered Logan's words and took one long breath. This was my audition, and I'd use it however I needed.

I began again. "Hello, everyone, my name is Charlotte Romero. In the musical *Gypsy*, the main character's mother gets her into the business of stripping. Yes, stripping."

Murmurs passed through the crowd.

My pulse throbbed. I took another breath. *Empty theater, empty theater, empty…* Not working. I was just going to have to push past it. People were here, they were listening, and I needed to get this done.

"I'm not in the business of stripping. But my…my…um, biological father was."

Gasps. Shouts. Moans. They filled the auditorium. But I wasn't done.

The piano kept going. Kat playing her part.

I needed to keep playing mine. "So my mother, who is the straightest-laced person like ever, did this super crazy, one-time thing and got with the male stripper who performed at her friend's bachelorette party."

One "whoa!" came from the back right. Followed by a string of laughter.

Heat seared me all over, cheeks to toes. But oddly, it didn't feel like fear. It was…anger.

I shifted toward the voice. "Just wait for our twenty-year high school reunion, and I bet plenty of you will have your what-was-I-thinking moments to share. Some of you already have them."

The audience laughed, right as Kat added a piano flourish.

"So yeah," I said, "I'm the daughter of a male stripper. But whatever. We don't get to pick our parents."

Someone near the front said, "No kidding," and more laughter came from that section.

"But if I could have picked my parents," I continued, "I would have definitely picked my mom, who not only gave me permission but encouraged me to share what had been her biggest secret."

Whistles and applause went up in the auditorium. Unexpected praise for my mom, or just good parents everywhere.

I grinned, big and proud. "We all have 'em, right? Our secrets. Like my boyfriend is totally freaked out by spiders."

More laughter.

"Well, now you know my secret." I cocked my head at Kat, and she shifted her playing toward the final chorus.

When the next singing line arrived, I belted it out like I was performing at the Kennedy Center, growl in my voice and all. Nausea swirled in my stomach, heartburn press against my chest, bile rose in my throat. I reached the last note and spread my arms out in the final finish. I was swaying before the music stopped. I dropped to my knees and felt the spasms.

I heard the gasps.

Dizzy's footsteps running.

Kat's voice yelling, "Charlotte!"

But my stomach couldn't wait. The contents of my stomach came up in full force.

*Ew*s and *blech*s came from around me, but my body didn't give a flip. It was on all fours, letting out my stage fright in the only way it knew how.

The spotlight faded, and someone yelled, "Lights."

The house lights went up, and Miss Holt's voice came next. "Theater closed. Everyone out. Now." The last word was *don't mess with me* serious.

The clamor of people leaving became static in the background. My vomiting had stopped, but my heaving hadn't. I kept my head down, praying I was done.

My mother was there right away with a towel I recognized. Had she brought that from home? She rubbed my back, cleaned up the mess, but didn't say a word.

Just what I needed.

Miss Holt's feet appeared in view. "Take your time, Charlotte. I'll ask the janitor to take care of this. You did well."

I huffed out a laugh. This moment did not feel *well*. But I had made it through—both the song and the secret.

49
CURTAIN CALL

The next week was eventful, and not. Even I hadn't realized how much pressure the contest had been on me. KHAL's Jenna O'Farrell-Fine had requested an interview, but I'd said no. I'd had enough of the limelight for a while. With the dares done, a weight lifted, and I could just breathe better, deeper.

Reactions to my audition were mixed—some smiles and encouragement, some grimaces and disgust. But no one seemed to care about my secret. In fact, several people hunted me down to say I'd inspired them to open up about their own secrets.

On Friday afternoon, Miss Holt asked me to stay after class.

Logan hung back too but waited on the other side of the stage, out of earshot.

I stood toe to toe with Miss Holt.

Under the A/C vent, her caftan flowed around her like a spinning kaleidoscope. "Charlotte, your voice and performance were stellar. I didn't know you had that in you. But sadly, I can't give you the lead this time, and I wanted to explain why."

I smiled. I hadn't expected a role after my puke finale, but the word *stellar* would stick with me for a while. "I think I know why. You can't send a mop out after every song I sing."

She gave a mentor's nod. "I'm glad you understand. But next year, I'd love to cast you in a big part. I know a psychologist who has helped several singers work through performance anxiety. I'd be happy to give you her information."

"Thanks," I said. "I'll let you know."

My chest warmed. She was offering me hope. But hope also cost money. Or at least psychologists cost money. If money wasn't an issue, I'd never have entered the contest.

"In the meantime"—she tapped my shoulder, like *listen up*—"you're in the chorus. I think you can handle that, and I want you on stage as much as you can do."

I swallowed hard. "But what if I—"

"You won't." She winked one false-lashes eye at me. "Strength in numbers. You'll be okay."

I nodded, both anxious and happy to be cast in a musical again. Even if it wasn't the lead. It was enough to be in front of the curtain.

"All right," Miss Holt said. "Guess it's time for you to go and for me to lock up. Or"—she raised her volume and ping-ponged her gaze between Logan and me—"one of you could lock up with your own keys."

Logan and I traded shocked expressions. How did Miss Holt know?

She smiled. "Enjoy it while you can. The locks are getting changed next week." Then she walked away, muttered, "Kids," and snickered to herself.

As we left, Logan asked, "What did Miss Holt want?"

"She said I'm good enough to lead but can't cast me until I overcome my stage fright."

"Ouch."

"Nah, it's okay." I slid my hand into his, and we walked down the hall together. "She's putting me in the chorus. I would have made the same decision, and now I know that's the only piece keeping me from what I want. If I can stop vomiting, I can start singing for real."

"Good. Because..." He pushed open the door that led to the parking lot and sunlight.

Deedra was standing outside. Like a dark cloud blocking the sun.

She pointed at me. "You wanna know results? Follow me." She spun on her heel and started walking, then called back over her shoulder. "Not Logan. Just you."

Something low in my belly quivered.

Logan nudged me forward. "Go. Find out, then come back." I jogged to catch up, and Logan's voice trailed me. "I'll wait right here."

Deedra led me around the school perimeter to a recessed nook between walls. Alec was already there. Just the three of us—the contest host and the two final contestants.

Alec looked as nervous as I felt.

"Hey," I said. "Whatever happens, you've been great. I'm sorry about your arrest, but if you win, I'll be happy for you. Really."

He shrugged a shoulder. "Looks like the criminal case will be a bust. They're not that interested in charging me for a childhood mistake that didn't hurt anyone. It's the civil case my parents are worried about. We could owe a lot of money for property damage."

Deedra sighed and shook her head. "I shouldn't have done that to y'all. I wrote the dares long before I knew anyone's secret or who would end up in the final round."

"Don't apologize to me," Alec said. "That secret had been weighing on me for five years. Maybe they're right about the truth setting you free."

"Same here," I offered. "I mean, I don't think you should have done it, but the outcome has been much better than I thought."

"Still, I'm well...you know." Apologetic as she was, she still couldn't bring herself to say the word *sorry*.

I'd take it, though. It was progress. "Thanks, Deedra. I appreciate that."

Deedra laughed and raised one perfectly plucked eyebrow at us in turn. "Okay, but this bittersweet moment does not make us besties. You two are still my social inferiors."

I started to object, but then she looked down and smirked to herself. As if she knew she was playing a part, a drama queen role that wasn't her real self. Or at least, not all of her.

I shut my mouth.

"Results?" Alec asked.

"It was close." Deedra looked up again, chin high. "Difference of only three votes in the end."

My lungs tightened. "Which one of us?"

Deedra's gaze danced between us, as if drawing out the suspense. Then she landed her eyes on me. "I think you had cinched it with your tryout, right up until the moment you..." She gestured vomiting with a wave her hand in front of her mouth.

My jaw went slack, my shoulders dipped. I'd given it my all, I'd been ahead, and my stage fright had cost me the contest.

"Yes!" Alec hissed and pumped his fist. "Sorry, Charlotte."

I smiled, a wan smile that I pulled up from somewhere. "Congratulations. You deserved it."

She pulled an envelope out of her purse and handed it to him. "Five thousand, as promised."

"Sweet," Alec said. "This'll pay for both chemistry *and* space camp." He walked off, charming smile on his face, defined muscles on his body, but the same science-geek brain in his head.

I started to leave, but Deedra stopped me with a hand on my arm. I turned back, expecting to see another haughty look.

Instead, she wore a thin-but-honest smile. "Actually, you deserved to win too."

"I did?" Her words took me off-balance. Shouldn't she be relishing my defeat?

"With your help, I surpassed my mother's social media numbers, and we came to a compromise last night. I'll major in fashion marketing, and she'll release some funds for me to start my business on the side." She flutter-rolled her eyes. "My dad showers cash on me, but Mom hoards it for college expenses."

Sounded like a good problem to me. But then, I also knew Deedra's bigger problem was her relationship with her mom in general. I wouldn't trade my problems for hers.

"Also," she continued, "I got some extra income through my site. So..." She drew a second envelope from her purse and handed it to me. "It's not as much as Alec's prize money, but I think you'll be happy."

I peeked inside to see a check for three thousand. My jaw dropped a second time, lower, harder.

Deedra turned and started to walk away. Then she turned back and looked right at me. "Oh, and don't worry about the repairs. Dad covered them."

Jaw, meet ground.

I just floated for a few minutes. The check in my hand and the canceled debt topped five thousand. I'd lost, but I was going to New York.

My heart beat once, twice, three times in my ears, then stuttered.

I pulled out the check and stared at it. I was holding enough money to fulfill my dream of going on the theater department trip to Broadway. Wasn't that what I wanted?

The truth hit me like a spotlight. Yes, I wanted to visit Broadway. But on my own terms—a different plan altogether.

I ran to find Logan.

50
ENCORE

Logan and I stepped into his den, where Kat, Jeremy, and Dizzy were waiting for him for practice. Logan spoke first. "We have news about the contest."

All heads turned toward us.

I took a deep breath. "I lost. By three votes."

Stunned faces stared back at me.

I looked directly at my self-appointed manager. "I'm sorry, Kat. Really."

She winced. "Whatever. I hated this contest anyway." She grabbed her drumsticks and tapped her knees. "The people you should worry about breaking this to are Charlotte's Angels. Georgia might launch a You Were Robbed campaign."

"That's the bad news." Logan grinned. "Now tell them the good news."

"Deedra rewarded me for helping her get followers with a big prize of my own." I pulled out the check and held it up.

They just stared, taking time for the message and the number to sink in.

Then Kat stood and raised her fists, victory-style. "New York, here you come!"

"Yes, and no."

She dropped her arms.

"Yes, I'm going to New York, but I'm going to invite my mother to take that trip with me. I don't want to go with friends that aren't y'all, and she deserves a break. Deedra also canceled my debt, so any money I have left, I'm putting toward therapy to deal with my stage fright. Miss Holt's casting me in the chorus, but I want a principal singing role. Someday."

"Now you're talking," Jeremy mumbled from the couch, where he was slumped, sprawled, and settled.

Logan put his arm around my waist. "We wanted to talk about that. Charlotte, we want you to join the band. Sing vocals. I'll still sing some, but you're better than I am, and adding a female voice expands our playlist options."

My face flashed heat. "But you heard me—I can't sing lead. Not yet."

"So what," Kat said. "You play a mean tambourine and can sing backup. Take lead when you're ready."

Jeremy snorted. "You're more fun to have around than Hendrix."

"Leave my cat alone," Dizzy protested.

I laughed. "So five of us, huh? You sure that's not too many?"

Kat rolled her eyes, exactly the way Deedra had done before. Not that I'd tell her that. "Five worked just fine for The Rolling Stones, AC/DC, Aerosmith—"

"One Direction," Logan added with a smirk.

Kat pierced him with a scowl.

I nodded confidently. "Fine. I accept the invitation to join your nameless band of five members." And then it snapped into my head, the last jigsaw puzzle piece. "Wait. I have an idea."

Kat turned her scowl to me. "We are not playing any One Direction songs. Or boy-band music. Or anything that even smacks of pop. We will not be sellouts playing stupid songs that stoke the sexual fantasies of teenage boys. I for one am—"

"And Kat Jamison is back." I grinned at her.

She straightened and preened. "She never left."

"My idea is about the band name."

"What is it?" Logan asked.

Deep breath. "I'll understand if you don't like it, but we wouldn't all be together but for this contest. This contest for five thousand dollars. What if that's the name? Five Thousand, or"—I paused and spread out my arms, *Cabaret* emcee style—"Five. Grand."

I waited for the annoyed glances from band members.

Instead, they paused, considered, and broke into smiles.

"That's it!" yelled Jeremy.

"Yes!" Dizzy added.

Kat bumped my shoulder. "See, you're already an asset."

"Love it." Logan pulled me into an embrace and kissed me. A kiss to rival the most romantic musicals I'd ever seen.

From the corner of my eye, I saw that Jeremy had taken that as his signal to kiss Kat.

Dizzy simply muttered, "I need to get me a woman."

♡

Remember when Charlotte said two girls
tried sharing boyfriend the year before?
Read that story in Sharing Hunter.

And sign up for my newsletter to get
deleted scenes, sneak peeks & more!

Also by Julie Glover

Be sure to check out my other stories!

YA Paranormal

My Sister's Demon – short story

My School's Vampire – short story

My Stepmom's Ghosts – short story

My Team's Fairy Godmother – short story

My Neighbor's Shapeshifter – short story

My Paranormal Life – box set

YA Contemporary

Sharing Hunter

Changing Chloe – sequel short story

Supernatural Suspense (under Jules Lynn)

The Muse Island Series

Mark of the Gods – Book 1

Power of the Song – Book 2

Rise of the Storm – Book 3

Finn's Call – prequel short story

Curse of the Night – Book 4

Heir of the Chaos – Book 5
Gryla's Gift – holiday short story

Charlotte's Playlist

"Supercalifragilisticexpialidocious" from *Mary Poppins*
"Don't Rain on My Parade" from *Funny Girl"*
"Cell Block Tango" from *Chicago*
"If I Were a Bell" from *Guys and Dolls*
"On My Own" from *Les Misérables*
"I'm Gonna Wash That Man Right Outa My Hair" from *South Pacific*
"Helpless" from *Hamilton*
"I Could Have Danced All Night" from *My Fair Lady*
"Don't Tell Mama" from *Cabaret*
"Any Way You Want It" from *Rock of Ages*
"As the World Falls Down" from *Labyrinth*
"You're the One I Want" from *Grease*
"Defying Gravity" from *Wicked*
"Come What May" from *Moulin Rouge*

All the Musicals

Here's a list of all the musicals mentioned in *Daring Charlotte*. Many, but not all, have been made into movies.

42nd Street

Aladdin

An American in Paris

Annie

Beauty and the Beast

Bye, Bye, Birdie

Cabaret

Cats

Chicago

Evita

Funny Girl

Grease

Guys and Dolls

Gypsy

Hadestown

Hair

Hamilton

Labyrinth

Les Misérables

Lion King

Little Mermaid

Little Shop of Horrors

Mamma Mia

Mary Poppins

Moulin Rouge

My Fair Lady

Pajama Game

Phantom of the Opera

Rent

Rock of Ages

Seven Brides for Seven Brothers

Show Boat

Sound of Music

South Pacific

Sweeney Todd

The Addams Family

Tommy

West Side Story

Wicked

Wolff

Actually, *Wolff* is a figment of my imagination. But if anyone wants to stage it, give me a call. I have most of the plot worked out and a couple of songs written. [wink]

Acknowledgments

First up, I have to thank Lori Freeland, fellow young adult author (whom you should totally read), who was already an amazing friend and then invited me into her excellent critique group. Speaking of that group, thanks to Katie, Lori, and Teri for the fantastic feedback and encouragement to keep editing and get Charlotte's story into readers' hands.

A big thank you to Kathryn Crawford, whose feedback and Spanglish knowledge really helped me sharpen this story.

To all of the high schoolers out there who came up with some great senior pranks, you inspired me. Yes, I googled all about it to get ideas!

And of course, Christina Delay, you are *mi mejor amiga* and the best critique partner an author could ask for.

Finally, my husband deserves something—pat on the back? Kiss on the cheek? Roll in the pigpen hay? He can have all of them, if he wants. After all, he takes care of a lot of our household while I write and lets me know that I'm not half-bad at this book thing. Thanks, hubby. *Te amo siempre.*

About the Author

Julie Glover is an award-winning author of teen novels and mysteries. She loves to both read and write quirky stories with intriguing characters, fresh humor, and lots of heart. Her debut YA novel, *Sharing Hunter*, was a Romance Writers of America Golden Heart® finalist.

Julie is known among close friends for her surplus sarcasm, her growing collection of boots, and her willingness to grab a karaoke microphone at the slightest nudge. A born-and-bred Texan, she now lives in the Lone Star State with her wonderful husband and a loquacious cat.

You can visit her online at: julieglover.com